INTERNS & VOLUNTEERS: Taylor Yeomans, Nolan Boomer, Alex Bauer, Zack Grossenbacher, Frances Cannon, Erica Plumlee, Jessica McHugh, Taylor Wallau, Shoshana Akabas, Nate Rogers, Amanda Arnold, Sally Weathers, Aralyn Beaumont, Noah Pisner, Paolo Yumol, Ian Delaney, Valerie Snow, Yannic Dosenbach, Laura Ceron Melo, Ilaria Varriale, Jess Bergman, Lara Sichi, Will Gray, Alec Joyner, Madison Wetzell, Olivia Judge. ALSO HELPING: Andi Mudd, Sam Riley, Rachel Khong, Clara Sankey, Dan McKinley, Daniel Gumbiner, Brian Christian, Ruby Perez. WEBSITE: Chris Monks. SUPPORT: Sunra Thompson and Jordan Karnes. OUTREACH: Isaac Fitzgerald. ART DIRECTOR: Brian McMullen. COPY EDITOR: Phyllis Fong. ASSOCIATE PUBLISHER: Adam Krefman. PUBLISHER: Laura Howard. MANAGING EDITOR: Jordan Bass. EDITOR: Dave Eggers.

Cover art by Ryan Mrozowski; interior art by Wesley Allsbrook.
Printed in Michigan at Thomson-Shore Printers.

YOU HAVE TO SEE THIS

PORTRAITS OF LAWRENCE WESCHLER

CURATED & EDITED BY RACHEL COHEN

with Errol Morris, William Finnegan, Lauren Redniss,
Bill McKibben, Ben Katchor, Wendy Lesser, Geoff Dyer, Bill Morrison,
Riva Lehrer, David Hockney, Jonathan Lethem, Peter Vermeersch,

DEAR MCSWEENEY'S,

I came, a recalcitrant thirty-six-year-old mom, to Des Moines, Iowa, which is like America's dream of an America where no Kennedys ever died. The best coffee shop has a flavor called "Jamaican Me Crazy."

"Is Iowa in the United States?" asks my older son, strapped securely behind me in our car-seat-laden Suby. Yes, technically, I say. Des Moines is a metropolitan city and all, but from where I am, I can stand up and see two unlocked bikes parked in a garage that does not even have a door on it— which, after fifteen years in Chicago, just seems like perversion. Iowa the reality is much like the Iowa of my imagination.

That night it is so silent that we cannot even walk around our rental, the creakiest home ever to be offered to overnight guests on the internet, for fear of waking our sleeping children. There is almost a druggy novelty to it, all the silence and safety tipping us out of reality, like too-stoned teenagers exiting their dorm room and finding the mundane world to be "weiiiiird." My husband and I huddle in the kitchen and slowly open a bag of chips. We keep our crunching deliberate.

I came, a wary visitor. I had never heard my sister so upset and over-the-phone comfort did not feel like

enough. So we packed up the children and all their supplies, which included a folding mini-crib, toys for chewing, cars small enough for in-car use, a stuffed dog that has been dressed in a preemie diaper and onesie for the last week, and books for long and short attention spans, and embarked on our six-hour odyssey.

It is always nice to get out of the city, but this trip was not about that. My sister was sobbing because her friend had been shot six times, as had her friend's boyfriend, who had been lying on top of the girl to protect her from the gunman, who happened to be the girl's mother's abusive boyfriend. This man then shot and killed the mother and himself. The mother had been attempting to move out of the home they shared. She was a family friend, had dated my stepdad after he and my mom split up. I was eighteen and out of the house, then, out in Los Angeles, and so my memories of her are vague—she was blonde and nice and seemed to be a comfort for our dad. The papers in Minneapolis called it "femicide," which bothers me, as it seems to imply women being killed by their husbands or boyfriends is some new, novel thing—that it needs a separate designation.

We've come to Iowa to be of service. We have two little boys who are valuable as a distraction and so we are here to deploy them like those comfort dogs they bring to colleges during finals week. Children can pull you back from grief. William, very nearly three, has of late been engaging me on the topic of why don't I have a penis, then running down a long list of people/animals/relatives in his life and telling me whether they do or do not have a penis themselves. Sometimes he offers, as if to console me, that "one day" I will grow a penis, a butt, and a beard; that one day I will be a daddy. It is like living with a teeny-tiny Freud, all this talk about a penis it is assumed I wish to own. Meanwhile Jude, the Younger, has a small arsenal of party tricks, impressive given that he is one year old—some rudimentary harmonica skills, the tendency to yell "POW!" when he gives you a high-five. They are too young to know how much they salve us with their very existence.

The drive was fine; even the people in the car who are allowed to shit their pants didn't. I lobbed a few questions at my husband, who went to college here and lived in Iowa City for a time. The Iowa I know is his telling of it—which is mostly oriented around his impossibly gross stories of working in a surgical pathology lab, an unfortunate jazz recital where he sat in with Wynton Marsalis, and his job driving a campus bus. We drive through Iowa City, pit-stop at the co-op, and then drive around until we lay eyes on it. See, William? This is the bus that made your father a man.

Within hours of our arrival in Des Moines my mom comes down with an illness that, in another era, probably would have landed her in an iron lung—charging my sister with the care of our bedridden mother as well as her small menagerie of impossible dogs and a smush-faced kitten who has a problem with life and so never ceases meowing. Which is to say we spent most of our time without either of them, puttering in a funny orbit around Des Moines for a weekend. We eat at my mom's favorite restaurant without her, a Vietnamese spot incredibly named A Dong, which we know of from her many excited and earnest check-ins on Facebook, with their accompanying posts about how much she loves eating A Dong. This is all true, *McSweeney's*.

The place we stayed had no wireless internet—the hostess's explanation being, simply: "My son is fifteen." I looked at the pictures of this boy around the house and thought about the things we do to try to keep boys good. The events that brought us to Des Moines had me dwelling on that, on all we do in hopes of raising good boys, on living in quiet fear of whatever it is that turns a boy bad.

The boy who lives in that house, this internetless boy, he looked like a good one. He had an agate collection and a Chinese workbook and dinosaur sheets on his bed where my own good boy was asleep.

On the long drive home we talk about Iowa's idyll—we consider it. A little house with a long lawn where the boys could run shoeless and free. While stopped (again) at the co-op in Iowa City, alone in the car with the baby sleeping, a miniature Carnaval-style children's parade passes by me in the rain, trailed by a salsa band crammed onto a flatbed. It feels like a dream; I am the only one who sees it as they cruise past. A moment later, as I start to explain to William what he missed while they were in the store, a mom dressed as a tree walks past and shakes some ginger candies out of her crudely formed treetop hat for him.

I think I fell in love with Iowa a bit. Yours from Paradise,
JESSICA HOPPER
CHICAGO, IL

DEAR MCSWEENEY'S,
I recently returned to Brisbane, on the east coast of Australia, after a series of trips away to get over a girl in my hometown whom I liked too much. While trying to forget her in Brooklyn, I was struck by the beards of both the older Hasidic Jews and the younger hipster males. This is beard-town, I thought.

Upon returning home I was struck again; these hipster beards, some kempt, some unwieldly, had apparently followed me 9,500 miles away from Brooklyn, into the southern hemisphere. We might have only 11 percent of the world's population down here, but a small number of that small number seem uncommonly alert to what is happening in Bushwick.

In my neighborhood, West End, there is now a small bar, The End, that is known as a hipster bar. It sells Rainbow rather than Pabst, and our nineteen-dollar-an-hour wages mean you don't have to tip a dollar a drink, but all of the boys behind the bar sport magnificent beards. No one here knows whether hipsters are a good or a bad thing. But one of these young men has put his hipster countenance to good use.

He is known universally as "Fake Ryan Gosling." He looks enough like Ryan Gosling, at a time in history when that is a distinct advantage, that people often make the comparison: "Hey, has anyone ever mentioned that you look like Ryan Gosling?"

It is made more quaint because the young man's real first name is Ryan. With so much going for him, he understandably attracts gossip, and he seems to do well socially.

Recently, though, while I was drinking at his bar, he began flirting with an ex-girlfriend of mine in front of me. At the time I didn't cut much of a figure, so I just let it play out: "My name is Ryan. A lot of people say I look like Ryan Gosling. I think that is what you call an irony."

She got him to roll her a cigarette. They talked about how her haircut looked like Anne Hathaway's new pixie crop. I looked at the way he looked at her, and then I looked at the way she looked at his beard. He stroked it—for all our sakes. I felt my own naked skin.

McSweeney's, I feel you are obliged to use your influence with the American hipster community to quarantine this new archetype of male beauty. What is wrought in Brooklyn should not be a threat to cultures and to women so far away. A smooth-skinned man living, in nature, south of the Equator should not suffer for want of a beard imagined first in the Adirondacks and then re-created in mainstream cinema. Please let me know what you can do.

STUART GLOVER
BRISBANE, AUSTRALIA

DEAR MCSWEENEY'S,
When I was in third grade, a children's book writer came to speak at my school. She read us a story about frogs. When it was time for questions, a student asked her why she'd written it. She laughed and said, "I needed to pay my rent."

After the assembly, our teacher sat us down for a meeting.

"I'm sorry you had to hear that," she said. "Real artists make art because they're inspired. They don't do it for the money."

Then she told us about Vincent van Gogh. He was so poor, she said, that he was always hungry. Sometimes, he had to decide between bread and paints. He always chose paints.

Years later, I looked up van Gogh on Wikipedia. It turns out he was actually from a wealthy family. His uncle and brother were famous art dealers and they supported him financially for years. That's how he was able to make paintings his whole life, instead of getting a normal job.

Another thing it said about van Gogh is that he liked to eat paints to get high.

•

My friend Ben is an improvisational comedian. I went to see him perform at a theater in Brooklyn. It cost $5 to get in. There were fifteen people on stage and only seven of us in the audience. When I saw Ben after the show, he looked embarrassed. "I guess you gotta start somewhere," he joked.

As I was leaving, I saw him hand some cash to the owner of the theater. I don't know how much it cost him to perform. That was five years ago. Ben still performs improvisational comedy but he also goes to medical school. The last time we spoke he was leaning toward becoming an oncologist.

•

I once wrote a joke about Tony the Tiger for a TV show. Just before the show aired, Kellogg's Cereal called to complain. They had bought a commercial on our show and they didn't want us to make fun of Tony the Tiger. My joke was cut. During the show, I drank whiskey with some of the other writers. I wanted to see the Kellogg's commercial, but it came on late in the broadcast and I must have been in the bathroom. At the afterparty, I asked my boss how much Kellogg's had paid for their commercial. He told me it had cost them $80,000. I recently reread my Tony the Tiger joke. It isn't as funny as I remembered it being.

•

When I was at Harvard, a Tibetan monk visited the school. He spent seven days in a roped-off corner of the Arts Center painting a picture with colored sand. At the end of the week, someone told me, he was going to scatter his picture into the Charles River. I couldn't believe that an artist would work so hard on something only to destroy it.

Each day, I passed the monk on my way to breakfast. His lips were always pursed and his eyebrows were always creased. He never looked up from his painting. He was really working hard on it.

A friend of mine was taking a course on religion. She explained to me that the monk was making a point about "process." By destroying his art, he was trying to teach us that achievements are ultimately hollow. We shouldn't live our life in pursuit of goals; we should live life just to live it.

I wanted to watch the monk destroy his work, but I had class that afternoon. I made sure to stop by the Arts Center in the morning, though, so I could see his finished painting. It was beautiful: an intricate series of circles, each containing a different pattern. When I thought about him scattering it, my stomach hurt.

As I was leaving the Arts Center, I looked back over my shoulder. I was surprised to see that the monk was holding a digital camera. He swiveled his head around, to make sure no one was watching. Then he aimed the lens at his work and snapped a bunch of pictures.

•

When I was six, I wrote an essay about what I wanted to be when I grew up. I forgot about it for years, until my twenty-eighth birthday, when my mom had it framed and gave it to me as a birthday present.

WHEN I GROW UP

When I grow up I wont to be a writr of kids books. I wont to write kids books becus you cood writ enefing in kidsbooks. rol doll is my favret writer. if he dinint assist I don't fingk I wood wont to be a writer. Good fings abat beeng a ritr: good ruvoos, a lot of mone and lots of fan.

The last sentence, where I list all the "good fings" about being a writer, has a lot of misspellings. My mom was able to decipher the first two things on my list: "good reviews" and "a lot of money." The third item, though, gave us trouble. Does "lots of fan" mean "lots of fun" or "lots of fans"? I wish I could ask my six-year-old self what he wanted.

•

I was hired to work on a movie for two weeks. People had been working on it for years by the time I got there. I had to sign a lot of forms before they showed me the script. The forms said I couldn't tell anybody what the movie was about. I signed the forms and they led me into a room where the script was. I read it twice, but I couldn't understand the plot. There was no main character and events seemed to happen at random. At one point, in the second act, somebody killed his brother. I couldn't figure out why he had done it.

The next day, I made some suggestions to the director and he yelled at me. He seemed to be under a lot of stress. He yelled at his assistant too and then disappeared for three hours to do hot yoga. They had already built all the sets for the movie and hired the main actors.

The director didn't want me to make any big changes to the script. I had signed a two-week contract, though, so I had to stay in the building for eight hours every day. I spent the mornings working on a love story that wasn't very good, although I didn't know that at the time. In the afternoons I walked around the studio, stealing Clif bars from all the snack tables. As soon as I got home, I took the Clif bars out of my backpack and put them in a drawer. By the end of my two weeks at the studio, I had nearly one hundred Clif bars.

It took me almost six months to eat all of the Clif bars. By that time, the movie had been scrapped and the people working on it had been fired.

•

The English painter Robert Haydon spent years on his final work, *The Banishment of Aristides*. While he was working on the painting, he fell into enormous debt. His wife and daughters begged him to stop painting and find employment, but he refused to give up on what he believed would be his masterpiece. He was nearing sixty, which was considered old at the time. This was in the 1840s.

When Haydon's painting was finally finished, he rented a hall in Piccadilly to display it. The hall was gigantic, and in order to pay the rent, he had to go into even greater debt. While he was setting up his exhibit, P.T. Barnum came to London. He rented the hall next door to Haydon's and displayed Tom Thumb, a popular seven-year-old dwarf. Haydon's and Barnum's exhibits went on simultaneously. During Easter week, twelve thousand Londoners paid to see Tom Thumb. Only 133 paid to see *The Banishment of Aristides*.

Not long after that, Haydon wrote a note saying, "Stretch me no longer on this rough world," and shot himself. When the bullet didn't kill him, he slit his throat with a knife. His daughter found him dead inside his studio.

I first learned about Haydon when I read a biography of Tom Thumb.

•

When I was twelve, my favorite hobby was to juggle. I taught myself about a dozen tricks. My best trick was to juggle two balls in one hand while kicking the third up with my foot.

One Sunday, I went to Central Park, put a shoebox on the ground, and started juggling. A small crowd of tourists formed around me. They clapped and put coins in my shoebox. I'd practiced for months in front of a mirror and I didn't make any mistakes. When I tried my hardest trick, though, the one that involved kicking, I dropped all of the balls. Some of the tourists walked away, but about half of them stayed. I thought about going back to my easier tricks, but the crowd had already seen those. The only trick they hadn't seen was the hard one.

"I'm going to try the hard trick again," I told the crowd. Then I took a deep breath and threw all the balls in the air. This time it worked and everybody clapped.

I juggled for about two more hours and then sat on a bench to count my money. I'd made $12. On my way home, I passed a vendor selling frozen lemonade for $3.25. I opened my shoebox and carefully counted out the right number of quarters.

"Good show," he said, as he handed me my drink.

"Thank you," I said.

As I left the park, my shoebox in

one hand and my lemonade in the other, I thought to myself, this is the happiest I've ever been, this is the single greatest moment of my whole life.

SIMON RICH
OAKLAND, CA

DEAR MCSWEENEY'S,

Do you know two lads from the Oklahoma City area, one by the name of Chase Barker and the other Joe Something? I'd like to thank them for not punching me in the face.

I drove to Moore, Okla., a few hours after the tornado hit, working as a stringer for the (I better not say which) newspaper. I had given up on the Flaubertian route—you know the one where your writing just rises to greatness, soufflélike, by virtue of your finely whisked prose? I was trying to Hemingway it up, to write from the balls, to bear witness. If you can't write something worth reading, do something worth writing. Right?

During previous catastrophes within driving distance of my home in Denton, I had kept my head down. I half-expected one of my journalist brethren to knock on my door and stick me with a white feather. With Moore closer to me than any of the newspaper's bureaus, I had no excuse.

The clouds over I-35 that evening almost made me flinch. These clouds were not your fluffy, inert jobs,

Macker. (Hope you don't mind the diminutive—mark of respect where I went to school in Ireland.) They were protean, plasmic; they glowed at the edges like burning coals. They were Turner seas, turned upside down.

All the roads into Moore that night ended in a police blockade. The gravity of my assignment made me excitable. But after two hours of traffic-jam hopping, I was slightly farther from Moore than when I first got off the highway, and I was getting frantic.

I saw a space for my car in a row of vehicles across the street, but I was too flustered to parallel park. Instead I drove straight into the roadside drainage ditch, thinking I could reverse up the hill and onto the verge without interrupting the flow of traffic. It looked dry, but it was, of course, drenched. Feeling the wheels lose their grip, I pressed harder on the accelerator, which only spun me deeper into the slush. I was soon stuck. I decided to ditch the car, which was actually a relief, even if it was a little too literal of a job.

Can I just say, *McSweeney's*: Betsy Randolph? Best source ever. Superhuman patience. This Oklahoma State Trooper not only gave me new information, she made sure my phone was charged to transmit it, despite some glowers from colleagues that were as heavy duty as their Toshiba laptops.

Even in the darkness, the destruction around the Plaza Towers elementary school was staggering. Stalin could not have scorched the suburban earth more brutally. The very trees were tonsured of their leaves and upper limbs. Those trees could have been mistaken for a petrified forest were it not for the muddy pieces of clothing that hung from the sawn-off branches. The houses were reduced to shipwreck flotsam. The school looked like a steel-and-timber version of a Celtic burial mound. The only structures still standing were the satellite masts rising from a flotilla of television vans on a side road perpendicular to the school.

A police officer scolded me for way-laying a fireman—mighty shoulders weighed down like those of Atlas—on his way back to search for survivors. I thought of defending myself with a line about how we, the media, had to tell the world what happened in Moore. The policeman probably would have decked me, and I probably would have deserved it. As it was, he marched me to the media area.

The local television affiliate reporters were just as warm offscreen as on-. While allowing me to charge my phone yet again in his van, one of them told me about a tornado that went past his own home. After the quiet and before the storm, he said, the rain came slanting from both directions at once. When a rival affiliate rolled up, he complained of how his channel had been ruthlessly outspent: "See that? They've got a picture of the talent on the side of the van!"

It was after 3 a.m. when I started back toward my car. On the edge of town, Joe Something stopped to offer me water. As soon as he'd heard about the disaster, he had packed his pickup truck with water and dry foods and driven down from nearby Oklahoma City to help out in any way he could. I got up on the bed of Joe's truck and he drove me back to my car.

We found Chase Barker a mile up the road, searching in vain for his own vehicle. Chase said his search-and-rescue team had found a man's body lying in a field, next to a car dangling like a Christmas ornament from a truncated tree limb.

"It won't bother you today, but tomorrow, it'll bother you," said Joe, who didn't want to talk about what he'd seen or have his name in the paper. If he stopped to reflect, he said, he might not get going again.

Joe and Chase strapped my car to the truck like it was nothing. My *sang* wasn't even *froid* enough to keep the steering wheel straight. Thinking the car was out of the ditch, I veered wildly, and almost dragged Joe's truck into the mire with me. But Chase and Joe never lost their composure.

There were people in Moore far more deserving of their help, but they did not blame me for that.

So here's to Chase and Joe, Macker. Heroes in the Hemingway mold.

ROB CURRAN
DENTON, TX

DEAR MCSWEENEY'S,

On a gusty spring day, I was driving south on Federal Boulevard in Denver to pick up Gabriella,[*] the young lady I was mentoring, when the trucks in front of me began to swerve. By the time I saw what was causing the disturbance, it was too late. An enormous tumbleweed appeared in my path and, as I hit the brakes, smacked into my car and attached itself to my license plate. It was so large that it extended across the entire length of my front bumper and halfway up my windshield, even as it continued to scrape along the asphalt with a disturbing SCREEEEE sound as I drove.

The tumbleweed hit me near the Alpine Rose Motel, nicknamed the "Motel from Hell," which would be shut down later that year, when fifteen people were arrested for running a kilo of crack cocaine out of it a day, and one for murdering a man whom the prosecution portrayed as a "disgruntled

crack customer." Most everyone on that part of Federal was driving a pickup truck, and traffic slowed to watch me in my Toyota Corolla with tumbleweed attachment. Luckily I was only a few blocks from Gabriella's house. I pulled off Federal and parked in her driveway, trying to formulate a plan. Gabriella came running down the stairs to meet me right away.

"I've got a tumbleweed situation," I told her. "Give me a minute."

Gabriella waited patiently. I suspected she already had her doubts about riding in my car, a dinged sedan from 1996. Her family owned an immaculate white Ford pickup truck and a little red Mustang that she planned to drive across town to school as soon as she was old enough for a license.

I walked around to the bumper and attempted to grip the tumbleweed where it looked least prickly. It must have been six feet tall and four feet wide: a truly impressive specimen. It detached easily, though; I was surprised at how light it was, given its size. But then tumbleweeds are by nature light, I told myself. Now I had to figure out how to dispose of it, and to do so in a fashion that would set a good example for Gabriella. Wasn't that what a mentor was supposed to do? I couldn't leave it in her family's yard; that wasn't right. Instead I picked it up, crossed the street, and walked down the block

[*] I've changed her name. She's suffered enough from her association with me.

toward Federal again.

I glanced at the neighbor's yard, a patch of overgrown weeds fenced in chainlink. But the neighbor, a skinny old woman with the pinched, wrinkled face of a lifelong smoker, had been watching me from her porch since I pulled in, and didn't like the way I was eyeing her yard. She shot out toward the fence. "Don't you put that trash here," she said, shaking her head. So I kept strolling with the tumbleweed, pretending that I hadn't been thinking of dumping the thing in Crabby's yard. Have you ever carried a tumbleweed down the street, *McSweeney's?* It's awkward. It doesn't feel right.

On the corner I encountered a yellow fireworks stand with a black cat hissing by its side. I was running out of options, so I tried to wedge the tumbleweed near there, next to a bush, thinking this was stupid and most definitely not a good example for Gabriella. Tumbleweeds are flammable, and here I was stashing it near a cache of low-grade explosives. But I shouldn't have worried; the wind took it from me then, tearing it from my hands. It rolled away as if it had somewhere to go. For all I know it's still blowing from car to car, now.

Your Little Sister,

JENNY SHANK
BOULDER, CO

DEAR MCSWEENEY'S,

Last night the mansion was full of drama. Emotions were running high. It started on the group date, in a pool on the rooftop of an LA hotel, where The Bachelor wasn't paying enough attention to Michelle. All she wanted was to feel special on her thirtieth birthday, and here she was on a date with fourteen other girls! Your thirtieth birthday is supposed to *mean* something. Not to mention Keltie was wearing the worst outfit ever. But The Bachelor's the type of guy where if there's a problem, he's going to address it, so a few nights later he gave Michelle the first rose. That sent a signal to the rest of the girls that you *have* to put yourself out there if you want to fall in love. Not in the way Melissa put herself out there, though—Melissa just popped up out of nowhere and was like, "I'm so, like, dadadadada, and I'm not normally like this," and it's like, Well, what *are* you normally like? "Basically I'm very spontaneous," explained Melissa. Raichel definitely felt like Melissa should go home. She wasn't being authentic and she wasn't being real. She was nothing like Raichel and she never would be. As if Melissa wanted to be anything like Raichel! From the day they got there, Raichel had been literally pulling the positive energy out of Melissa. But that was only because Melissa was like a toxic disease to Raichel on this journey. "It absolutely breaks my heart to see any woman cry," said The Bachelor. All the girls agreed: he was smokin' hot. "He's perfect. I love his suit. His face," said Raichel. "I never thought I'd fall so quickly for someone," said Ashley. The Bachelor had chosen her for one of the individual dates. The two of them spent the whole night just laughing, connecting, being themselves, just letting go and having fun and living in the moment. Ashley made it easy for The Bachelor to open up: *her* father hadn't been around much either, and it definitely didn't hurt that she looked *amazing*. She *felt* amazing. She felt like a princess. It was a perfect night. A few nights later The Bachelor went on a date with Jackie; "I feel like a princess," she said. But The Bachelor worried she might not ever really let someone in. "Because at the end of the day this is very real," he said. "I know," said Jackie: "I'm here and I see it." She just had trouble making herself vulnerable. That was part of what made Jackie Jackie, unfortunately. The Bachelor wondered if she'd ever be able to throw caution to the wind. Still, they had the time of their lives. She was on cloud nine. It was a perfect night. The bachelorettes were seriously bringing it, and The Bachelor

was well on his way to finding a wife.

The tulips and daffodils have given way to poppies, roses, and, as of yesterday, tiger lilies. Paul built a little one-person swing for our front porch, and a trellis for the grapevine out back, which is thriving. Liza, still the joy of my life—when will you meet her?—is at work on an essay on Virginia Woolf. May your life be as full as mine is feeling these days, *McSweeney's*. Your friend,

ANDREW PALMER
PORTLAND, OR

DEAR MCSWEENEY'S,
This is a strange pet-peeve to have, but I'll say it anyway: The Jonestown Massacre involved Flavor Aid. Not Kool-Aid. It's true. So, from now on, whenever you hear someone say, "Hey, I bet that [so and so] drank the Kool-Aid," I'd like for you to do the following: take that person gently by the elbow, lead him or her to a quiet spot, and then (without malice) say, "It was actually Flavor Aid, not Kool-Aid. An entirely different brand. Okay?" Then lead him or her gently back to the conversation and make sure that before you leave, you hear them say: "Hey, I bet that [so and so] drank the Flavor Aid." Smile. Nod. Walk away. Job well done, sir.

MIKE SACKS
POOLESVILLE, MD

THE GUSHER

by REBECCA CURTIS

Dear Don Abrax,

Hi. How are you?

I imagine that you're staying inside your apartment in this rain. Also, yes! I'm sure you've your extra-large umbrella to keep you dry, should you be forced into the torrent by any particular need—for, say, the Sunday *Times*, or a chicken burrito from Chipotle with extra salsa.

So why am I writing you a letter? I know I could tell you anything I cared to in person. But you're right that sometimes it—talking—is easier for me with a pen in my hand.

And I've been thinking, since our conversation about women who don't like the physical union between a man and a woman, but who, in order to win a husband, will pretend they do, about a woman I forgot to mention: an aspiring Afghan diplomat, with whom I had an impactful encounter when I lived with her in a high-rise on Manhattan's southern tip. I'd like to say up front that the woman represents neither womankind, nor Afghans, nor left-handed red-headed ENFP B-blood-type Aquariuses. Also, given the political and economic upheaval happening in the world now, I'm afraid that to describe something trivial—the trajectory of a schemer who, to boost a career, deceived her fiancé—is tawdry. I've hesitated, too, because this story may make you think poorly of me.

Nonetheless, Don Abrax, I've thought about Cybill a lot lately. I've changed as a person this past year, since meeting you—though most of that has nothing to do with you. I believe I understand Cybill better now. And because, as a talented, hardworking O-blood-type New Yorker of forty-nine who fears being trapped in a loveless union, you asked about deceptive women I know, I'll tell you the story.

When I met Cybill, I was twenty-two years old and starting a master's program in English Literature at New York University. I planned to live on loans, had eighty dollars in cash, and didn't own a credit card. I'd never been to New York City and I aspired to write poetry.

When I arrived, I was determined to find my own housing. The university rates were high—$1,300 a month to share a studio—and I hated sharing. I found a 10' by 10' room with a mattress in a German-client-only realtor's office at Clarkson Street's end, by the water. It was cheap, and once the realtor left, I could use the kitchenette or shower in the tiny bathroom stall. But the realtor worked from nine a.m. to midnight, roaches scuttled through my room, and the two interns, who slept on blankets in the reception area, showered a lot, so the bathroom was always steamy. By day, when they answered the phones, they seemed to sneer at me, and they didn't speak English, so I couldn't befriend them.

Aside from poetry, my guide was my boyfriend, a tall, beautiful African-American JD-soon-to-be-MBA who lived in San Francisco and to whom I spoke, while standing on my fire escape, for an hour each night, using the cordless phone he'd gotten me before I left San Francisco. He was older than me by twelve years, smarter than anyone I'd met, and when I said I might get university housing after all, he said that was a good idea. Isaac was something of a visionary, an Aquarius like Cybill, and his advice and assessments of people and circumstance had always turned out to be correct.

When I first called University Housing, they said it was too late—it was October, the housing was gone. Not a slot left for a mouse, not a bed in any dorm, not a cot. The next day, though, they called back. NYU was expanding—they had hotels in Chelsea, suites in YMCAs, and now studios in a high-rise in Battery Park. That was where they had space, the representative said. One non-smoking spot. I was relieved. Thrilled, even.

One thing, they said. I'd joined the lottery late. The other occupant—the woman—several roommates had already moved out. There'd been complaints.

Just mind your own business, my boyfriend said. You never wanted to be close to a roommate, anyway. I should never eat her food or use her shit, he said. If I minded my own business, I'd win.

When I entered the marble-tiled lobby of the building, dragging my luggage—a suitcase filled with books and two trashbags of clothes—and said "24D" to the doormen, they shook their heads.

"Que lástima," one said. He was slender, with curly hair. His two fellows were tall, slope-bellied, and round-faced, and one had a beard.

The woman in 24D had ousted five roommates in one month, they said. They looked me over. "No offense," one said, "but *you* won't last a week."

I asked the doormen what it was the woman did to make people leave.

Oh, nothing, one said. She was imperious. "Here, grab *this*," he said in a high voice. She was difficult, he said. No one in the building liked her. The other men began to imitate her, too, speaking in that voice as they grabbed my luggage, over my protests that I would carry it myself, and dragged it to the elevator.

* * *

When I entered the room, the first thing I saw was the room: a ruby oriental carpet covered its expanse, and beyond three windows at its end, the Buttermilk Channel and the Statue of Liberty gleamed. By the door was a blue slate-tiled kitchen; in the middle, a loveseat and coffee table faced a mahogany cabinet; near the windows stood two desks, two night tables, and two pillow-topped, ivory-linen-dressed beds.

Cybill sat at the kitchen's breakfast bar. She wore leggings and a tight T-shirt. Maybe she'd been to the gym. Her ginger-red hair was in a ponytail. One yellow-tinged elbow was planted on the counter, and her long fingers held a lit pink cigarette.

She put the cigarette in a dish, stood, walked toward me, smiled carefully, extended her hand in a manly fashion, and said, "Hi, I'm Cybill."

She had a heart-shaped face with high cheekbones, an aquiline nose, broad pink lips, a high forehead, and hazel eyes. She was tall, with small breasts and wide hips. Altogether she was striking, but she walked like a duck.

We shook hands, and I introduced myself. She offered to help with my bags, but I dragged them myself toward the room's far end.

As I put my things away, she said she was an older student: twenty-nine. She'd put herself through college, and studied a lot. She had to earn straight A's to keep her scholarship, and to graduate at the top of her class in order to become a diplomat so that she could help her country. "My country." Those were her words. "I'm Afghan," she said. "My country is Afghanistan." She had grown up in New Jersey, I'd learn, had been to Afghanistan twice in her adult life, and like everybody else on this planet, she was a collection of quarks and energy, a lump of flesh that happened to appear in one spot and would decay and disappear in another. But like so many people, she felt a psychic pull toward whatever she believed was her country.

She spent, she said, her days in the library. "You seem serious," she said. "I think we'll get along."

"Thanks," I said.

She offered tea; I was charmed. I was aware of tensions in Central Asia—my father flew refuelers in the Gulf War—but had little knowledge of individual nations. When Cybill said "Afghan," my head filled with images of long-snouted, fluffy white dogs. When she served tea from a silver pot and delicate, cinnamon-topped biscuits, the tea tasted denser, sweeter than other tea. Later I'd learn it was Lipton's she added cardamom to, the biscuits 79-cent Lieber's from the bodega. When I bought them myself, they tasted like lard. When Cybill served them, they tasted divine.

"I hope you don't mind if I smoke," she said in her low voice, as I ate. "I only smoke *these* cigarettes." She gestured with one. "They don't smell much." She added that she burned incense after, and the smell never lingered. Her disclaimer was baloney—cigarettes are cigarettes—but I acquiesced.

After we'd chatted—I said that I was earning a master's in literature, and Cybill that she kept a neat house—she said, "There's something I haven't mentioned."

Cybill had a secret fiancé; the room was the only place she could see him. Cybill's uncle was the diplomatic liaison to Afghanistan at the United Nations, and Adibe—the fiancé—was a forty-one-year-old Afghan diplomat who worked at the UN, too; but they, Adibe and Cybill, were of *different sects*. When Cybill said *sects* I heard *sexts*. I smirked. Their *sects,* Cybill said, were opposed. Adibe's was conservative. But he was progressive, *for his sect*. The Afghan-American diplomatic community was small, though, and if they were seen together, it would cause political tensions. Adibe came from a well-known family. Cybill couldn't go to his apartment, because his building was rife with Afghans who would gossip.

This month, Adibe was in Kabul. When he came back, he'd be over one or two nights a week, *if* I acquiesced. He might sleep in Cybill's bed, but they wouldn't "do" anything—Cybill blushed—just sleep. Was it okay?

I guessed this had driven the other roommates away—the prospect of a conservative old Arab staying over. But it meant nothing to me. I'm a deep sleeper, and if they fucked in the night, I thought, maybe I'd have better dreams. Also, I believed, if I let Cybill have her *forbidden sext* fiancé stay two nights a week for ten weeks, then when Isaac visited from California, I could ask Cybill to leave, and put him up. Isaac had put me up scores of times, in his place, in hotels, and in friends' empty houses; he'd cooked and shopped for me, and I wanted to host him.

"No problem," I said.

*   *   *

Ignore them, Isaac said. I was sitting in the gigantic walk-in closet. It was exactly 10' by 10' and had a ceiling light. I liked to talk on the phone there, or read books in its corners after Cybill went to bed.

All this shit about *sects*—Isaac didn't buy that. Cybill had some reason for wanting her fiancé to come over while I was home, he said. Whatever it was, I should focus on my studies.

Her real name was Basira, she told me. But it sounded like *basura*, and in middle school, all the other kids called her "trash." At fourteen, she changed her name to Cybill, because she loved *Moonlighting* and its star, Cybill Shepherd—the coolest actress on TV.

I don't recall how her father came up. I must have asked whether her parents still lived in New Jersey, because I remember her saying, while seated at the breakfast bar, that her mother and father were separated. Her parents married young, she said, because they were in love. Cybill's father had been secular, at the time. Soon after, he became religious. He made Cybill's mother quit school, wear a veil, and follow Islamic codes. When Cybill was six years old, her mother called Cybill's uncle for help; the uncle wasn't rich, but his assistance allowed the two of them to move to America and find an apartment in New Jersey. Cybill's mother had worked in a clothing factory for twenty-two years now. That was why Cybill had to succeed—to help her mother. Also, so she could help her country. Afghanistan's government had changed from secular to religious, the Taliban had *ruined* it, and Cybill wanted to help change it back.

I asked her if she ever spoke to her father. She said no; not since she was six.

She was her mother's only child. Her mother had not dated since leaving Afghanistan. Cybill volunteered all this information. All I did was ask about her father and it came out, like a fountain.

*   *   *

If I didn't obey Isaac's strictures, it wasn't entirely my fault. Cybill bombarded me with invitations—to come to the library, to get lunch, give blood, hit the gym. Also, I'm attracted to anything foreign. I grew up in New Hampshire, whose inhabitants were largely repulsive to me, being ham-hock-colored, narrow-faced, dull-minded, and having narrow interests and ranges of thought. They were certain of themselves and aspired only to own a home, have kids, drive a better car than their neighbor's, vacation in Bermuda, and ensure that every winter they skied. Cybill's considerations of life extended beyond her own good, and if they were silly and deluded, they were also compelling.

She was open-armed in other ways, too. I was welcome to borrow her clothes, she said; my breasts were bigger but—she looked me over and spoke in her low, frank voice—she thought most of what she had would fit me. She made big batches when she cooked, basmati rice and Chicken Sib Chalow or Quorma, and said she could never finish the pot. "Just take what you want," she said.

It felt rude to refuse *everything.* So I tried some chicken, when she asked me to, and agreed to study in Battery Park one afternoon.

In the park, she lay on her stomach in shorts and a white tank, stared at a tome, and highlighted. But sporadically she'd flop over, observe the taffy-like clouds passing through the blue sky above the grass, and say something like, "Who's your fantasy guy that you would get together with if you could have anyone?" Hers was George Clooney.

"Who's George Clooney?" I said.

She pushed her book aside. Propped herself on her elbow.

"You don't know who George *Clooney* is? Haven't you seen *ER?*"

I had not.

I would love *ER*, she said. She and her mother watched it together, and they *both* loved George Clooney.

What about Adibe? I asked.

All around us, students picnicked on the grass. Joggers ran by on the promenade. Ivana Trump's yacht was parked at the pier. The tangy smell of shish kebab wafted from the vendors.

"I love Adibe," Cybill said, in a low voice. And, she continued, she'd never cheat on him. But it was okay to fantasize. Say she met George Clooney at a party. He could do anything to her, even—she said a phrase.

I looked at my textbook, a treatise on Beat Poets.

I'd understand if I saw *ER*, Cybill said. She yawned, flexed her long cadmium-gold body on the blanket, and rubbed a finger down her aquiline nose. George Clooney played a doctor, she said. He had this handsome face and big brown eyes. Watching him, she wanted to be sick, so he could operate.

I didn't like white guys, I said. At least not Christians.

She shrugged. Neither did she, she said. But George Clooney was different. He was manlier than most white guys. Also tanner. Maybe he *went* tanning, she conceded. But he was the best actor. She'd show me *ER* sometime.

I liked my boyfriend, I told Cybill. I didn't care about celebrities.

"Me neither," Cybill said. "Just George Clooney."

For thirty minutes, I read about the whiskey-drowned life of Allen Ginsberg.

She remarked to the sky that she'd had girlfriends in college with whom she'd used to study, just like this.

I said nothing.

She meant, she continued, that they'd take blankets and snacks, and study together each day in the park, on the grass.

I read about Richard Brautigan's suicide.

"Have you ever made out with a girl?" Cybill said.

I said I hadn't.

She had, she said. She and a friend had French-kissed while studying, to ensure that when they made out with boyfriends, they'd get it right. "Nothing serious," she said. "Just making out."

I told her that I'd never practiced kissing with a study partner and had no interest.

"Well I wasn't *suggesting* anything," Cybill said, her voice nasal.

Later that week, I entered the apartment to find a man drinking my orange juice. He was stocky, perhaps 5'9", with broad shoulders, a square face and jaw, and a plump underpad, signaling that he might go to fat. He had olive skin and a mop of black hair I assume he dyed. He set my juice carton on the counter and yelled in Pashto at Cybill.

She yelled something back—jabbed a finger at the map of Central Asia and the Middle East that she'd taped above her bed—the man shouted angry words—shook his head—Cybill uttered apologetic sounds, and the man put the carton to his mouth and chugged.

"Hello," Cybill said. "We're discussing politics."

I nodded and went to my desk.

"When we talk politics, we speak in Pashto," Cybill said anxiously. "It's easier."

"Speak away," I said. "Use any language you want."

"Adibe," Cybill said. "This is Cassandra."

"Hello," Adibe said. He nodded in my direction; I noticed his face looked like a frog's, probably because it had a green tint. His mouth turned down at the corners. He was bow-legged.

"Cassandra studies poetry," Cybill said.

"Very nice," Adibe said, in the tone one might say, "Very displeasing." He sat down at Cybill's desk and opened a book. "I like Rumi," he said.

When he left, Cybill seemed relieved.

There were problems in their country, she said. Adibe dealt with disasters every day at the UN.

I assured Cybill that he'd been polite, as he had—although privately, I was upset he'd drunk my juice, because it was expensive.

Thereafter, six nights a week, I'd come home from class to find Adibe reading at Cybill's desk. He farted and burped a normal amount, but he often drank my juice, and when he was hungry he'd say "Basira, I'm hungry," and Cybill would say, "What would you like to eat?"

She'd list dishes she could serve, he'd assent to one, and she'd make it and bring it to him.

The first time this happened, she told him Sib Chalow with chicken and basmati rice was available, and he nodded eagerly, but when she opened the pot, it was gone. I'd taken to eating her chicken dishes, and this had been a good batch. I'd eaten it for lunch and dinner five days running. Cybill was one of those B-blood types who have suppressed self-hatred and continually cook the one meat that for them is poison—chicken—and then, when it's ready, take a few bites, feel sick, and conclude that because the meat makes them feel ill they must have cooked it badly. Cybill, I'd learned, cooked enormous batches of rice and chicken every week, and never ate them. She always said that she wasn't a good cook, that her chicken tasted unsavory, that I should taste *her mother's Lamb Kabuli Palow*, and that someday she'd make me a real Afghan meal, and every week I ate her chicken. But I hadn't banked on Adibe. When Cybill said, "It's all gone," his face darkened.

Cybill added brightly, "I guess it went faster than usual!"

Adibe looked confused; then he looked at me. He glowered.

"There's plenty of *rice*," Cybill said. "I've got eggs. I'll make you—" she named some Pashto word.

Adibe said he didn't want the Pashto word. He wanted chicken. An argument ensued. At length Cybill cooked him a different word, which he ate.

When she asked, I told Cybill that Adibe's living with us was fine. I did this for one reason: Isaac was coming to New York soon, and I still believed that my letting Cybill's *secret opposite-sext fiancé* stay over for forty-plus nights was the equivalent of Cybill's vacating for two. This assessment seemed so reasonable that I saw no need to specify it.

When Adibe was over, I went in the closet to speak on the phone, and studied there because I liked it. Whenever I emerged to make tea, Cybill and Adibe would be reading. When I emerged again at midnight, the room would be dark and one motionless lump would be in Cybill's bed. By the time I woke, they would be gone.

As for my "work," I attended classes and studied. I'm not sure now why I wanted to write poetry, except that I liked the poetry of the ancient Japanese courtesans, who were always lamenting seasons, and that of the ancient Greek poetesses, who hated life, humanity, and men; also, I was unable to express my feelings, and the syllabic, metric, and length requirements I imposed upon myself guaranteed that I'd never have to. What

I wrote was obtuse, elliptical, and over-metaphored. Once Cybill asked to see some of my poems. I was nervous to show them to her, but I had a few my classmates had called "okay." I gave them to Cybill. I went into the closet. When I came out, the papers were on my desk. Cybill had her spectacles on.

"I didn't like them," she said.

I nodded.

"Here," she smiled. "I'll show you *real* poetry." She crossed the room and handed a hardcover to me. It was Rumi.

I never saw Cybill's work—the thesis she was writing about conflict resolution in the Middle East—or bothered to ask for details. I know she attended talks given by political luminaries, over and above those required by her studies, and assiduously read several newspapers. I was impressed by her dedication to something so complex.

I'd set my stuff up in the—what I thought of as "The Hotel Room," because of its oriental rug and damask drapes—quickly. I had no jewelry and few talismans. From my grandmother a quilt, from Isaac the cordless phone and a stereo with tiny but powerful speakers. I've been accused, in my life, of being autistic—I don't cry at funerals or weddings or during crises in relationships. Perhaps because I am, like you, Don Abrax, an INTJ. But on my desk I placed one framed shot of my brothers and one of Isaac. The one of Isaac was of him about to take his shirt off, lifting it up so you could see his abs. I'd found it among his things. He was smiling in the picture. You could see his dimples. I didn't think twice about putting the photo on my desk.

Night after night, I studied in the closet while Adibe argued in Pashto with Cybill. To me their arguments sounded like:

Gibberish, Gibberish, Hezbollah! Gibberish, medical supplies, Gaza Strip! Gibberloo, embargo, Gibberish, Palestinian Authority, Taliban! Gibberish, Gibberish, Gibberish, Gibberish.

Listening to them made me ashamed. I was aware that people suffered, that my worries were insular, my thoughts ignorant, the losses I'd suffered in my life tiny in the cosmic scheme.

His name is A-Dweeb, Isaac said, when I tried to describe their fights to him. Isaac also suggested that I tell Cybill to tell Adibe not to come over. We could rent a hotel room when he came. There was no need for me to suffer through weeks of A-Dweeb just so the two of us could stay for one weekend at 95 Battery Place.

At the same time, I knew he'd be pleased if I put him up.

I don't mind it, I said.

If I had critiques of Cybill, she had hers of me. What were these bloody tissues in the trash? she asked, and I admitted I had residual bloody nose from doing cocaine with Isaac in San Francisco. She hoped I didn't *still*, she said. I didn't, I said—Isaac and I had given it up. What, she asked, would I do with a degree in poetry? Secretly, I believed I'd write a book of poems and sell it for $50,000. This money would fund me for several years, and I'd write a second, similarly successful, book of poetry.

Teach, I told her.

Cybill nodded, but her face was skeptical, even fearful.

Didn't I need a PhD, she asked, to teach?

Yes, I said. I might get one, I added.

The first time I found the picture of Isaac on my desk turned toward the wall, I was confused. I guessed the maid had placed it backward by accident after dusting. The second time I came home and Isaac faced the wall, I was annoyed. I asked Cybill why she'd done it. She waved her hand as if swatting a fly. No reason, she said; looking at it made her uncomfortable. She'd meant to turn it *back* around before I came home; she'd forgotten.

Why, I asked, did the picture make her uncomfortable?

She stacked texts on her desk. It just *did*, she said. He was taking his shirt off; she didn't want to have to see his chest. How would I like it, she asked, if Adibe walked around when I was home with *his* shirt off?

I blunk. He had, once, post-shower. His chest was hairy, fleshy, wet—who cared? It'd been Cybill who'd frowned. A line had appeared between her eyebrows. She'd said, "Adibe! Cover up!" He'd looked surprised, said, "What?" his eyes wide. I'd liked him, in that moment, for the first time.

"We can all see your chest," Cybill said, "and no one wants to."

Adibe had put a shirt on. I reminded Cybill of this. Oh yes, she replied; but she'd *stopped* him.

When I found Isaac turned around once again, I was exasperated; but Cybill apologized. She'd gotten used to the picture, she said, and didn't mind it now at all; she'd moved it because Adibe had come over to see her while I was at my seminar, and she didn't want Adibe to think the picture watched them while they had sex. She wanted to show Adibe respect.

"She unsettle you yet?" the shorter doorman asked me once. Whenever I walked through the lobby, the three of them would grin at me.

I shook my head.

Did he remember the morning—the bearded one poked him—when she'd walked out with the umbrella, and it was supposed to be sunny all day?

The short one demurred.

It *poured* later, the bearded one said. *Poured*. A real *gusher*.

Occasionally we were both home during lunch, and one day Cybill asked me what I thought of Adibe.

I said he seemed nice.

I should give my full, frank opinion, she said. She wanted to know: did I find him attractive?

That was all it took to break down my courtesy.

I said, "He looks like a frog."

Please note, Don Abrax, that I'm not saying all Afghan men look like frogs. I happen to find most Middle Eastern men attractive—but Adibe must have been froglike, because when I said it Cybill looked down at her flip-flops, then said he *did*.

I felt confused.

Did she mean, I asked, that she wasn't attracted to him?

Not *physically*, she said. What she admired about Adibe was his intelligence and his capacity for working hard.

I asked: didn't she want to date someone she was attracted to?

Cybill lit a cigarette. The Afghan diplomatic community in New York City was small, she said. She had to marry well, to succeed in her career, and she preferred to date and marry someone *like her*: someone Afghan. Adibe treated her better than past boyfriends had. She displayed her diamond ring: it was *clear*, she said; no flaws. She and Adibe understood each other intellectually and philosophically. The physical wasn't the most important aspect of a relationship. She didn't like sex much, to be honest. Adibe would be—I remember every drop of her modulated voice saying this, as if it were liquid gold falling into a pitcher—*an important man* someday. Plus, she loved him.

Okay, I said.

"But I don't get excited with him," Cybill said.

I looked at the clock, and decided to head to school early.

Cybill walked to the window. In order to get her excited, she said conversationally, he had to use her *thing* on her.

Hastily, I tossed books into my bag.

She got it out of her desk drawer and insisted on showing it to me. It was a flat black disk. She made me hold it against my palm. When you flipped a switch, it vibrated.

Cybill made Adibe use it on her, she said—or, if she knew he was coming over, she'd use it herself secretly, to prepare for his visit. Otherwise she wasn't at all—her word—excited.

I gave her the disk back.

Did I want to know, she asked me, the number-one guaranteed way to make a man fall in love with me?

I shrugged. I didn't, particularly.

She lowered her head, inhaled deeply through her nose, and said, "Tell him he makes you feel good."

I said something incredulous.

"Trust me," she said. She sat on her desk. She cradled the black disk in her hands. "I have married friends, I've talked to other women, and I've read books." She stared at me, her hazel eyes wide. "You never pressure them, never ask for a ring, never nag. Just say 'You make me feel good.' Men are flattered by that. It makes them love you." She paused. "You have to say it after sex—'You make me feel so good.' And sometimes when you're hanging out, just say casually, 'I feel good when I'm with you.'"

"Really?" I said.

She nodded.

"Does Adibe make you feel good?"

She stroked the disk. "No. I told you. I don't get excited at all. And sometimes he makes me depressed."

I zipped up my backpack, walked to the closet, and put on my coat.

Her desk drawer opened and closed.

What about me, Cybill wanted to know. Did I... *have* anything?

I slung my backpack over my shoulder. Sure, I told her. But I didn't use it.

Cybill looked at Isaac's picture.

"And I know that's your..."

"What?" I said.

Nothing, she said. She was just surprised that I had a black boyfriend. I seemed to have a good head on my shoulders. She was open-minded; she wasn't racist. But black people thought differently and had different traditions. She wouldn't date a black guy, she told me. It was her culture.

"That's fine," I said. "You don't have to."

Then I told Cybill that Isaac was coming to visit soon. He missed me, and he'd found a cheap last-minute ticket, I said. I asked if she'd stay across the hall, in a friend's room, for two nights, when Isaac came.

Her eyebrows knit. She didn't know, she said. She'd never asked *me* to leave...

I waited.

She'd think about it, she said.

*　　*　　*

So maybe you're right, Don Abrax, that attraction between two people is always destined, with familiarity and time, to dwindle and die, and that women angle for security in relationships by feigning fondness that is no longer there. I've polled my married friends, and certainly none of them have much sex. But I have come to think our society's notions of romantic compatibility, in whatever sense—personality, passions, outlook, sympathies, habits, hobbies, blood type—are trite. Maybe it's difference (among other things) that keeps attraction alive. At least in the case of Cybill, she wasn't bloodless; she was more complicated.

I should, at this point in my story—which is only for you, Don Abrax—admit two embarrassing circumstances around my relationship with Isaac, which may have affected the impact of his visit to New York City to see me.

I'd spent the previous summer with friends, two lesbian couples, in San Francisco. Our plan was to live together—one woman's father owned a temp agency that shuffled out well-paid gigs. This was how I'd make rent. But when we arrived in town, there were no three-bedrooms available, and the temp agency rejected me because I failed the Microsoft Word tests and couldn't type. I found a room in an apartment with strangers, and after getting rejected from three waitressing jobs, got a job delivering artisanal pizzas. I liked the job. I had a little white Beamer, an '87 convertible I'd bought from an out-of-work actor for $2,500—"car money," the last gift, my father said, he'd ever get me; he warned me against the Beamer, saying it would break down and I'd never be able to fix it—and I loved driving that thing around San Francisco. I never bought a road map. I liked to get lost. I made the pizza place give me directions and tried, through the city's twisted streets, to follow them—it was like a game. The pizza place sold pan pizzas—four inches of gourmet cheese and heirloom tomatoes, with toppings like smoked venison and pheasant sausage—for $20 to $30 each. I wore a white lab coat with the pizzeria's name on it—*Zelda's*—but otherwise I could work in T-shirt and jeans. Something about driving around the hills and crazy, senseless roads of San Francisco satisfied my inexplicable loneliness that summer. My hair was always a mess from driving top-down. I often got tipped $20, even when I arrived late. I was young, it was 1998.

Silicon Valley was booming. Lots of guys who'd ordered a pizza asked me if I felt like taking a break and having a slice with them, in a friendly way, and I always demurred—I hate pizza—and drove away feeling like I was experiencing a lesson about the essential isolation of each mottled example of humanity.

Isaac was such a guy. I carried his pizza up his front steps, and he came to the screen door wearing a T-shirt and gray sweats, his fat orange cat pushing its head against his leg. I remember thinking he was good-looking, for a black guy—and that's not even why I'm ashamed. He invited me in casually, pointing to the pizza—a half joke—and I declined. Was on the job, I said. Needed to earn money for grad school, where I was headed in the fall.

He later said he fell in love with me then, seeing me there in my black dress—I'd been out of clean shirts and wore a loose scoop neck, a $15 Gap sale-rack job one of the lesbians had given me, and the night was so nice I'd left my lab coat in the car.

What did I make an hour, he asked, delivering pizzas?

$8, I said, plus tips.

So he offered me $40 an hour to sit with him while he ate. It was Sunday and he'd read textbooks all day, hadn't spoken to another human being; he could use company, he said. I protested that if I stayed, I'd get in trouble with my boss; he said I could say I got stuck in traffic. He seemed pleasant, and if he wanted—and I did find it pathetic—to pay me $40 an hour to chat with him, I didn't see why not. We chatted; he told me about his current work, and I told him about my aspirations in poetry. He told me about the white yuppie woman who'd gotten pregnant on purpose with his son, for whom he now paid for a "manny" and private school in London. I'm not sure how to express that we simply got along. I was interested in what he had to say, and I felt—it's a horrible cliché, but "alive," talking to him, because of his unusual way of thinking. For example, when the English "manny" refused to give his seven-year-old son a shoulder ride, Isaac's son said, "You're *paid* to do that"—something Isaac had told him to say. Yet, I soon learned, he was polite to waitstaff, cabbies, and maids, and he gave money to homeless men. He could be intractable. When he threw a barbecue so I could meet his friends, he only had two, and one was the next-door neighbor. He told me he'd gotten a perfect LSAT score, even though he'd smoked pot the night before and only taken one practice test, and that the test company made him retake a section to prove he hadn't cheated. When, after three years of doing well at a law firm, he overheard two partners say he'd never make partner, he quit the next day and signed up for an MBA. He loved technology. When he took me to work with him in Palo Alto, his excitement about the product—a cell phone that could check email—was palpable. Did I want one? he asked. He could get me one, he said, his huge brown eyes wide, his arms around me. It was going to be big, he said. He was director of business technology, or something like that.

No thanks, I told him. In the end he got me the cordless phone instead, and a CD player with tiny but very powerful speakers. I didn't care about technology. But I trusted him. He gave good advice. When I told him about my father's rage fits, he said he wished he could be a fly on the wall—because it sounded funny. I liked him because I didn't ever have to censor my thoughts with him, and his mind was as fast as a machine.

At the end of that first hour, he wrote me a check. The next two nights in a row, he ordered a pizza, requested that I deliver it, and paid me to stay and chat. On the third night, he walked me to the door, took me in his arms, and asked if I wanted to return later, and I decided that I did. I drove to his place most nights after that. He wanted me to move in with him, but I wouldn't. I had six weeks before I left for New York. We were happy, the things we did together weren't even datey—I shopped with him for shoes for his son, we went to the gym, had sex, made food, went out to eat, slept. Sometimes we drove north to Bodega Bay or Santa Rosa, or south to Monterey, where we stayed in bed-and-breakfasts or hotels, shopped in the local squares, ate at road stands and cafés, and went swimming.

The problem—the part that I am ashamed of, and which may have factored in events to follow—occurred when I deposited Isaac's third check. It bounced. I couldn't understand this. He was meticulous about balanced checkbooks. When I queried Isaac about it, he said he must have accidentally removed some funds from that account. But he didn't offer to write a new check. I asked if he would. Yes, he said gruffly. But he'd have to do it later;

he was out of checks. I felt embarrassed for him. Of course I'm appalled, now, that I asked. I see that having one's girlfriend ask for back pay for chatting could twist like a worm in the gut. Everything seemed cut and dry to me, at the time—the pizza-girl transaction separate from the interlude that followed. At any rate, I soon forgot about it.

The other incident was that he asked me to marry him, before I left town. He took me to dinner, and afterward, he sunk to one knee in the grass outside the restaurant, held up a closed, blue-velvet box, and spoke. I was shocked, but Isaac was more so.

He said, "Oh my *God*."

I said, busy being surprised, "What?"

He looked up at me.

"You just got such a look of horror—of revulsion, of *disgust*," he said, "on your face. I've never *seen* a look like that."

I felt angry at my face. "Yes," I said. "My answer is yes." I'm not sure why I said yes, since at that point I'd never loved anyone, not a single person in my life; but I liked Isaac better than anyone I'd met, and had the sense I was about to lose something good. "Show me the ring, please," I said.

It was too late. Isaac pocketed the box, refused to show me the contents, and said his question had been *a test* and that the box contained not a ring, but a note saying, *This is a test*. We never spoke of marriage again.

With the advent of Isaac's coming, Cybill got testy. She'd noticed I'd worn her red silk tank, she said, and my breasts had *stretched it*; the shirt cost $900 and was the only designer piece she owned. In future, she'd be pleased if I'd not stretch it. I would appreciate it, I told her, if Adibe didn't drink my orange juice.

Cybill said she hadn't known he did. But if so, didn't I eat the chicken she made? Didn't we have a shared kitchen? I did eat her chicken, I said, but her mother bought it by the twenty-pound bag at Costco—the juice, I bought myself from the expensive deli. Adibe should chip in a few bucks a week for juice, I said. Cybill had never *heard*, she said, of anything so petty. Making a fuss over orange juice—incredible.

She was in the right, of course—I did eat her chicken.

"Don't eat her chicken," Isaac said on the phone. "Christ, I *told* you. Why were you eating her food? We're getting a hotel when I come, that's it." He was an adult, he said, and didn't have time for squabbles. "Listen," he went on. "She's a foreign Afghan bitch. She doesn't think like you think." To be honest, he said, she was *beating me*. I was lying there every night while beside me she pleasured herself with a vibrating doorknob so she could hump her frog, in the *hopes* I'd get two nights of privacy in my own place.

"Stay away from her," Isaac said. "Don't eat her chicken."

The next day I told Cybill that we should have separate food.

"Okay," she said, her face blank. "If that's how you want it. No dirt off my shoulders."

But the day after that, she made a request: her mother was coming from New Jersey to visit for a week—a surprise visit—and needed to stay in the room. Cybill looked glum. She'd have to entertain her mom, though she needed to study. She realized it was an imposition. If I agreed, Cybill's mom would sleep on the loveseat. They'd go out every day. Her mother, who somehow had never done it, wanted to ride to the top of the Empire State Building and visit the Statue of Liberty.

Cybill waited.

I'd be happy to have her mother stay, I said, *if*, when Isaac came, Cybill would vacate—completely—for two days. Normally I *liked* guests, and would have been happy to have Cybill's mother stay. But I saw opportunity.

Okay, Cybill said; she would try.

Not "try," I said—do.

Fine, she said. But she wanted me to know it would be hard on her. Because of her tests.

I was sorry to hear that, I said. But surely in her friend's apartment across the hall, she could study.

She looked at me limpidly. She had her hair in a ponytail, and was in leggings and one of her cutoff shirts.

She had one, tiny, request, she said. Would I mind taking my picture of Isaac down? Her mother was conservative, and she wanted her to think well of me.

I was taken aback.

I hoped her mother liked me too, I said. But I wouldn't take down Isaac's picture.

That night, while walking through Washington Square, I heard a man hiss, "Dime bag." When my friends said it meant "pot," I was thrilled, because I'd never realized pot was so cheap. I told the man I'd take fifteen. When he said that "dime" meant "ten dollars," I was too embarrassed not to buy one. I normally wouldn't have, because ten dollars meant something to me, and I'd never smoked pot. When Isaac called, though, he was pleased—he hadn't smoked it in years, he said—so I hoped I'd done something right.

Cybill's mother was a short, plump, gray-haired lady who little resembled tall, red-haired Cybill, and who made clear, through gestures and mono-syllabic words, that she was pleased her daughter had a good roommate. "Other girls *bad*," she said, referring to the five roommates Cybill had done in before me. She held my hands in hers. "Thank you for taking care my daughter," she said.

As promised, Cybill and her mother were gone much of the week.

Only one portentous thing happened during Cybill's mother's visit. The two of them were watching the Arab news stations together, cheering at reports of turbulence in the West Bank; I was surprised, as Cybill was sophisticated and advocated peaceful solutions to conflicts, but I guessed her mother's presence influenced her. Cybill encouraged me to sit with them, which I did, to be polite, and after a bit, she put on a video of her belly dancing with twelve cousins during a visit to Afghanistan—they danced on a stage in shiny, voluminous gowns. And then it was back to TV, and for some reason the video of the police chasing O.J. Simpson through Los Angeles in his Bronco was on. Cybill seemed bizarrely excited by it.

"Go, O.J., go!!!" Cybill yelled at the TV.

"O.J.'s *hot*," she said. "I'd be his woman."

Cybill's mother and I stared at her, shocked.

"Cybill," Cybill's mother said. "O.J. BAD man. BAD."

"O.J.'s a GOOD man!" Cybill yelled. "I'm for O.J.!"

"He killed his wife, you know," I said.

Cybill's mother nodded vigorously.

Cybill leaned forward on the loveseat. The fingers of her long hands clasped her knees. The Bronco surged forward.

"Nicole Simpson? That wench? *I* don't care. She *deserved* to die. She cheated on O.J. with Ron Goldman!"

"O.J.," Cybill told the TV, "if *I* were your woman, I would never cheat!"

"Cybill," Cybill's mother said. "O.J. *bad* man! *George Clooney* good man! O.J. bad!"

Cybill didn't look away from the screen.

The Bronco leapt two red lights.

"George Clooney's a peaceful shmuck!" Cybill yelled. "I'm with *O.J.*!"

I didn't know why Cybill was acting crazy; I gathered books for class. But as I walked toward the door, Cybill's mother's hand gripped my arm and squeezed hard.

"*You* think O.J. good?" she said.

I said I did not.

Cybill's mother stared at Isaac's picture on my desk. I saw the white hairs sprouted above her upper lip and smelled her breath: yogurt, yeast. "O.J. BAD," she said. "George Clooney *better*." She patted me.

During her mother's visit, Cybill didn't mention Adibe once—even to me, while her mother slept. I supposed she was a good actress, able to store inconvenient feelings until the time and place would arrive when they could be released.

Her mother never made Lamb Kabuli Palow. But one morning after they'd left to go clothes-shopping, I found a piece of toast with melted mozzarella and basil sprinkled on top on the kitchen counter, and even though I knew it wasn't mine and I don't like cheese, I ate it; in part I think because as I'd lain in bed that morning, I'd heard Cybill and her mother chatting happily as they readied themselves for their day, and something about their chatter made me sad. Later, when I confessed to Cybill that I'd eaten her cheese-toast, she said with a certain condescension that the toast had been *mine*. Her mother had left it for me.

When Isaac arrived, a week later, he conceded that the room was better than a hotel. Cybill had taken the books, clothes, and toiletries she needed across the hall, and the only sign of her was the big Middle East map above her bed. To celebrate, we pushed my bed next to hers and made them face the TV.

After a while the first "disaster" happened. I'd bought filet mignon, fresh pasta, leafy greens, Scotch, avocados, everything Isaac liked, and planned to cook. But Isaac knew I was a bad cook; he was tired from his flight, he said, and hungry. He wanted good food served quickly. I could cook for him the next night, he added more kindly. So we took a cab to Beekman's, a steakhouse where he'd always wanted to eat. The restaurant was empty, but our orders weren't taken for thirty minutes. The food took another hour to arrive; by then the two white couples who'd entered after us had eaten, paid, and left. Isaac's steak came bloody, though he'd asked for well-done. Our waiter was an old man—tall, British, dignified. Isaac felt we'd been treated poorly because he was African American and with me, a white woman. I thought the delay coincidental, and said so. I wasn't sure what else to say. He seemed upset.

When we got back to the apartment, I made tea, trying to make it as Cybill did; Isaac placed pot-rolling supplies on the coffee table and showed me how to pick the nubbies out of the pot. It was midnight by the time we were stretched out on the loveseat, watching TV, and a knock fell on the door.

Isaac looked at me.

"Did you order something?" he said.

I studied him. I knew him to be devious, fully capable of any number of things. "Did *you* order something?" I said.

His big brown eyes went wide. His hands spread in the air. "No," he said. "Not *me.*"

The knock came again.

Isaac said I'd better answer it. It was my place, he said.

I shrugged. I just didn't know who it could be, I said.

Isaac flipped channels on the TV; he wasn't happy with anything he'd found. We could ignore the knocking, he said. If I wanted to. Did I want him to answer it?

No, I told him. It was my house. I'd get it.

I walked through the room, past the kitchen to the heavy front door.

I opened it.

Cybill wore a gauzy blue negligee. Her gingery red hair was down. The robe over her negligee was sheer, and I could see the nipples on her high, sideways-pointed breasts.

"I'm sorry to bother you," she said with quiet dignity. "I realized I forgot my blow-dryer."

I asked her to repeat herself; I was furious that she'd broken our agreement.

She needed to dry her hair in the morning, she said, before she went to class; if I wouldn't mind, she would just enter the room, grab her blow-dryer, and leave.

I let her in. I went to the couch. Cybill went into the bathroom and emerged with the blow-dryer. Then she approached the couch.

"I got my blow-dryer," she said.

I stared at her.

Isaac was reclined on the loveseat, his long legs stretched forward, wearing sweats. He seemed relaxed for the first time that night.

I felt, with Cybill standing in front of us, that I had to introduce her to Isaac. I supplied the barest introductions, just gave each the other's name. Cybill put the blow-dryer down on the coffee table, stuck out her hand, her breasts swinging under the negligee, and said, "Nice to meet you."

She asked Isaac if he'd come from San Francisco; he said he had. She asked about his flight; he answered, still watching the TV behind her, and me.

I remarked that Cybill had her blow-dryer. She nodded, picked it up, thanked me for allowing her to fetch it, and said she'd leave. She assessed the room, the two beds pushed together and the nubbies and ashtray on the table.

"What are you doing?" she said.

"We're smoking pot," I said.

Then I did a foolish thing; something pushed me; I believe it was a dratted New England mandate that had been drilled into me from an early age, to feed guests. My father put NO HUNTING signs for miles around our woods in fall, evicted bikers who camped in our hayfields, and ordered tourists who'd stopped to photograph the view from our hill to drive on, but whenever strangers got stuck in a blizzard and knocked on our door, he always let them in, and fed them. I was exasperated, expected her to refuse. I said, "Would you like some?"

Soon Cybill was high as a kite, sitting next to Isaac on a chair she'd pulled up, chatting—she was glad we'd invited her to smoke a joint, she hadn't had one in years, hadn't realized how she'd needed to relax, this was fun—and with each point she made, she placed her hand on Isaac's arm. I don't remember what was discussed; I only recall Isaac relaxed on the couch, watching Cybill in her negligee move toward him, with an expression of I-am-enjoying-this-negligeed-woman-with-her-nipples-pointing-SE-and-SW-leaning-over-me-but-it-is-not-my-fault-and-I-am-not-lifting-a-finger-so-do-not-be-angry-at-me. Soon two hours had passed, Cybill claimed to be hot, took off her robe, and then, with girlish enthusiasm, offered to show us the belly dance she'd learned in Afghanistan.

Isaac looked at me.

I suppose I wanted to see her embarrass herself, or else to see a belly dance; I said, "Okay."

She stood up slowly from her chair and walked to the room's middle. She faced us. Her shoulders dropped. She seemed nervous, and I pitied her. Isaac and I watched from the couch. Cybill frowned, looked to her right and her left, then announced that she needed music, and put on her Cousins video. The twelve cousins in their voluminous, shiny gowns appeared on the TV screen. Cybill stood in the middle of the room once more. Strident lutes played from the television's speakers. Slowly, awkwardly, Cybill's hips rotated under her negligee. She craned around to watch the screen. When she turned toward us, her mouth quivered. Her hips moved more quickly. Isaac watched from the couch, face blank. His hands rested on his knees. Cybill looked down at her hips, frowned, moved them in a weird fast circle, then looked up at Isaac. She said, "Do you like this?"

He shrugged: "Sure."

Cybill glanced at the screen. Her cousins' voluminous gowns had come off; they now wore tasseled bras and low-slung, shiny pants. In a flash, Cybill's fingers went up to her shoulders: her negligee fell off. Her small yellow breasts bobbed; she wore a blue T-string. I was shocked. I'm not sure why, but I was: I stood up, red in the face—a cold New England square, I suppose—and said, "You have to leave."

It wasn't that I'm against the things that happen between a man and a woman—or even a man and two women. But—as I essentially already told you, Don Abrax—when I find one of the few things I feel is valuable in life, I get possessive. I hate sharing.

Cybill stood stubbornly. She looked at Isaac.

"Isaac wants me to stay," she said. "Don't you, Isaac?"

He didn't blink.

He said, in his deep voice, that it was up to me.

"You need to leave," I said. "Isaac wants you to leave."

Cybill's face turned pink.

"Isaac," she said. "Do *you* want me to leave?"

He glanced at me then, his huge brown eyes boyish, slight color on his brown skin, his high cheekbones and expressive lips tinged—that face that I sometimes could die for. Cybill watched him, shoulders lowered, chin up, hands loose at her sides.

"If Cassandra wants you to leave," he said, "then I want you to leave."

Cybill turned red. She looked at the clock, exclaimed surprise; stated how important it was for her to study, thanked us for the pot, and left.

We went to sleep; not before I accused Isaac of failing to oust Cybill. He became angry, saying I was blaming him for failing to do what I should have done myself. In the morning I tried to cook Isaac breakfast, and burned the fried eggs, then put sugar in them to make them taste better; Isaac said the eggs tasted shitty, as if someone put sugar in them. I said

I *had* put sugar in them, and he told me no one puts sugar in eggs. I replied that I'd never made eggs before, and he got angry, saying he'd lied about finding a cheap plane ticket, that the ticket to see me had cost $1,800, and he hadn't paid $1,800 so I could experiment on him. We walked to a breakfast buffet. At the buffet he encouraged me to take twelve packets of Equal, to which I was addicted, and put them in my purse; "You like them," he kept saying, "here, take them, stock up, put 'em in your purse," but the instant I'd done so, the tall, white-haired maître d' came over and said, "Ma'am, you cannot put those in your purse; they are for *use*, not for stealing." After I put them back, red-faced, Isaac said he'd *told* me not to steal; did I *see* what I'd done? Whereupon I accused him again of encouraging Cybill to stay in the room, and he said "Take some responsibility"—*I'd* opened the door and let her in, *I'd* offered her pot, *I'd* failed to send her away. Sure, he said, he would have slept with her if I'd let him—he wasn't particularly attracted to her, but he could have done it. Instead, he'd done nothing.

At least, I said, it was over. We'd have two days of peace.

We returned, through fog and bay-mist, to the apartment, mired in our shallow woes, and decided to take a nap, then go shopping. Isaac needed a suit. He had job interviews back home coming up.

The phone rang.

It was Cybill.

We needed to talk, she said. She couldn't stay away from the room another night; Isaac and I had to leave.

I told her we'd made an agreement.

She wasn't asking, she said.

I refused.

Isaac and I should get a hotel, she said.

I told her I'd put chairs against the door; our argument devolved into absurdity. I berated her for coming over in a see-through nightie.

I knew I was lost, felt my pettiest self arise.

"You threw yourself at him," I told her. "He doesn't find you attractive."

I heard a dial tone.

*   *   *

One hour later, a loud knock came at the door. I opened it to three police.

They'd come to escort Isaac from the building, they said, because he'd sexually harassed and physically threatened an NYU student.

Isaac stood. His body had gone rigid. Two of the policemen approached Isaac, arms lifting slightly from their sides. I knew that as an African-American Stanford-Berkeley-trained JD-MBA, Isaac's greatest fear was getting arrested. They'd escort him out, the cops said. They all stepped toward him. "Don't touch me," Isaac said, a bit aggressively, I thought. He was an attorney, he added. They drew close. He knew his rights, he said; he'd leave, but they mustn't touch him. Reluctantly, they lowered their hands. Isaac asked if he could gather his belongings; they refused.

In the lobby, the bellhops stared. The cops followed Isaac out the door and into the pouring rain.

"Great," Isaac said. "It's raining on my only set of clothes. It *would* be pouring."

At the Marriott, inside a 10' by 10' room, scarcely big enough to contain the stiff white double bed, Isaac lay on his back and stared at the ceiling. He wouldn't let me touch him.

An hour later, we'd laughed—a little—and showered. We blow-dried our wet clothes. Isaac gave me a cell phone he'd brought me. We spent hours playing with it. He had a friend who'd started a restaurant in the village, and he wanted to take me there. But first he wanted his luggage. When I called the room, Cybill answered.

Before I said anything, she said, she wanted to say something: she'd done what she had to. She needed *to study to keep her scholarship*.

I told her Isaac wanted his luggage.

Cybill said she and Adibe had been studying. They'd leave now, for two hours. She'd tell the doormen that Isaac could return—in this window only—to get his things.

When we entered the room, nothing had changed. But when I went into the bathroom, floating in the toilet was an enormous turd. It's too petty to put in the story, but because it was the largest I've ever seen, a foot long and round as an eggplant, and because this is all *true*, I must mention it. I was shocked not by the gesture, so much as by the turd—how had this come out of a human body? Cybill, or Adibe? It had to be Adibe, I thought, but—really? It seemed oddly coincidental, that at the moment he needed to express his contempt, he had this cantaloupe-sized turd.

At length Isaac asked why I was standing in the bathroom.

I called him in.

They probably just forgot to flush, he said; and he did.

I don't know if our relationship was doomed from the start, the $40-an-hour pizza-delivery chats, if my anger at Isaac's failure to oust Cybill cut him, or if it was the fact that a month later, after I'd moved to midtown hotel-housing, I invited a young Cuban guitar-player-dishwasher up to my room for a drink, and Isaac called, and the old Chinese concierge, who'd met Isaac and admired him, announced that I had a friend over. Isaac and I had what I felt was a good relationship. But it's true that most of the time we'd been together, he'd been too high to have sex. He was wilder than I; the experience gap between us was great, and I was not mature. Something motivated me, generosity or vengeance. Perhaps I just wanted vengeance. Because, Don Abrax, I come to the thrust of my story.

A few nights after Isaac returned to California, I sat in the walk-in closet, talking with him. A studio had opened in a midtown hotel, and I'd move there in a week. Cybill was in bed, reading a book. Adibe had not come by once since Isaac's visit. Cybill was not her old self; she didn't bother to make tea, or chat, and barely ate. Isaac and I were speaking as friends again—he'd recovered from the visit. Ha ha, I said; I had an idea.

"What?" he said.

Ha! I said.

"I have a feeling I'm not going to like this," Isaac said.

I wanted him to talk to Cybill, I said. He should speak to her on the phone, patch things up, make her feel comfortable, and say nice things. Even though she'd claimed he physically threatened her, I knew her dearest wish was for him to flatter her. But once Cybill admitted that she was attracted to him, I said, Isaac should—and I knew this was cruel—announce that he didn't like her.

"That's mean," Isaac said.

I reminded him about the police.

Well, Isaac said, if I really wanted him to, he would. He could be boyish. I heard the seeds of mischief in his voice. "I bet I could get her going," he said.

He paused. Asked whether I'd be angry at him if he did it.

"I swear I won't be," I said.

Of course, I had no idea what would happen.

I entered the low-lit room, told Cybill that Isaac wanted to speak to her, and held out the cordless.

Cybill looked surprised. She said, "To *me*?"

I nodded.

"Why does he want to speak to *me*?"

Her hair was in a bun. Her blanket up to her waist. She had reading glasses on and wore a blue cotton nightie.

"I don't know," I said. "I think he just wants to speak to you."

She took the phone.

I went back into the closet.

I sat in the dark. I'd closed the door, but I could hear Cybill's voice. I heard surprised intonations. I heard questions, like, "Really?" "How?" "What?" "Well," "I don't know," "Are you sure?" "I don't think so," "Now I'm..." "I never," "Okay..." I read my book. I was studying for a test in Russian literature. I had read an entire Gogol story called "The Nose" when I realized how bad my idea had been, realized they were still talking, felt myself growing irate, irrationally, but what is reason? I heard very few *words*, I realized suddenly—I'd become afraid, I don't know *what* I was afraid of, but I felt an urgent desire to get the phone back right then, to interrupt whatever was happening. I burst out the closet door.

The room was faintly lit by Cybill's lamp; Cybill lay in the bed, her long blue nightie pulled up to her waist, her knees wide, hands in the realm of her panties, and I wished I hadn't emerged, just then, because I saw the most shocking sight, as I entered the room: a yellow stream of pee shot from Cybill's nether region and sprayed the wall where she'd hung her map. I stared. Cybill saw me and pulled her nightie down. She held the phone, told Isaac she had to go. Her voice was low, intimate, and happy. "I have to go," she said. "Cassandra is here."

She gave the phone to me.

Later, I told her again that Isaac wasn't attracted to her. The phone chat, I said, had been a plot to make her admit she liked him. When I told her this, she turned to the wall in her bed. Her body shook. The next day she said that what I'd done to her was the meanest thing anyone ever had.

When I asked Isaac why he'd taken things so far, he said he'd done as I asked; I retorted that he'd only needed to speak to Cybill for five minutes. One couldn't just stop in the middle of these things, he replied; it was ungentlemanly. Furthermore, he said, I was breaking *my* promise not to get angry at him for doing as requested.

"Isaac," I said, "she *peed* the *bed*!"

He said, "She did?"

"Yes," I said.

"What do you mean?" he said.

I shrugged. Looked at the dark closet around me. "Like a boy," I said.

Well, Don Abrax, that's the tale. Please excuse the lack of depth. I know that lack of depth in the world has plagued you in your life. I wish, for myself, that I had a higher capacity for emotion and thought. I aspire to grow more open, and to become more receptive to the world, and to whatever in it is best.

There is a postscript. I heard once more from Cybill. It was on September 11, 2001. I was in Syracuse, New York, where I'd moved to pursue a degree writing fiction. That morning I hosted, in the living room of the Victorian flat where I lived, a dozen graduate students who were watching the video of the towers falling on TV and crying, although they did not know anyone living in the city. Some were trying to call people they knew who lived and worked in New Jersey, to see if they were all right. I was pleased to have guests. At some point, I asked someone why they were crying, and then my boyfriend, a former district attorney, took me into the flat's kitchen and told me I was being an ass, that people had *died*; I responded that tens of thousands of people that none of us knew had died in Kosovo, but that no one had cried; he responded that these were *Americans*; I shrugged, and then my boyfriend said, "My God, my GOD"; he'd thought of my father. My father, he said, an American Airlines pilot who flew out of Logan, could be *dead*, it was *his hub, his route*; I had to call him *immediately*, because he could be dead. The odds were against it, I responded. Besides that, I knew he wasn't; I didn't say I could smell him, somewhere on the earth, but I could. Still the DA insisted that I call; I demurred, my father flew reserve, I said, and never took a flight unless low-man-on-the-totem-pole; he flew six days a month, and the rest of the time sailed his boat. There was no need for me to call, I knew, but upon the attorney's insistence that I *must*, and his announcement that I was a cold, heartless wench, I picked up the cell phone that Isaac had given me, which I never used, and as I turned it on, it rang, and it was Cybill.

I'd forgotten about her.

She was sorry to bother me, she said. She was taking a trip, and she'd packed some things, and couldn't find her red silk tank top. She wondered if I knew its whereabouts.

I didn't, I said.

That was true, insofar as I didn't know my longitudinal coordinates on earth; the top was in my closet. I remarked that Cybill might find delays at the airport. Yes, Cybill replied, in a nasal tone, she would not be flying out of JFK but from a private airstrip; some men from the FBI had come to her house and wanted her and her mother to take the trip. It seemed her father had been involved in events that morning. I turned toward the couch; my boyfriend jerked his thumb down to say, Call your father!; on the television, smoke plumed. I'd later learn that my father was seated at home with his feet in a bucket of water, my mother's idea, because he'd become incontinent, because they'd offered him the trip, and he'd been second-to-low-man, and passed, and another captain, his friend, got it instead; he deserved to die, Cybill said as I passed into the kitchen, if he *was* involved, and he doubtless was; what happened was a terrible crime. I closed the kitchen door. She wasn't defending her father, she said. But she'd watched the TV, and she wasn't sure that Al Qaeda was this organized, to coordinate the attacks so perfectly by themselves. Ah well, I said. I was pleased she wasn't pursuing the tank-top line. I asked where she was going on her trip; she didn't know, she said. Her voice was flat. She asked whether I'd seen the TV; I said I had. Why did I think, she asked, Building 7 collapsed so completely? I didn't know, I said. They were saying, Cybill said, that debris did it. They'd invade her country, she said. I asked, did she mean Afghanistan? Yes, she said. I sighed; she began to rave: she asked, did I believe debris made Building 7 collapse? I allowed that I did. "Then you're an idiot," she said. "I thought you were smarter than most Americans. I guess you're not."

The kitchen door opened; the DA said people wanted more coffee and bagels. I shooed him away.

I was glad she was safe, I told Cybill. I am never sure how to comfort people, and I'd realized that she was crazy, and that I had not been kind to her.

"They won't tell me where I'm going," she said. The odd thing, she continued, was that aside from her mother and uncle, no one in America knew who her father was. She was unsure how they'd located her, in her mother's apartment in New Jersey, where she'd lived for the past few years while writing her dissertation. She spoke about her father: he was lazy, disorganized, cheap. "Like you, Cassandra," she said. I asked what she meant. You could stop him on a dime, she said. If I had her tank top, she said suddenly, I could keep it; that was what she'd called to say.

I put beans in the grinder and ground them.

She was going to give it to me, she said, if I hadn't taken it. It looked better on me.

Thanks, I said.

So, she said. She had to go.

Okay, I said. I sliced bagels.

"Do you ever," she asked, "see or speak to Isaac?"

I told her I didn't.

"He came back to see me," she said softly. "In the spring."

I felt the heat of rage—ridiculously.

It was after he and I had broken up, she said.

Isaac wasn't particularly interested in her, she added. He came because he was in town for more job interviews; she guessed he'd had nothing better to do. She'd never been assigned another roommate. She'd skipped her classes. Isaac had delayed his return flight, she said quietly. He had stayed in the room with her for six days.

There was a pause.

"He wanted to see if he could make me pee again," she said.

I put bagels in the toaster.

"Did he?"

"None of your business," she said.

I said it didn't matter.

She'd ended her engagement not long after, she said. She'd realized— she trailed off.

I said nothing.

Isaac had said some things about me, she said. He'd said I was cold. He said I was a pretty girl, she added, but that I had the emotional heft of a toad.

I see, I said.

Personally, Cybill said, she liked me fine.

I see, I said.

At any rate, she said, since she was leaving the country, and was not sure when or whether she'd return, she thought she'd say goodbye.

"Okay," I said. "Goodbye."

"Good luck," she said.

I never heard from her again. Many of her siblings are in Iran, I read— but what interests me is not Cybill's patrilineage, Don Abrax, as I hate patrilineage, as no girl can choose her face, father, skin, the antibodies in her blood, or the stars visible when she's born, but rather the fact that a woman, even a scheming, possibly schizophrenic B-blood-type Aquarius—in the presence of the right—I don't know, for lack of a better word, *attraction*, although I want to use a stronger term, like *heat* or *genuine cellular interest*— can go from cold to hot, dead to alive, solid to liquid, stone to flesh.

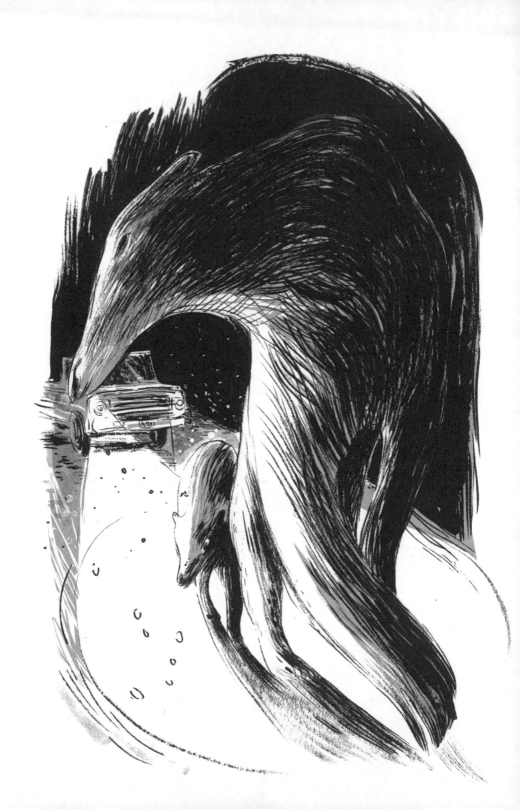

ANIMALS

by JOE MENO

t the height of the storm, in between one unimportant reverie and another, Gabe looked up and saw a polar bear marching past the parking lot. He did not move, only held the paper cup of cloudy-brown coffee in his hand. It had to be a female, he guessed, as a short-legged cub—only a couple of months old—was patiently trailing behind, the two shapes made hazy by the disruption of the slowly falling snow. Gabe peered around, wondering if the other AA regulars had noticed, but no, it didn't appear so. Big Bud Hawkins, the front of his flannel shirt rubbing against the podium, was complaining about how he was still stuck on the same step because his ex would not allow him to make amends. He was on his third attempt with her now, and getting sick of seeing her so often. He said he thought he might have to marry her again just to be forgiven. Everyone laughed, except for Gabe. He hadn't been paying much attention.

The court, which had taken his driver's license away, had thrown him in with the drunks, even though what he had was a narcotics problem, not a drinking one. There was no NA anywhere near here. He had pleaded to a lowly Misconduct Involving an Illegal Substance in the Sixth Degree and a DUI, had already completed his community service, and had eight months of probation left at his job, during which time he was supposed to be a model employee, stay focused, and get himself clean.

For the last four months, he had been focused. He had tried to be a decent employee. But just before the bears' appearance, he had been in the middle of the same thought he had whenever he went to a meeting, which was: Don't you think you're just kidding yourself?

Don't you?

It didn't matter now, anyway—the answer to that particular question—because tonight he was on call and the bears were going to be a problem. Besides Gabe, there were two other full-time employees in the Department of Streets and Sans in Ada, Alaska: the department manager, Burt, and a fifty-eight-year-old supervisor, Jeff. Both of them were down at a strip club in Fairbanks called The Pleasures of the Orient. There was no local Department of Wildlife agent here, nor a Bureau of Animal Control, and so it was Gabe's duty as assistant shop supervisor to see that the snow got cleared, to attend to any water mains that might break, and to take care of whatever animals might happen to make their way into town. The protocol was this: Gabe was supposed to call the part-timers, usually old Henry Tsosie or the twins—Frank and Gene Leonards, two twenty-year-old cousins who looked identical with their pug Irish noses and raw, freckled faces—and tell them what streets needed to be plowed or where there was a water-main break or if there was an elk that needed chasing off. Then they would take care of it while he stood looking over their shoulders, nodding lamely. Ever since the DUI, though, each time he gave one of the part-timers a job to do, somebody would make an embarrassing snorting sound while someone else delivered some waterbrained joke about Gabe's cocaine problem. Here he was forty-one years old and still being reminded of the major fucking mess he had made of his life.

He was sitting up, now, the folding chair tilting forward with his weight. The bears strolled quietly toward the Conoco station. They were like an apparition, the two of them, their bodies stark white against the green paint of the gas sign. Gabe had never seen a live polar bear before, not in the wild nor anywhere else. There had been plenty of brown bears, elks, and lynxes around, in his youth, but not a single polar bear. There was a photo of one, shot dead, hanging on the wall behind the bar at The Well; it had been taken in 1970 or so. By Gabe's figuring, these two bears were maybe a couple hundred miles away from home, maybe even a thousand, which made his bad luck even more obvious.

He turned and squinted out the side window, watching as the bears strode closer and closer to downtown, then stood as quietly as he could, apologized his way to the end of the row of folding chairs, and walked toward the back of the room. He pulled his cell phone from his coat, trying not to make a ruckus. If everything was going right, the twins would be on the east side of town at that very moment, plowing the roads right down to the police station. But there was no way of knowing with those two.

He flipped the phone open and gave Frank a call. It picked up on the first ring.

"Where're you guys at?" Gabe whispered. The phone chirped its response:

"Over on Elk. We're about halfway done over here."

"Good. I got another job for you to do."

"What? You need us to make a run?"

"A what?"

"A run. A drug run. You seen all that white powder piling up and decided you wanted a fix?" And here Frank began sniffing wildly.

Even with the static, he could hear that other idiot Gene cackling, too. Gabe sighed. He squinted hard out the window, watching the two bears disappear around the corner of the distillery.

"Forget it. Just get the roads cleared. You can start on the west side when you're done with that."

"What about this other job you got?"

"Never mind. I'll call Tsosie."

"Tsosie's out."

Gabe had forgotten; the old-timer had been sick with the stomach flu the whole week.

"Fine. Just forget it," Gabe said, feeling flustered.

"You're the one who called us."

"Never mind that," Gabe growled, and then, "Just get the goddamn roads plowed." He hung the phone up and muttered "Idiots" louder than he would have liked. Pastor Dan at the front of the community center gave him a stern look. Big Bud Hawkins went on at the podium with his tale of woe, uninterrupted.

The bears were now nosing through a pair of garbage cans on the far side of the road, the mother getting a snoutful of what looked to be discarded hot dogs. Gabe pressed his forehead up against the cool window and stood there watching, hoping to see them get their fill and turn back to the woods. When he took a step back he saw his own reflection in the window, watched his breath fogging up the glass, and thought for a moment about how everyone, including Margaret, was right about one thing: he did not look any different. He didn't even look like he had quit doing coke. It had been four full months, and the capillaries in his nose and eyes were still red and broken; his skin was the color of a corpse. Even with his hair greased down, he still looked like shit.

The mother bear was moving on from the garbage cans, quicker now, shoulders rising and falling. The cub dodged in and out of her shadow. They made clean white tracks in the snow, the cub's identical to its mother's, though smaller in size—the two of them ambling right down Patanka to where Main Street ran.

The rule was once they were on Main, they were fair game.

He thought that even if he hustled now there was a good chance some idiot with a .22 stowed in his gun rack, who just so happened to be sitting in front of The Well, would look up, see the bears, and get to them before he did. Or maybe the bears would stumble upon a pair of heavy drinkers and tear off an arm or two before disappearing back into the woods where they belonged. And then whose fault would it be?

He thought for another long moment and finally decided he would take care of the bears himself.

Having apologized to the pastor at the front of the community center, having charged through the double doors, this thought carried him as far as the breezeway, where he slowed to find Margaret sitting with her feet up on an adjacent chair. Margaret, waiting to take him home.

It hurt to see how much she was like her mother, even the way she took to reading a book. Feet up, pen in hand, the book in her lap, sixteen years old, furry jacket on, hood pulled up, her snowboots leaking water all over the other seat, not even noticing him coming her way. She was so focused on it that it was only when he looked down, standing over her, that he realized she was working in a coloring book. Margaret had made a number of lewd comments and drawings around the pictures, which seemed to be of Jesus and his disciples. "Where are all the bitches?" is what the Apostle Luke was asking the Romans.

"Nice," Gabe remarked, shaking his head.

"What?" she asked, smiling. "Pastor Dan gave it to me."

"You get your homework done?"

"Yep."

"Good," he said with a frown. "Listen. I need your help. It's okay if you want to say no. But I don't got a lot of other options."

"What are you talking about?"

"Do you think you can drive in this?"

The girl nodded, her whole fur-lined hood moving, searching for the silver keys in her pocket.

"Why? Where we going?"

"There's a mother and a cub out there taking a stroll. I think maybe they're polar bears. We got to go."

"Polar bears?"

"Yep. We ought to try and chase them off before they tear something up. You feel like taking a drive?"

Margaret looked up at him and smiled, which made her look not like her mother at all. It was a rare thing these days, that smile, and the feeling it gave him was something altogether separate and painful. How could she not be embarrassed? Other kids, their dads were coaches, lawyers, even a judge. Him, he had to have her drive him to AA meetings.

"Okay," she said.

"Okay," he said, and then thinking on it, thinking of the danger he was putting her in, said, "Are you sure you want to do this?"

"It's no big deal. We'll be inside the car, right? I mean, we've chased off elk before."

Gabe nodded. "Okay. But don't tell anybody, all right?"

She gave him a goofy grin as she packed up her things. Then she paused.

"Wait a minute. What about your meeting?"

It irked him a little, her thinking she had to check up on him. Gabe decided he didn't care for it.

"The pastor saw me. They'll count it."

The girl nodded, and threw her book bag over her shoulder.

The thing that killed him was that she was not his own. They weren't even related by blood, technically; she had been three years old when Gabe had married her mother. He had done the right thing, and gone through the courts to have her adopted, but even now, seven or eight years after he and Virginia had split up, he had a feeling that once Margaret turned eighteen, she'd want nothing to do with him. There'd be no way to force her to come spend weekends, no way to keep her from disappearing from his life. What they had now was the most temporary sort of relationship, one where she'd come by whenever Gabe needed a ride somewhere or whenever the two of them, her and her mom, got in a fight. In a few months, whenever he got his license back, she wouldn't even have a reason to stop by anymore.

"Watch the ice. And bundle up," he said, as they trudged out into the snow, before noticing that she already had.

Why had he left the meeting? He could have called Dale Beavers, he thought—why not call Dale? Dale was the sheriff and the only other person in town who would sometimes handle this sort of thing. He was also an Indian, but couldn't make up his mind on what kind. It changed, depending on what story he was telling. Dale had been Gabe's AA sponsor, but recently, a month or so back, he had fallen hard off the wagon, right after winning his re-election. People around here had voted for him in hopes that it would keep him sober, but it hadn't done much good. Dale had called Gabe a week afterward and said, "Who do you think I am? Me, I know who I am. I'm a drunk. So what are we kidding ourselves for?"

Gabe looked down at his watch. It was a couple minutes past eight o'clock; Dale probably wouldn't even answer. He pulled out his cell and gave him a ring anyway. When no one picked up, he dialed again, then a third time, listened to the tone, listened to Dale's garbled message, and slammed the phone shut. Off on a bender, Gabe thought, and then he wondered again what he was doing trying to get anyone else involved.

It was too late to change his mind now, he decided. The bears had trailed off somewhere near the hardware store; they were almost downtown, and something had to be done about it. Margaret started the station wagon and put the car in drive. He got into the passenger seat.

"Where am I supposed to be going, anyway?"

"Just go straight. I saw 'em go down that alley near the hardware store."

"Okay," the girl said, letting the station wagon creep forward. She got them going slowly, inching over the ice and snow, both hands placed exactly at ten and two on the steering wheel. Eyes locked straight ahead.

"Who taught you to drive like that? I get a stiff neck just looking at you."

"Mom did," she said, her eyes still fixed on the snowy road. He looked over at her, hunched like that, pretty serious. Margaret looked like her real father, a man Gabe had never even met. She had the same high forehead and dark eyebrows. Not a knockout, not like her mom, but those looks didn't last long.

"Things been quiet at home?" he asked, and, before she could answer, he said, "Go on. Put on your wipers."

Margaret nodded again, searching for the wiper arm without lifting her eyes from the road.

"Pretty quiet," she said. "She's out on a date tonight. Some new guy."

Gabe nodded and thought of Virginia. They had met back in high school, back when Virginia was drop-dead gorgeous, and had dated on and off. After sophomore year, she had stopped going to school and began going around with roughnecks, refinery guys who would come up from Fairbanks on motorcycles. She had wanted to start a rock 'n' roll band. They met up again years later; by then, Virginia had a coke-nose and a three-year-old daughter, and was doing all she could to re-create the looks she'd had as a freshman, with some success. They had all hit it off. A few months later, he asked Virginia if she wanted to get married; her answer was, "Why not?"

As far as Gabe knew, she still smoked a lot of dope. This gave him a strange, incomplete feeling, something not quite like sadness.

"I want you to know I don't hold a grudge," Gabe said. "Not for anything. I just wish I had the willpower to stick it out with her."

Margaret seemed to ignore this. Her eyes were glued to the windshield, to the snow blowing back and forth across the station wagon's hood. Gabe leaned forward, seeing the bears making tracks uphill.

"There. They just turned the corner near Brackett," he said.

"Least they're staying away from the middle of town."

The bears—the female bounding upward, the cub scuttling through its mother's tracks—were moving toward an area that hadn't been built up: there were two or three trailers and a couple split-level houses, but not much else. This was going fine, he thought.

"Okay, let's pull up beside them over there. By that embankment. We'll try and scare 'em."

The girl nodded, opening her mouth a little as she spun the wheel toward the side of the road. Gabe thought it was the goddamn loveliest thing he'd ever seen, her forgetting herself, opening her mouth as she turned the wheel like that for no good reason.

"Lay on the horn," he said.

Margaret looked over at him, then back over at the two bears, and pressed both hands down against the steering wheel. The station wagon—a mid-nineties, four-wheel-drive Subaru—had a horn that sounded like some kind of waterfowl. It squawked loudly at first and then grew more and more quiet, until finally it became a sore-sounding, electric groan. The bears turned toward them for a moment, eyes flashing silver in the car's headlights, then darted up toward a row of blue and tan houses—all halted mid-construction—perched along the side of a hill.

"Okay. Now what?" Margaret asked, turning toward him again.

Gabe frowned.

But wasn't this just like everything?

"Well, I guess we could go by my place. Get a gun and go scare 'em off with that. What do you think?"

"What gun?"

"An automatic. A friend of mine loaned it to me. What do you think?"

The girl was silent. He knew what she was thinking: What friend? And what was he doing with an automatic? When he got arrested for waking up the whole town with it, wasn't he going to blow his court supervision? Wasn't he going to finally lose his job? Wasn't he just going to foul things up again? But there was no other choice, and even Margaret seemed to know this.

What she said was, "I think we should do something before they try and eat somebody."

The girl was right, like always.

"Okay, let's go get the gun," he said. "Go on, shake a leg."

Margaret put the station wagon back in drive. They crawled back along the icy street, the snow coming down a little heavier now.

The gun he was thinking of using had been given to him by a Canadian, a soldier named Ray, whom he had smoked cocaine with a couple of times. It was an AR-15, a machine gun, way too powerful to hunt anything with. But it was the only gun of his that had ammunition. It was shoved in the front closet, beside some old coats, clothes he had been meaning to give away. It had been there for some time, before he had gone off his nut, before he had wrecked his truck, before he had lost his license. What had happened was he had driven into the side of a tree while trying to do a line of coke. It had been after one a.m. on a Saturday night and he had gone home from The Well alone, and had not wanted to face the disaster of his empty apartment on his own. The two deputies who pulled him from the wreck had looked at the cocaine exploded across his face and laughed. There was so little of it left, and the sight of him standing dazed in the road gave the cops such a distinct pleasure, that they booked him with the measly Misconduct and a DUI, which led to three days in jail and a fifteen hundred dollar fine. He had not been fired because there was some sort of law that protected state workers with drug problems, which he thought funny and also kind of ridiculous.

"Take a left on Oregon."

"Okay."

The station wagon slowed up in front of the apartment complex he had been staying at for the last year or so. He opened the passenger door and said, "I'll be right back."

He trudged up the steps to the front of the building, found his keys, beat his boots on the second-floor landing, and got inside his place. A moment later he was staring down at the rifle and remembering the smell of burnt cocaine. It made his sinuses ache and reminded him of the bloody nose he'd caught off some of the garbage Ray the Canadian had sold him. He stared at the gun for a while longer and then thought of Margaret downstairs in the car, waiting, and the bears, and how he was on call and ought not screw anything else up. He hoisted the gun up to his chest, checked to be sure the clip was fully loaded, then locked his place up and came clambering back toward the station wagon through the ankle-high snow.

"What the fuck is that?" Margaret asked. "Is that an actual machine gun?"

"No," he said, though he did not know what the point was of trying to lie.

"Where the hell did you get that?"

"I don't know," he said, pulling the passenger-side door closed. "Come on," he said. "Let's go."

"Aren't you going to get in trouble for shooting that off?"

"Why? Maybe. I don't think so."

The station wagon was making its way back along the S curve toward the hill.

"Are you going to shoot them with that?"

"No," he said, and until he had said it, he had not realized that this might be a possibility.

"We're just going to scare them, right?"

"Right," he said, and knew again that he was lying.

The station wagon's headlights swung over the hill, picking their way among the willows and pines.

"Maybe they went back home," the girl said.

"Maybe."

They drove on a little farther and saw nothing but the snow falling there along the unplowed street. They inched ahead, tires rumbling, getting caught, then spinning free. The girl, on her own, decided to stop, holding her foot down on the brake, scanning the windshield from left to right, the two of them doing their best to try and listen to the night. Gabe noticed he had a runny nose but did nothing about it, just stared off into the snow, searching for a sign of the two bears.

The snow was coming in barrelfuls now, flakes as large as moths, tumbling down from the low-hanging clouds. Finally he wiped his nose and was startled to see the girl staring at him. She looked ghostly, as serious as a pope.

"What?" he asked.

"Are you stoned?"

"What?"

"Are you?"

"Are you kidding me? Jeez, Margaret, come on."

She kept staring at him, and then nodded, satisfied by something in his terrified, unshaven face. He looked away from her, saw the snow coming down even harder, then glanced back and saw that she was still studying him. Something, whatever device it was that leads girls to place an ineffable trust in the men who attempt to be their fathers, was no longer alive and working in her. He was a bad bet, and she was finally beginning to figure that out.

"Have you gotten high? Since you've been going to AA?"

"What?"

"Have you?"

"No."

"Do you think it's helping?" she asked.

"What?"

"Do you think it is?"

"Do we have to talk about this now?"

"We do."

"Oh, come on, kid."

"You come on."

He groaned and then nodded. "I don't know, babe. Maybe a little."

"A little?"

"Like I said, I really don't know. I don't want to talk about this with you."

"But you haven't gotten high."

He shook his head. "No. But that doesn't mean shit. All I am is scared right now. Once that wears off, who knows what'll happen."

The girl nodded again, turning away from him. He looked over at her, seeing she was done looking him in the eye.

"Anyways, you don't have to check up on me," he said.

"I know," she said, and didn't even try to hide the fact that she didn't believe it.

He cleared his throat. "Those bears are probably holed up on the other side of the highway by now. We can head on back. I got a frozen pizza we can pop in the oven. How's that sound?"

"Okay," she said.

"Okay, let's go," he said, and she shifted the car back into drive.

Before they were back on the road below, Gabe heard the dog barking. He held up his hand, motioning for her to stop, the two of them sitting there listening, Gabe pressing his ear against the frosty window. It was some kind of retriever, baying like it had treed something.

"Go that way," Gabe said. The girl turned the wheel to the left, her mouth making the O shape again.

The station wagon skidded to a halt in front of several half-filled trash cans that had been strewn across the road. A pair of plastic garbage bags lay like two bodies in the snow, claw marks bisecting their near-translucent skin. "Wait a second," Gabe said, and climbed out of the car. The snow was falling in uneven clumps. There were no bears anywhere around.

He squatted down beside the garbage cans and saw the female's footprints, as large as dinner plates, angling away from the torn-up bags and back toward a residential part of town. The air was cold. He thought he could taste burnt cocaine in the back of his throat. He heard the dog baying again and climbed back in the car, feeling exhausted.

"Try that way," Gabe said, and the station wagon rolled on, angling down a short decline toward a cul-de-sac of newly constructed homes.

They pulled up in front of an expensive A-frame, its wide lawn aglow with milky floodlights. There were no bears, but Jerry Wogan was standing on his front lawn in his pajamas with a look of terror, holding a newly oiled Winchester rifle like he meant to use it. Gabe opened his door and hopped out, slipping in the snow a little, trying his best not to drop the machine gun. Once he got his footing again, he held up a hand, doing what he could to summon some kind of authority.

"Jesus, Gabe, were those bears?" Jerry asked, eyes wide with excitement.

"Go on back inside the house, Jerry," Gabe said.

"They looked like polar bears."

"Go back inside."

But Jerry didn't move. He looked down at the AR-15 and winced.

"Whoa. That's an awful big gun, Gabe. Do you want me to call Willie Lafitte? He won the turkey shoot the last four years running. He's the best shot in the county."

The howl of the dog echoed again through the empty trees and both Gabe and Jerry turned toward it.

"Just stay here," Gabe said, and climbed back into the station wagon.

"What happened?" Margaret asked, blowing on her hands. "Did he see which way they went?"

"I don't know. But he'll be on the phone to every hothead in the town. We got to find those bears quick. Try that way," Gabe said. He rolled down his window. After a few moments they heard the dog barking again.

"There, go down there," he said, and the station wagon swung west down a dead end. The hollow sound of the dog's bark got louder and louder until finally, Gabe spotted the animal—a big black Lab—chained in front of a split-level house, some thirty feet away.

Then he could see it—the female bear—snarling and swatting at the retriever. It was enormous, like a bull or some other kind of livestock, and the cub, standing a foot or so behind, was the size of a full-grown dog. The mother bear charged forward and the black Lab yelped, lunging defensively, then retreating, getting choked by its chain, losing its footing in the snow.

"Wait here," Gabe said, and climbed out of the car.

He took an uncertain step forward and slid backward in the slush, the silly machine gun flying up in the air, his boots going out from under him. Just another example of how he was hell-bent on doing harm to himself, he thought. He got to his knees, then, leaning against the side of the car, made it to his feet.

The bear roared, striking again, pinning the dog under one of its giant paws. Gabe got the rifle up, pointing it at the bear and realizing that he had never shot it before, had no idea where the safety was or what was going to happen once he pulled the trigger. Why had Ray given him the gun? Why had Gabe taken it? Margaret was staring at him from the driver's seat with an urgent look on her face. She looked like a nun. It made him feel guilty all over again. All he could do now was surprise her by not fucking anything else up. He braced himself, feeling the butt against the inside of his shoulder, and then aimed at the sky, pulling the trigger hard.

The AR-15 sounded like a helicopter crash, a high whine and explosive growl that shocked the dog into silence. The bears moved a lot quicker than animals of that size should have been able to, bounding off without even looking back at what had made the awful sound in the first place. The Lab swung its head around so fast it nearly jerked itself off of its feet. Seeing the two bears had flown, the dog started up its howling once more.

Gabe held the gun away from his body, watching as the snow melted against the muzzle. The bears were nearly gone, hurrying past the small line of houses back into the forest. He imagined them making their way through the woods and back over the highway, back into the wilderness where they belonged. He switched the safety on and turned back to the car.

He slipped again, climbing in, banging his knee on the gun. Margaret was looking at him with the same smile her mother used to give him, a narrow little smirk—one that let you know you had only done as good as she thought you should have in the first place. But it was a good smile, and he decided to take it for what it was worth. He closed his door and huffed, a little out of breath. They sat there in the dark for a couple of moments, Gabe deciding if he was having a heart attack or not. Margaret watched him, still smirking, then put her hands back on the wheel.

"Are we good?" she asked. Gabe squinted, seeing no trace of the bears, the snow coming down even harder now. It was like they had never even been there. Some of the lights in the houses nearby had come on, and a few folks were standing on their porches in pajamas or longjohns, searching for the source of the rifle fire. He got the seatbelt over his belly and nodded at her.

"We're good," he whispered, and then wondered how many times he would have to say it before the both of them believed it.

THE OCEAN OF AIR

by JIM SHEPARD

As a boy from the highest hillsides above our town I watched the winds depart our valley empty and return laden with spoil, and I came to know the sky's upper reaches as a domain of tempests and whirlwinds from which poured torrents and hail and other phenomena that suggested Nature's combat with herself. Pliny urged us to consider the marvel of the heavens, that immense space where the vital fluid to which we give the name of air flows in all of its diffusion and mobility, and so I followed the ascension of clouds that rose like capitals on invisible columns of air, and imagined even then an aerial machine that might take advantage of the prevailing currents of the higher atmosphere the way sailing ships plied the trade winds.

Life in the countryside and solitude left me well fitted to the study of natural phenomena. I was congenitally retiring, and neither conversation with my peers nor my increasing age further emboldened me. I felt as if I were dark to all the world, or like the amphibian, disposed to live in two antithetical realms, the first within my fancy and the second forever pulling me toward society. But from my earliest days, my capacity to speculate and to imagine resolved me to the heavens.

My brother and I are Jacques-Etienne and Joseph Michel Montgolfier, the fifteenth and twelfth of sixteen children born to Pierre and Anne Montgolfier. Etienne was always entranced by what he imagined to be the magical space of my imagination, and I always assumed I would submit all of my ideas to his more mature discernment, despite his being five years the younger. He was esteemed for his capacity and reliability whereas I seemed to be forever indulged for my fecklessness, and so we envied each other's positions. But we always understood that in those tasks and explorations that we contracted to undertake together, we would never refuse our time, begrudge our thought, or deny our care.

I had been intrigued even as a boy to read what I could about the discoveries concerning the constituent gases of the atmosphere. I was sent to school first at Annonay and then, when that failed, to the Jesuit college at Tournon. The latter institution drove me to such active rebellion that at the age of twelve I stole away on a barge down the Rhone before being retrieved.

My teachers were always citing me as a way of impressing upon the group the limitations of human knowledge. One theorized that I had absorbed less theology than any other charge with whom he'd had the misfortune to work. But in my secret folders I had already systematized for myself the nature of various forces and the structures of matter, and my self-education proceeded by the experimental verification of various propositions, though my development was impeded by my having had to evolve my own methods of calculation, the Jesuit Fathers having rejected the utility of mathematics.

I made my first balloon in Avignon when I was supposed to be studying law. One cold winter morning I sought to warm over the hearth the shirt I was to wear, and noted that the fabric billowed and lifted with the heat. The image stayed with me, like the sun's warmth brooding on the waters, and a rainy November evening a few weeks later I found myself examining a print I'd tacked to the wall depicting our country's futile siege of Gibraltar. The fire in the grate below it carried its sparks upward through the flue beyond. Why couldn't that force be confined and harnessed? No access could be gained to the fortress by either sea or land, but my shirt's behavior reoccurred to me, and I thought: why couldn't a force arrive by air?

I constructed a machine of silk stretched over the slenderest of wooden frames, a polyhedron, the next morning. It would be made lighter than the air it displaced by the expansive power of heat. It was half my height with an internal capacity of forty cubic feet. I burned paper for its heat source. Soon after I lit the paper the assembly floated from its cradle and hovered beside me before rising further to bump along the ceiling to the window. I immediately wrote to Etienne that if he laid in a supply of silk and cordage, I could show him one of the most astonishing sights in the world.

Therese Filhol was my earliest memory and model of a sensibility that consorted and sympathized with all things. One of my first images of her was of a tanned and glossy-haired seven-year-old wearing behind her ear an intricate flower made of paper and crouching naked in a pond to examine a leech she'd laid along the top of her hand. Five years later I spent an afternoon alone with her and her schoolbooks, the pair of us curled in a set of her mother's armchairs. At one point she remarked that the Greeks believed Olympus to have been so high that it never rained on its summit and that instead the air there was always still. She was four years my junior. I almost never spoke to her. She seemed to cherish her own contradictions, as if she did not want to throw any part of herself away. When three years following that afternoon we finally kissed and I asked if she'd been aware of my interest, she swept her hair back, her eyes half-closed and her mouth half-open at the thought, and said of course; everyone had.

We were first cousins, and married when I was thirty and she was twenty-six against the wishes of my father, who found such consanguinity indecent.

She maintains on our bed table her own private cabinet of rarities, including a miniature painting of a sea-meadow on the ocean's floor, and with such gestures she reminds me that we carry with us the wonders we seek throughout. She pursues within me all those evasions I assay in the realm of the spirit and the heart, and she demonstrates with her daily attention the way participating natures can unite across incomparable distances, and the way we can build and sustain the bounty of our compact, even in the face of my profligacy, just as, at God's bare word, all of creation started up out of nothing.

Whispering in the dark, she has conceded the various ways in which I remain a mystery even as she has celebrated the shared and preternatural transparency of our enjoined hearts. She fancies in me a diffused benevolence and interest in others that they appreciate no matter how distracted I appear.

My father has said I am so absentminded that upon retiring I once tucked the cat into bed and put myself out the door. In various travels I departed one lodging house without my horse and another without my wife. In the latter case it had only been two weeks into our marriage. I had arisen before dawn for a constitutional and had so entangled myself in thought that I had walked straight through to our destination, only remembering I had left Therese asleep in the inn's bed when our hosts, upon my arrival, had asked after her.

My letter arrived in Etienne's hand at a propitious moment. For two years he had been negotiating to make the Montgolfiers the first papermaking concern in France to adopt the new manufacturing machines developed in Holland, and the laborers, frightened for their livelihood, had organized a strike, whereupon he'd locked the strikers out. He wrote me back that he would be pleased to take up a project that wasn't endlessly vexing, and that might also bring credit to the family name at a time when that name was being slandered in the streets.

I hastened home to meet him and we began work on larger models. Therese was called to her father's side to help with his faltering ribbon factory, and for three months was a presence only in her letters. Did I miss her during the course of my days, she wanted to know? Etienne and I lived in

our little workplace, hardly coming round even for meals. We investigated
the lifting potential of every vapor, and especially considered steam and
hydrogen, before settling on the dilation of ordinary air by heat as the sim-
plest and most inexpensive technique. We realized there was much to be
learned by the burning of various materials, and so ignited an array of woods,
wet, dry, and decomposed, as well as sodden straw, chopped wool, old shoes,
and rotten meat. We had the best luck with a fire of straw and meat, perhaps because of the greater lifting power of the combination of mephitic and
inflammable gases. All of this I explained to her. Her letters in response were
enthusiastic, if not all that I had hoped.

Our machines rose well, as anticipated, but the force doing the lifting
soon dissipated, as the gas was lost through minute holes and imperfections
in the silk. My brother was no more discouraged than I, though, since from
the tenderest age he also had refused to put any measure to his hopes, and
we spent two weeks experimenting with methods of sealing the fabric. We
dreamt our designs, but it was only when we put our calculations into physical form that we could judge the practicality of what we had imagined.

Paper-backed taffeta proved the most successful solution, and on a
bright December morning in which even the carriage wheels were covered
in frost, we repeated the Avignon experiment in the seclusion of the new
garden just north of the house with the entire family gathered round. Our
little polyhedron rose eighty feet into the air and rode the breezes to the
southwest for a full minute. Once it returned to earth, my brother and
I repaired immediately to our workroom, where for the next three weeks
we fabricated a balloon three times the size. It rose with such vigor that
it broke its tether and disappeared over the trees to the north, only to be
destroyed where it landed by some alarmed passersby.

The new garden is one of the few spaces near the house large enough
to accommodate the entire family. Our dining table seats forty. While
unmarried daughters might avail themselves of the religious orders and
younger sons might attempt a commercial venture or enter the priesthood,
those of our relations who find no place for themselves in the world—the

ne'er-do-well, the artist, the widow, and the plainly discouraged—are all granted their shelter in our household.

Family tradition claims the Montgolfiers have been producing paper since the twelfth century, our ancestors having apprenticed in the art in Damascus during the Second Crusade. One hundred years ago another pair of Montgolfier brothers married the daughters of a rival papermaking family and settled in Annonay. The region had ready access to markets and raw materials and a climate mild enough for sizing paper the year round. They built their mill deep in a ravine through which the Deume pours from the surrounding hills before it reaches the town, the river's water clear and soft and fine for rinsing rags and pulp, its pitch powering the mill wheels with commendable vigor except in the summer's driest months.

Pierre, our father, was one of nineteen children and as the eldest surviving son, succeeded to his inheritance at the age of forty-three. He has maintained his place at our table as patriarch for thirty-nine years since. Under his hand the firm has earned the patronage of the King, and the seal as Royal Paper Manufactory.

The factory is really a series of additions to an ancient farmhouse, and as toddlers we thrilled at the thundering of the mill wheels and the flume on the massive wooden blades, and the groaning of the cyclopean joists and axletrees. It was only when we were permitted to forage sufficiently upstream and deep into the woods that we could hear ourselves think, or listen to the wind in the poplars.

Our father rose every morning at four and performed his ablutions out of doors in the millrace whatever the season, and for the rest of his day oversaw everything. Any and all deficiencies would at some point be uncovered in his sight. He retired every evening at seven following supper, and until he did, light conversation was forbidden.

He seemed particularly pained by the sight of me. Etienne, as the youngest son, had gone off to study architecture in Paris, but the death of our brother Raymond meant that each of the elder brothers was now either in ill health, the holy orders, dead, or temperamentally unsuited to business, and so Etienne renounced his dreams so that he could become head of the concern.

We harbor no illusions in our family about one another's qualities, and ask of each other what we do well, not what we do not. We avoid the unkindness of requiring more of a loved one than it would be reasonable to expect. From my earliest memories of the factory floor, and hearing the nursery songs of the women and children sorting rags, I knew that when it came to the affairs of commerce I could not persuade myself to honor that which practice demanded. I continued to search for success with no notion of which way to turn my face to find her.

Etienne was, unlike me, well-educated in mathematics and self-discipline, and not hopeless with the affairs of commerce. Having escaped the Jesuits, I had drawn on my experiments for my first commercial venture, that of fabricating dyes which I'd hoped to sell at fairs and markets. When this proved unsuccessful, my father had installed me, along with another of my younger brothers for whom no one could find a useful sinecure, with a lease on two small paper mills in Dauphiny, but to that concern I had also remained inattentive. Even in the study of law at Avignon I had mortgaged enough credit to have spent a week in debtors' prison. And yet my home remained open to me, as it remained open to all those who caused my parents pain.

Even before our little balloon had landed, Etienne had expressed to me his anxiety that we might be cheated of whatever advantages our invention might be made to yield. He wrote to an influential friend in the capital to ask that our ascending machine be registered with the Academy of Sciences, and the friend wrote back, baffled, to suggest Etienne send an adequate drawing and a more detailed account. My brother responded with more details about our success, and added that our novel speculation likely could ferry very heavy weights at very little cost, and that it might be immediately useful for sending messages or supplies into cities under siege. He further stipulated that he would refrain from providing any additional particulars about our next, much bigger machine until we had tested it.

Our entire family was then drawn into the project, our father suffering the machine to be built only on the condition that we swear a filial oath never to ascend in it. It was arranged that our brother Jean-Pierre, the second eldest, whose health had improved, would assist in the daily business of the mill, and our brother Alexandre the Abbé at Lyons, who liked to say about his career in the Church that it remained unmarked by either devotion, success, or chagrin, would oversee all correspondence and sales.

We were six months constructing the machine for the first public demonstration. We determined that a spherical form would provide the maximum internal volume, but soon discovered that shaping sheets of taffeta of the necessary size, before lining them with paper and enjoining them together with thousands upon thousands of buttons and buttonholes, was something no seamstress had ever attempted. The monster was assembled out of segments that together formed three lateral bands and a dome fitted over the top, all reinforced by a net of stout ropes encompassing the entire exterior. The ropes converged beneath the envelope in a frame securing the iron brazier that would hold the material to be burned. In a test we conducted in late spring in the privacy of our garden, two laborers let the cords fly through their hands and two others were pulled aloft until they released their grips and fell back to the earth with panicked cries. We retrieved our machine undamaged from the next property over.

It debuted in our town square on the morning of the 4th of June in the year of our Lord 1783, with the provincial assembly among the spectators gathered. It was raining while our laborers worked. The extravagant mass of the taffeta was piled on a wooden stage beside the bridge over the river, with two detachable ropes, one each running over a wheel set atop a mast, fastened at their ends to an eye sewn into the center of the fabric. At our instruction the laborers positioned the envelope's maw over a hole cut in the stage, beneath which we'd set ablaze in a furnace a great quantity of wool soaked in alcohol, and the balloon's upper reaches were then hoisted in preparation of its inflation by means of the ropes running through the eyelets in the masts. Within minutes our creature was bridling at its restraining lines, and commenced bucking and twisting like a fairground animal while four of our burliest laborers endeavored with all their weight to rein in its fury. Then Etienne and I together ordered its release, and the great sphere bounded upward and spiraled to a fantastic height.

As it rose, the congregation's discordant minds were aligned in a state of astonishment that held sway until the silence that we had created ended in a roar of acclamation. All present described the ascent as majestic and beautiful beyond compare, and many were amazingly affected. A small boy yelped and slapped at his face again and again, and an old woman beside me clutched at my arm and wept. If savants could achieve such a miracle, she said, what else might they accomplish?

The currents of the wind carried the machine a half league to the south while we all gave chase, before it finally came to grief on a stone fence, where coals from its brazier spilled across its envelope and set the entire mass afire.

Therese had requested I hold the ascent until she had been able to arrive, but I had been so taken up with solutions to various vexations that I had neglected to do so. Her expression upon her arrival was so dismaying that Etienne was forced to take over the account of our triumph. And even as I stood listening to his exultation and gazing upon her unhappiness, I was served with three promissory notes for which I was badly in arrears, and about which I had told her nothing.

That night in our bed I marveled at how close upon one another tread the footfalls of exhilaration and frustration and misery. She said she understood that my childhood had been one of indulgence, and that I had imagined I could endlessly have everything a home could provide. She understood, as well, that unlike many of her friends, she had been spared a life with a husband who differed from her so materially as to prevent the free exhibition of her happiness. She thanked God there were so many mornings in which she found she desired nothing different for the morrow, and so many nights in which under my hand she savored all the felicity a woman was allowed. She said that every marriage was a story of indebtedness, and that she tried to tell herself that when considering my irresponsibility she was looking at the wrong side of the picture, and that if she just turned things around, or balanced the accounts between the two sides of my behavior, she would still find ample reason to be joyful. She reminded herself that I had jokingly urged her during the period of our engagement to bear with me, for I knew that some day I would come out all right. She understood that there were husbands who needed to be managed as well as obeyed, and that sometimes it was her duty to remain silent even when she found me in the wrong, and that married life was not about choice but about living with choices already made.

But days like this one demonstrated that I was one of those who granted themselves endless absolution in advance, believing themselves to be weak but never wicked. I acted as if the everyday in my mind was veiled with dread. She was supposed to model excess when it came to affection and restraint when it came to our household affairs, while I seemed to believe myself to be discharging a task well suited to my natural generosity when I squandered what security we might achieve. What a sense of obligation she had to lie under, because of this most generous of men!

Such was her state of agitation that I twice had to restrain her from leaving the room. We squabbled the long night through. Eventually I entreated her forgiveness. I told her I cared but little what came to cheer me if she drew away. I promised to repay each of our creditors monthly until all were satisfied. She asked where we would find the money and I reminded her that the very next day Etienne intended to petition their lordships of the Estates to formally acknowledge our success and establish our priority and thereby persuade the King to support our project, since we meant to improve our design in order to make it useful. I urged her to imagine no end to the amount of wealth that might be generated. She was quiet for some minutes and then finally murmured that whatever funds we received would be instantly devoted to reimbursement for our machine's expenses and further development. I pledged I would set some portion aside to address her distress. After another silence, she reminded me that in a family if one suffered then so did all.

"You chide me for taking no delight in things and yet you force me to keep our accounts," she said.

I was sorry to make her weep, I told her.

"And then you return to my bed and I'm supposed to be seduced by you once again," she cried.

I understood her disappointment, I conceded. Perhaps this was a matter of age turning bad dispositions into worse habits. We attended a commotion from our stable-yard that featured donkeys and our terriers, who always set up a fearful barking whenever something turned up outside the gate.

"I expect you to govern our household as if you cherished it," she said, and I promised I would. And through such resolutions we seek access to the mansions of our restored selves, even as we fail to banish those unanswerable doubts that torment the wisest understandings.

Eventually in her exhaustion and sadness she fell asleep, and I took her hand, listening to her breaths. I know now what I knew then: that I loved my wife even before myself, which was not to say I loved her enough, and that I still failed to fully credit the extent to which I carried my own domestic enemies within.

We were informed that the Academy of Sciences had appointed a committee to study the matter of our machine, and that the committee included Lavoisier. It was decided at a family council that Etienne should go alone to Paris to secure our fortune, since I was too unworldly to be of any help there, and that I should remain behind to continue our experiments and oversee the construction of new balloons.

Mention of our machine had already appeared in Paris: the *Feuille Hebdomadaire* had printed a description of the flight provided by one of our neighbors, an account that was neither good-natured nor accurate. Still, it was said that the Controller General of Finance himself had had his imagination fired by the thing.

The morning post held a special fervency for us. Etienne had left his wife seven months pregnant, and only two of her previous four girls had survived their infancy. It was agreed that he would produce two sets of correspondence: one of more general developments that could be read in our father's presence, and another addressed to his wife containing news about the machine, which she could share after our father had retired for the evening. Among those more general developments stood our hope to capitalize on our machine's fame to win further privileges for our mills. As Jean-Pierre put it, why compete if we could fix the game?

Etienne wrote that he found himself contending for the right to pursue our discovery with J. Charles, the young man whose laboratory in experimental physics had had such a string of successes that the American

Franklin was said to have remarked of his performances that Nature could not say no to him. Charles's balloon was only twelve feet in diameter but was filled instead with hydrogen, which he generated in a barrel through a reaction of iron filings and oil of vitriol.

Etienne's letters expressed mostly his fears that he was out of his depth as a provincial businessman in such a great capital. He claimed to have little aptitude for the calls to be paid to the ministers and the courtiers, and little feel for in which salons he should play the lion and in which the lamb. He reported to be afflicted by turns with irritation and depression, and Alexandre wrote him to counsel more patience, reminding his younger brother that patience was a drug impossible to overstock. He added the further reassurance that Adelaide was keeping up her spirits but that her condition made her sleepy in the mornings. Jean-Pierre appended a post-script urging Etienne to obtain some American orders for paper from the famous Franklin.

A month later Etienne wrote to report that Charles had released a teth-ered balloon that had ascended one hundred feet into the air, and that two days later it had been set free on the Champ-de-Mars before an estimated fifty thousand spectators, where it had risen until it disappeared into the clouds, and that Franklin, having heard someone remark that the inven-tion was of no practical value, was said to have responded, "Of what use is a newborn babe?" Etienne added that it had been put about that he had been turned away from the demonstration for want of a ticket.

Left to my own devices, I spent my weeks drawing up plans for a balloon one hundred and fifty feet in diameter and one hundred feet high. It might cost sixteen thousand livres. But why settle for less? I conveyed to Etienne my excitement, and urged him to suggest, if the commission balked, that we might take our invention to England. There were plenty of wealthy patrons there.

He responded that the commission had undertaken to pay our expenses, but only to the extent of supporting a machine of the size he had proposed: about two-thirds the height of my leviathan. The Controller General had indicated the King's interest and had authorized those at court who could arrange a demonstration at Versailles before the royal family to do so. The exhibition was to be mounted on the great patio before the chateau on 19 September, with a private trial to be staged for the Academy a week earlier.

Even for a machine that size we had anxieties about the durability of the taffeta and paper. I proposed silk coated with varnish, but Etienne rejected that option due to the expense. I wrote him back that only Etienne would make economy a point of honor after having been accorded carte blanche.

It was decided that this time we would not be content to match the spectacle of the Charles balloon with a grander machine of our own; this time we would bear into the air some living beings. But which animals should go aloft? Etienne first proposed a sheep, but I wrote back that a sheep might go unnoticed. What about a dog, whose barking would better make itself heard from high above? Or what about a cow?

I inquired if I should come at once to the capital to assist in the preparations, and Etienne answered that his patrons had provided him with all of the assistance he required, and that I was of the most use at home, where I was. The entire family went silent when Adelaide read that passage from the letter.

Construction took place at the Réveillon wallpaper factory, and Etienne wrote upon the balloon's completion that when it came to its design, I had approached it like a visionary, he had approached like an architect, and Réveillon had approached it like a decorator. The result he depicted as a truly splendid object, seventy feet tall and forty-five in diameter with an intricately patterned exterior of cerulean and gold, a machine he pronounced fit to float above a king. In order to align the edges and conjoin the seams, his workers had spread the fabric out in the factory's courtyard entire, since there were no spaces in its interior sufficient to accommodate the task. When rain or wind threatened, everything had to be refolded with excruciating care and hurried back under shelter.

On the 11th Etienne and Réveillon conducted a trial themselves that went perfectly. On the 12th it rained. The commissioners failed to arrive at the appointed time. Once they had assembled themselves, the rain had increased. Etienne made the decision to proceed. In what became a down-pour, the paper peeled from its backing and our unhappy machine dragged its gaiety dismally into some nearby trees. Two months of work disappeared in a morning. He wrote in his letter about the disaster that the spectators were sympathetic.

I reminded him in my response that every success sowed the seeds of failure, and that any change in a system might introduce a new way in which the system could fail. Understanding came from failure and success came from understanding. We needed only to own up to our roles in the disaster, and in that way achieve our absolution. All hope of improvement had its roots in our shortcomings. I refrained from any mention of my suggestion of the varnish.

With only a week with which to work they constructed a new and smaller machine, fifty feet tall. It would ascend with a wicker cage holding a sheep, a duck, and a rooster. Etienne's letter about that great day, when it finally arrived, described the arrangements at Versailles, with the enormous crowd surrounding a great octagonal stage, below which an apron painted to resemble a velvet curtain concealed an iron stove as tall as a man; Etienne had been privileged to explain the preparations to the royal family before the noxious smell produced by the material being burned had forced them to retire from the machine's immediate proximity. He described how electric the atmosphere among the spectators had become when the great fabric had begun to stir and rise. And how the balloon had taken to the air, drawing along behind it the first aeronauts. The flight had covered two miles, and the King himself had invited Etienne to observe its landing through his own spyglass. Astronomers had used a quadrant to estimate its altitude to have reached one thousand five hundred feet, not nearly as high as we had gone before, but the animals had all been recovered in fine shape, although the sheep had pissed in the cage.

Etienne was now negotiating countless invitations to dine, including with the Queen, who had requested a detailed account of our invention. And the King, upon the first mention of the possibility of sending a man aloft, had suggested a condemned criminal, to which the Marquis d'Arlandes had responded that no such honor should be afforded a wretch bound for the gallows, and had proposed himself. Etienne ended his letter with the galvanizing news that the King had agreed to the notion.

I wrote him back our congratulations and an account of our jubilation, and added the further happy news that Adelaide had delivered to them another daughter, which she had not yet named.

Once it was common knowledge that men would take to the sky, a mania engulfed our nation, with all manner of objects being produced featuring balloon motifs. Etienne sent home to the family four bottles of Créme de l'Aérostatique liqueur, the labels of which featured fanciful images of both our machine and our faces. All conversation seemed to turn on flying machines and the means of managing them. All one heard in Paris, Etienne reported, was talk of inflammable gas and journeys through the clouds. Miniature *montgolfiers* of scraped animal membranes were sold on every corner.

The first upon the scene at our downed balloon in Versailles turned out to be Jean-Francois Pilatre de Rozier, who had already made a name for himself at the age of twenty-six by having provided to the young ladies of fashion demonstrations of chemical and electrical effects, accompanied by various gallantries and levities. He had a passion for offering himself up to scientific causes, and in a kind of rubberized coverall had descended into one of the foulest sections of the Parisian sewers in order to successfully test for thirty-four minutes a breathing apparatus attached to an enclosed barrel of air, an invention that had been acclaimed for the lives it would save, since those workmen tasked with cleaning the tunnels had been so often overcome by the mephitic gases. The morning following our flight he had publicly announced his willingness to accompany the Marquis d'Arlandes aloft, and since he enjoyed the patronage of the comte and the comtesse de Provence, the King's brother and sister-in-law, Etienne wrote that he found the young man to be well qualified.

The ascent of the Marquis d'Arlandes and de Rozier was arranged for the morning of 20 November. It would take place at the Chateau de La Muette, a royal hunting lodge. Etienne wrote at the end of every day to describe the progress of our preparations. In our bed in the middle of the night, after I had thought she had gone to sleep, and after having heard, earlier in the evening, one such letter read in its entirety to the assembled family by Adelaide, Therese whispered to me, her palm cool and soft along my cheek, "How has he not sent for you? Why have you not gone to him?"

The machine would be our grandest yet, with Réveillon having assigned eight workmen to the decorative touches alone. The main envelope would be indigo and royal blue, with red and gold fleur-de-lis and eagles rampant, and the signs of the zodiac encircling the great dome. The aeronauts would ride in a wicker gallery surrounding the aperture for the burner, the gallery curtained in a lightweight cloth painted to resemble drapery. The entire contrivance including the passengers was calculated to weigh sixteen hundred pounds. The burner once aloft would be tended with straw by means of lightweight pitchforks. On our own experimental machines, constructed separately, we had determined the distance of separation required to keep the heat of the brazier from setting fire to the fabric above.

It was decided that some experiments with tethered flight might be a prudent prelude to a manned, untethered voyage, and so Etienne warned the public by means of a notice in the *Journal de Paris* that on 17 October some tests would be conducted that concerned only scientists. Of course the announcement created even more excitement, and he wrote a week before the tests were to occur to report with both pleasure and dismay that it was clear that many thousands planned on attending, and that a multitude had already arrived upon the site.

Our father's anxiety that Etienne himself would make an ascent became so intense and ungovernable between the arrival of his son's letters that both Alexandre and Jean-Pierre threatened to leave home. Jean-Pierre finally wrote that our father required that Etienne give him no further cause for distress and to absolutely warrant that he would not ascend in his machine. The old man countersigned the letter himself. "If he were to be lost, I do not know how I would carry forward," he announced to our assembled family at dinner the following evening, apropos of nothing.

On the appointed day the tethered flight took place before a vast assemblage and under threatening skies. The American Franklin, whose residence in the Hotel de Valentinois was nearby, was there in attendance. De Rozier ascended alone, first, to eighty feet, with a one-hundred-pound sack at the opposite end of the gallery to balance the weight; my mind's eye beheld him soaring on rapture's white wings. He said as he drew near the earth that it seemed the whole country was alarmed.

The following day a heavy wind prevented him from rising any higher. The day after that he floated at some two hundred and fifty feet for eight minutes, and as for Etienne's reports of the remaining two flights on that great day, the first climbed to over three hundred feet, thereby becoming visible to the entire city, and the second finally included the impatient Marquis d'Arlandes, who upon his descent predicted aerostatic ships that would one day carry guns and strike down our enemies from above.

In my exile from the invigoration and euphoria of those events which all of France save myself seemed to have witnessed, the dreams that took shape in the solitude of my workshop filled vast sheets with unrealized extravagance: a rectangular balloon two hundred feet high and capable of lifting a horse and wagon. A cylindrical machine six hundred feet long that would float by burning two hundred pounds of wood per minute. Vessels without equal in size in the world's existence. Etienne with an air of distraction noticeable even in his letters praised my ambition and suggested I attempt some small-scale models. Though, he joked, he feared that my notion of small was not that of other men. When I wrote that I was constructing a machine that would ascend far higher than any previously had, he wrote back that my fantasies might be well and good if we were both twenty and without responsibilities, but that Therese had informed him of my financial situation, and that we could no longer be certain of an endless supply of funds. Our father had privately made clear that he would do no more to enable my profligacy, and even in England the rich didn't toss their wealth out the window any more readily. He suggested I instead devote my energies to searching for ways to improve the impermeability and lessen the weight of the envelope.

Subsequent to the Marquis d'Arlandes's remark, my brother had been calculating the military applications of our invention, including the possibility of ferrying bombs over walls to be dropped onto fortified positions.

He had always been upset by the complaint that aviation ministered only to the vanity of scientists. Because of us, the skies were now as open to exploitation as the seas. What most excited him, though, were the opportunities for commerce, the lifeblood of the ordered world, especially for the transportation of bulk goods at low cost.

I wrote him back confessing that what drove me now was no monopoly, but a community of learning. He apparently found the suggestion to be of such pitiable naïveté that he chose not to respond to it in his next letter.

But trade itself is nothing more than a galaxy of the imagination, wheeling about a marketplace of services and commodities. Confidence and anxiety, each utterly ephemeral, are infinitely more powerful than solid materials. Consider credit, with its ghostly power to buoy and carry forward its servants, even as they register how diaphanous it remains—only a vapor—when grasped.

I relate this conviction to Therese in the middle of the night, and, having been pulled from sleep, she concurs in order to be left alone. "You still have to pay what you have to pay," she murmurs, her back to my front.

On such nights, having once again renounced the arms of my wife, my sleepless and prowling sadness unsettles me. I'm struck by the way the conceits of this world may be as dreams to those of the next, just as the phantoms of the darkness give way to the clarities of the day. Therese seems even more herself in her sleep, and even more worthy of my devotion, and so I peer down at her expression in repose and remind myself of our intimacy, despite all of the obstacles I have strewn in its path, the way a memory of a troubled dream relates to the awakened mind a confused and broken tale of what has passed.

We continue to fall short, like the objects we create. We can only pray, on our rounds, *Let me not injure the felicity of others.* And wait for sadness to grow tired of her office, and to provide us some respite. And for labor to vibrate more forcibly on the chords of our heart than the most harmonious music.

I wake Therese again and she sits up in the cold of our bedroom, as drowsy as a child but concerned enough about her husband to counsel herself to patience. Her forbearance itself is an indication of the intimacy about which I fret. "Go to Paris if you want to go to Paris," she tells me, believing she anticipates the cause of my distress. A better man would awaken her more fully to what's coming, but this one only sees to her comfort with a blanket, and sits beside her until she eases back down into sleep. So that even the clarity with which I can discern the ongoing pattern of my withdrawal refuses to occasion in me a shift.

I have often fancied that man in his relation to the sky resembled marine organisms confined to the ocean's bottom, and that in order to discover the true conditions of the atmosphere it would be necessary to observe them at considerable heights. We live in the depths of an ocean of air.

Etienne writes that the Marquis d'Arlandes urges all speed in readying our craft for its first untethered flight, since Charles is now also at work on an improved hydrogen balloon for the same purpose, and the Marquis confides that persons of the greatest eminence have made clear that being the first to launch a man in free flight would attach the final seal of glory to our invention. Jean-Pierre has written to remind Etienne that he should accept no distinction that did not apply equally to me, and when Etienne wrote to reassure me on the subject, I told him that if the King had only one ribbon, it was Etienne who should have it, and Etienne who would no doubt put it to better use. As for me, the more I am informed of the pleasures of society, the more I am drawn to my solitude. Jean-Pierre showed me a letter Etienne sent to him privately, in response, in which he noted that apparently the success of my experiments had elevated my imagination to such a height that I could not easily lower myself to attend base considerations like providing a creditor with payment. He also accused me of playing Achilles in my tent.

I have used all of the funds remaining at my disposal, including those I pledged to Therese, to complete my own improved machine. Under cover of darkness, with the household asleep, I have made all of the final preparations for ascent, with only the terriers as my spectators. My balloon is much smaller but its envelope is reinforced with varnish, and my brazier and fuel supply are double the size of Etienne's.

It is very late before I'm ready. The terriers circle below the ever-expanding fabric above them, wary but quiet. When the balloon is filled to capacity and the restraining ropes vibrate with the tension of its demand,

I slip the knots and feel myself leap upward into the darkness. One of the terriers barks and I hear two others pursue me for a short stretch the way children might a butterfly, but then they fall away below.

At three hundred feet the tether arrests me with a thump that knocks me to one knee. Once my little basket stops swaying on its ropes, a stillness reigns over the air. I can hear the increasingly hoarse and far-off barking of the terriers. Then they cease and even the wind is hushed to a calm by the canopy of constellations above. I gaze upon new and unheard-of stars. I can make out the glow of furnaces from the blacksmith's in town. Otherwise a black plunging gulf surrounds me on all sides. I sip some water and drop the empty bottle out of the basket and hear it whistle as it descends. I remain as still as I am able, laboring under the grandeur of the moment, until just before daybreak, when the cultivated fields begin to materialize below, bordered with embrowning hedges.

In the gray light of morning, smoke begins to rise from various chimneys. Highways and rivers appear just as if laid down on a map. Rising hills to the east afford pasturage to dotted flocks of sheep. My father is already awake and about, and no doubt puzzled by the ropes and tools in the courtyard.

The barometer stands at twenty-eight and the thermometer at thirty-one. I untie the tether, which helixes away below, and vault upward. The act makes me the first in the world to engage in untethered flight.

I can gauge from the horizon the accelerating speed of my ascent. The balloon spins gently on its axis. I close my eyes and turn my face to the sun and imagine somewhere down below Therese has done the same.

The barometer now stands at eighteen, having fallen an inch since my release. The temperature has dropped to twelve and seems to be decreasing uniformly with the height. I pass through thinner and more striated cloud, and don the sheepskin from the bottom of the basket. I wait. A van of mallards passes over the far-off river. According to the barometer and my timepiece I have achieved an altitude of over eight thousand feet in just under nine minutes.

At some point I give a small shout of relief and joy before covering my mouth in surprise. The mallards, now almost invisible, continue on their way. Finally, with a cord attached at a valve, I release some of my store of heated gas and halt my ascent.

The balloon pendulums alarmingly, and then stabilizes. The wind picks up and I pass horizontally through yet more mist. From the fabric's shape it's clear that the rarefication of the air has diminished the envelope's volume even further. I imagine Etienne's expression were I to tell him of all this.

Therese will wake to my absence and find all the evidence of my departure among the chagrined and confused terriers. She'll wonder if what I've done is possible, and if I'd really risk such a voyage that could bring us to ruin. But we ride our lives' trajectories as if swallows passing from fair weather to foul, and at least, at my most self-aware, I have worked to remember that all too often the only world I choose to regard is myself.

The cold is sharp and dry, but not unbearable. When I survey the astonishing course of my life, I call to account the finger of God and the scepter of His mercies for having delivered unto me these gifts of my imagination and love and hubris and achievement. Posterity will applaud each of my brothers before they take their places in that perpetuity unto which all of us must finally relinquish the compass of our reach. But were I to be saved, and were Therese to forgive me, we would still pass away before we could witness, in the years to come, aeronauts departing on the trade winds for America or the tropics, to return laden with passengers and goods. The fruit of my machine is beautiful to imagine but not for us to sample. It's a tree planted for our children.

I remind myself that Therese is the patron who made me ready, in the happiness of being known, and through our common faith and cause, to assail such heights. Through what she has enabled I have been delivered all that I dare call happiness on earth.

The balloon, still shrinking, has begun its descent. My hands beneath the sheepskin are numb. My reasoning feels light-headed. There's a pain in my ear. I examine each sensation in tranquility. I stand in the center of my basket lost in the spectacle afforded by the immensity of the horizon at this height. So many below me remain in the dark where I left them. So many allied themselves to me only to see that they grasped at a wraith. So many farms and houses are still in shadow that the sun seems to have risen for me and me alone, gilding the basket and fabric above with its light.

HAPPY ENDING

by STUART DYBEK

The only one to arrive fashionably late for the Mogul's little soiree was the last of several rain-soaked bike-delivery kids bringing up Thai takeout. By midnight, the rain had turned into an unexpected, fluorescent snowfall wafting past the windows facing Central Park, and the dozen or so members of the show who'd been invited to the Mogul's suite at the Carlyle had nearly drunk their way through a case of Dom Pérignon. When no one moved to open the last bottle, the Mogul popped it himself.

"To the success of *EverAfter*," he said. "By the way, that fucking title's got to go."

Everyone raised their flutes and drank.

"I can order up more bubbly," the Mogul said, "but it won't be the same great year."

"Man, they're all great years," Nestor, the musical director, said and drank to that.

"Some are decidedly better than others," the Mogul said. "That's what you pay for."

Nestor bowed, corrected. They'd all witnessed, earlier in the day, what disagreeing with the Mogul could cost.

The Mogul had flown in from LA that morning in his private jet to watch the rehearsal. Wearing smoked-gray aviator glasses as if he had piloted the plane himself, he slipped into the theater unannounced and sat silently smoking in the back row. The cast didn't need the smell of cigarillo to know he was there. Gil had never seen the actors more jumpy. Even Renee and Tony Kayne—TK—the romantic leads, both with established careers, appeared nervous. They'd been working on the play for over a year.

No one called the Mogul "the Mogul" to his face. The nickname wasn't meant affectionately; it alluded to his reputation for being egotistical and ruthless. But it wasn't solely his reputation that put the cast on edge. The rehearsal was a make/break audition. If he liked what he saw, the Mogul was set to buy the film option and help bankroll the dramatic production. If *EverAfter* went on to Broadway, he would buy it outright for a film; and, if that happened, even the writers with their mere one-percent shares would score.

"You'll never have to teach again, Gil," is how Liam, the director, put it.

EverAfter was a sequence of three one-acts, each written by a different playwright, and unified by a musical score and by the ensemble of actors. Over the course of the evening, the audience watched the players changing identities and aging as the stories moved from youth to middle age to maturity. Gil had written the first act, *Youth*.

It was set in a haunted jazz club that back in the Roaring Twenties had been a speakeasy, and told the story of an affair between a coked-up chanteuse named Bea and a young trumpet player named Dex. Bea believed Dex was a reincarnated Bix Beiderbecke, and that in their former lives, when they'd been lovers, she'd been responsible in a way she could no longer remember for his mysterious death at twenty-eight. Now, back together in love again, Bea feared their fate would repeat itself.

Dick Jokes, the second act, involved a banjo-picking woman comic touring the Deep South during the Nixon-Kennedy presidential campaign. When *Dick Jokes* ended, the Mogul signaled for a break. He didn't return for an hour, and this time he sat close to the stage next to Liam, who, besides directing, had conceived of *EverAfter* and assembled the company.

Everyone in the company knew that the third act, *Visti di Mare*, had problems. Jeremy Spada who'd written it had disappeared into a Mexican alternative medicine clinic; the rumor was, with AIDS-related cancer. The act told the story of a couple trying to save their marriage of twenty years by taking a honeymoon cruise on the Adriatic. It opened in the ship's lounge during a storm at sea, with the Captain sitting down at the piano and singing "Slow Boat to China." Sven Nystrom, a noted Shakespearean actor, played the Captain. Halfway through the song, the Mogul interrupted. "Stan," he said, "hold on a sec."

Sven continued to sing until the Mogul stood and raised his voice, "Stan!"

"It's Sven," Sven Nystrom said.

"You're doing it like Sinatra," the Mogul said.

"Actually, Tony Bennett," Sven said. "The Captain's Dutch, but he always wanted to be an American crooner. You'll see that everyone on this cruise is acting out a fantasy."

"Try it like he thinks he's Michael Jackson," the Mogul said.

"He's *Dutch*. White, retirement age. Why would he want to be something so outlandish as Michael Jackson?" Sven asked.

"Maybe because the corny white lounge singer shtick's already been done to death. Here, have him put these on," the Mogul said, handing his aviator shades up to Sven.

"Wouldn't dark glasses be more Stevie Wonder?" Sven asked, taking the glasses and looking to Liam for support, but all Liam said was, "Nestor, take it from the start of 'China.'"

Sven sat down at the piano, put on the sunglasses, and resumed singing "Slow Boat to China." He halfheartedly grabbed his crotch a few times à la *Thriller*, but still sounded like Tony Bennett.

"Stan," the Mogul called. Sven ignored him and kept crooning.

"Stan!" the Mogul shouted. "Instead of parked on your heinie, you're supposed to be all but moonwalking behind that fucking keyboard."

"It's Sven," Sven said.

"Sorry," the Mogul said, *"Sven.* Do I have that right? Sven you can deposit those sunglasses on the piano as you leave the stage."

"Pardon me?" Sven asked.

"I have to spell it out? You're toast, Sven," the Mogul said

Gil was sitting beside Tina Powell, who had written *Dick Jokes.* She pulled him toward her so that her lips were beside his ear. "The Mogul just announced that he's bankrolling the show. And that he owns us," she said. "You may never have to teach again."

After the rehearsal, Liam waved Gil over. The Mogul wanted to meet him. "I knew I was going to back the play after I saw your first act, Gil," he said. "Brilliant, spooky stuff. Do you ever write about vampires? The third act totally sucks, though. Can you rewrite it?"

"It's not my play," Gil said.

"I can hire a script doctor," the Mogul said, "but I'd rather someone already connected with our project did it. I'm not even sure I know what the fuck it's supposed to be about. I get the everybody-has-a-fantasy bit, but that's not doing anything for me. Help me out here, Gil. What's there to salvage?"

"The fantasy motif isn't working for you?" Gil asked.

"I'm not Disney, for fuck's sake. You've seen the movies I make. There's got to be something that goes for the throat."

"Passion," Gil said.

"Passion?" the Mogul repeated. "Go on."

"The couple has lost their passion," Gil said.

"Gil, that's brilliant," the Mogul said. "Fucking love it."

"You do? Thanks. I mean it's a little clichéd, but..."

The Mogul cut him off.

"You know, Gil, a secret to success in this business is to understand there's a fine line between a cliché and a classic, so fine that—not to sound cynical—it's virtually invisible to most people in the audience. You're a classy writer, but you don't let it get in the way of life. Think about a rewrite. Passion. We'll talk more tonight. I'm giving a little soiree."

*   *   *

By the time a second case of champagne arrived, the park trees, ablaze for autumn, were flocked white. Flights of leaves, weighted with wet snow, gusted through the swirl of flakes, as if the park might be stripped bare overnight.

"The wind sounds like whale songs from up here," Tina Powell said. She and Gil stood together at a window, looking out and passing a bottle of champagne between them. "When it comes to beautiful illusions, this city still has a few tricks up its sleeve," Tina said. "Or is that just the booze talking?"

"Makes you want to be out there walking," Gil said.

"Not in these it doesn't." Tina lifted her skirt to give him a better look at her slender calves and violet open-toed pumps. "Wish I'd worn boots."

"Perfect footwear for a soiree," Gil said. "You look lovely tonight."

"Had I known months ago you only flirt when drunk on overpriced hubbly I might have insisted on Petrossian instead of Papaya King," Tina said. "Not that those weren't top New York kosher dogs. When the Mogul makes us rich, we can celebrate. We'll dress our wieners in beluga and get drunk as skunks."

"I'll admit to being a little buzzed maybe, but not drunk," Gil said.

"Too bad. I am, might as well be." Tina said. "What's stopping you? Tonight's a celebration of sorts, no? You'll never have to teach again. You can retire to a hut in Malibu and write that blood-sucker trilogy you've always known you had in you."

A bellman refilled the ice buckets, dimmed the lighting, and asked if he should also clear the food.

"Leave it," the Mogul said. "People are still nibbling." The Mogul had been drinking quietly as if brooding, or maybe his own party bored him. He sat beside an ice bucket as one might sit with a teddy bear, alone on a couch behind a coffee table barricaded with takeout cartons. Takeout cartons occupied almost every surface in the room—the tabletops, the desk, the windowsills. There were cartons balanced on top of cartons that had yet to be opened. The Mogul rose and began to open and reopen a few of them, jabbing his chopsticks in for a sample, then resealing each one.

"Just dipping your beak?" Tina Powell asked.

"Don Fanucci in *The Godfather*," the Mogul answered. "Best line in the movie."

The Mogul said that when he'd asked for the best Thai delivery in the city, three different restaurants were recommended. They couldn't all be the best, so to settle the question, he'd ordered from all three. But now, with the cartons mixed up, it was impossible to tell what had come from where. He had instructed the front desk to send up the delivery boys because he felt the best part of takeout was the ring at the door followed by the smell of steaming food. You knew the food was never as good as it smelled, but it didn't matter. The smell, he said, reminded him of the cheap Asian food he'd survived on when, with no prospects, he hitched his way to LA—his city of dreams—where young, broke, scuffling, literally picking cigarette butts out of the gutter, he'd determined to make his mark or fucking die trying. In those days when he was always hungry, the food had tasted as good as it smelled.

The Mogul sat back down beside the ice bucket and filled his glass.

Champagne was being popped all over the room. Debates broke out over the best carryout places in the city, Queens against Manhattan, until Liam announced that as far as he was concerned, the question wasn't what restaurant was best, but rather, which was most authentic.

"You can say the same thing about theater," Liam said.

TK took that as a cue to tell them all about the time he'd shot a film in Bangkok, and how the food there bore little resemblance to Thai food in New York. He'd especially loved the street food, and never once got sick, at least not from eating. Drink and drugs were another matter. He was partying hard back then. They'd start shooting at six a.m. and he'd clear his head by eating an incendiary curry for breakfast. Lunch was fruit delivered from the great fruit market on Pahonyothin Road: mangoes, young coconuts called *ma praw on*, and fruits TK had never tasted fresh before—mangosteen, jackfruit, lychee. There were fruits he knew only by their Thai names—*lam-yai, longkong*—and, speaking of the difference between smell and taste, sometimes a durian, a fruit so putrid smelling that the hotels posted signs warning it was illegal to bring one inside. Yet durians tasted like silky custard, like nothing you'd ever had before. They'd blend them into icy smoothies, and then TK would get a massage from a skinny woman who spoke no English but could cure a hangover by walking her fingers down his spine. He didn't think you could get authentic Thai in New York, though maybe a durian could be found in the wilds of the Bronx.

"Just don't try bringing it into the Carlyle," Tina said.

"Are those places that say 'Thai massage' authentic?" Renee asked.

"I have *no* idea," TK said.

"So, man, how do you ask for happy ending in Thai?" Nestor asked.

"Try, *I want happy ending*," TK said, "not that I am speaking from personal experience."

"Is happy ending what I think it is?" Garth, who had inherited the Captain's role now that Sven was toast, wanted to know.

"Man, everybody knows 'happy ending,'" Nestor said, his speech noticeably slurred.

"I don't," Renee said. "Is it animal, vegetable, or mineral?"

"All of the above," Nestor said. "Imagine instead of an actor, Garth's something real: a teamster driving a sixteen-wheeler down I-80 through the night in Nebraska, listening to Jesus radio, popping No-Doz, his back killing him, and suddenly there's a pink neon sign—not THAI MASSAGE. Just RUB DOWN. Five minutes later he's naked, blissed, as this pretty Asian woman slathers on oil and walks her magic fingers down his spine. And just as he's thinking it's over too soon, she asks, *Want happy ending?* That's not the moment to blurt *Miss, is happy ending what I think it is? Is it authentic happy ending?* You say, *Oh, yeah!* And she says, *Happy ending, fifty dollar extra.* And man, there in the darkness of Nebraska you've learned the authentic price of happiness."

"I was going to suggest changing *EverAfter* to *Happy Ending*," Renee said, "but now I'm afraid that would raise the wrong expectations in the audience."

"Wouldn't it be nice if life was that simple?" the Mogul asked. "If expectations were always fair and easily met? If all it took to find happiness was to know the right words for asking, and who to ask, and the going rate? Everyone wants to know the magic words, and there's no shortage of religions, philosophies, gurus, psychologists, politicians all claiming to be able to tell us. Take Nixon and JFK in Tina's play: Nixon's telling America, Here's my idea of happy ending, and Kennedy is saying, Well, here's mine. Of course Tricky Dicky with his grizzled face was one morose-looking dude, and Jack Kennedy you knew was getting happy ending eight nights a week, so bring on Camelot.

"Look at the talent in this one hotel room, the plays, films, music, books you people have produced. Isn't *authentic* Art—capital A—supposed to show us how to live happily ever after? I once went to a famous therapist, I won't drop his name or sticker-shock you with how much he thought his time was worth, and told him: I've got everything a man could want— power, fame, fortune—I could go through ten reincarnations and not spend what I've made in this one lifetime. I've got a mansion in Santa Monica, a chateau in Provence, my own Pacific island, the best food and liquor, women JFK would have singing Happy Birthday Mr. President for him every day of the year. I can feel the envy when I enter a room, yet I'm not happy. First thing the shrink advises me to do is read this novel he thought would help me. I say, Doc, I know the author, I brought him to Hollywood and like most Artists, capital A, he was one of the most miserable fucks on the planet. I'm supposed to learn something about happiness from him? So the shrink immediately retreats to plan B, his Socratic fucking question: How do you define happiness? Like I'm going to pay in time and money to play semantic games, just so he doesn't have to admit he doesn't have a clue. And here I am, tonight, surrounded by artists, intellectuals, the New York literati—can any of you come up with a better answer?"

In the quiet, it was possible for the first time in the evening to hear the classical guitar music that had been playing in the background.

"Liam," the Mogul said, "you put this whole show together. Do you have an answer? Renee, you're a glamorous, award-winning actress, how about you? TK, you've traveled the world. Tina, you're witty enough to do stand-up on TV. Gil, we haven't had a chance to talk about passion yet, but you're a hell of a writer. Anybody?"

The guests had formed a semicircle around the couch where the Mogul sat alone with his ice bucket. They looked down into their wine glasses, avoiding eye contact, sipping meditatively as if mulling over his question, drinking as if that disguised the embarrassing lack of response.

"I might," Gil said.

"And here I thought you of all people would shy away from the subject," the Mogul said. "Because, you know, happiness like passion can be a little *clichéd*. Let's hear it. An answer could be worth the proverbial king's ransom."

"I can't tell you why you're unhappy," Gil said, "because you aren't."

"Oh, I guarantee you that I am. I could produce some very famous people willing to serve as witnesses."

"It's not a matter of what others say, is it?"

"Well, if it's simply my word against yours, who do you think the jury will believe? Frankly, I'm going to be very disappointed if you're leading up to some semantic what-is-happiness bullshit, because I'm talking naked, Gil. Gut level."

"Gut level, absolutely," Gil said. "What if I can prove you are happy?"

Behind the carton-stacked coffee table, the Mogul leaned forward on the couch as if not wanting to miss a word.

"I went to college on a track scholarship," Gil said.

"And you look like you've stayed in shape," the Mogul said.

"Thanks," Gil said. "My event was high hurdles. I put a lot of practice into making my move out of the starting blocks explosive. When you see hurdlers racing, knocking down hurdles, it can look like a free-for-all, but it's actually a very controlled event. Every hurdler has the same number of strides between hurdles—usually three. That's about the distance between you and me. If you weren't expecting it, and why should you be, I could cross the room, hurdle the table, and before you could react, jam these chopsticks in your eyes, and after you finished howling, and your long hospital stay was over, and you were learning to feel your way with a white cane, you'd think back to tonight with the snow and the champagne and the smell of takeout that cooks sweating over spattering woks had ladled into cartons for a kid who probably can't speak English to bring us on his bike in the driving rain, and I bet you'd realize that you *were* happy. You just can't see it at this moment."

Except for Nestor's snoring, the room had gone dead silent. No one moved or spoke. The music had stopped.

"So, when do you say, 'Hey, just kidding'?" the Mogul finally asked.

The question released the tension in the room enough for Liam to rise— a little unsteadily—and, saying it was a great night but it was late and there was a rehearsal tomorrow, grab his coat from the rack set up by the door. A mass exit of guests followed him out into the hall, grabbing their coats without pausing to put them on, and packed into the elevators.

The Mogul stayed on the couch.

Gil rode down the elevator with Tina.

"I didn't know you ran track," she said.

"Artistic license, capital *A*," Gil said. "Third place in the state finals in high school was as far as I got."

"Where'd the chopsticks come from?"

"You know, until he said *gut level* I was actually going to tell a story about a Chinese poet friend of mine who's studied kung fu for thirty years at a dojo called the Sanctuary of Universal Peace. When he told me the dojo's name, I asked if he'd ever used kung fu to defend himself, and he said that wasn't why he studied. So what are you after? I asked, and he thought awhile like he'd never considered it, then said: To be able to say thank you every minute."

"And 'thank you every minute' turned into chopsticks. Inspiration will do that," Tina said.

They stood beneath the hotel's gold-lit marquee while, over the wet hiss of traffic along Madison, the doorman whistled for cabs. When the wind gusted, snowflakes caught in Tina's hair and melted glittering in the marquee lights. She did look lovely. From the little she'd mentioned about her personal life—a runaway daughter now living at a drug-rehab center, an ongoing divorce from a man she described as "a decent guy who still adores me"—Gil knew she was going through a difficult time. He wondered how she was managing to work as well as she was. He had told her at Papaya King, months ago, that her piece, *Dick Jokes*, and Nestor's musical score were the only really solid things about *EverAfter*.

"When I get home, just before I pass out, I'm going to think about tonight and laugh myself to sleep," Tina said. "Hopefully it will keep off the spins."

"Don't forget to picture Sven doing the crotch-grab while singing 'Slow Boat to China,'" Gil said.

"That's too ha-ha sad," Tina said, "But then maybe he'll have the final revenge after he incorporates some crotch work to rave reviews the next time he plays Lear."

A cab pulled up. "I won't bother to ask if you want to share a ride," she said.

"I'm going to walk in the park."

She kissed him goodnight lightly on the cheek and he closed the door of the cab after her and stood watching her pull away. The cab started and stopped. Tina rolled down the window. "Gil, one more thing. If I were you, I wouldn't be planning to give up my teaching job just yet."

She gave a wave and he waved back.

The cab started and stopped again. Tina rolled down the window. "One more one more thing," she called. "If you want to say it every minute, you have to start with one minute. Thank you."

THE DANCE
CONTEST

by WELLS TOWER

MEN OF THE DARK

One afternoon at the start of the rainy season, Captain Surongporn, warden of Thep Moob Men's Prison, orders all inmates to the Zone B yard to hear some jolly news. Surongporn is only four months into his leadership; the prison, a former military fortification built in the reign of King Rama V, has been in operation since the end of World War II.

Surongporn's leading feature is a compact balloon of abdomen, proudly snugged in a brass-button shirt cut from lemon-colored cloth. He is a sway-backed little fellow built like a jellybean. The fourteen hundred men sitting or squatting before him all wear underclothes or cutoff pants. Nearly all are barefoot and shirtless. A few vain fellows, aristocrats for whom a sun-tan spells disgrace, hunch beneath broken umbrellas. Captain Surongporn looks shyly pleased with himself. His mien of coy potency resembles that of a gifted seven-year-old gymnast readying herself for her first public walk along the balance beam.

"My friends," he says, "I hope all of you are having a mellow and productive day. Perhaps you feel surprised that I say 'friends.' Well, you deserve to be called by that word. Three months ago, I came to you seeking assistance with several problems. Inmates doing bodily harm to each other was a problem. Drug casualties were a problem. Another problem was videos filmed on contraband phones, videos which referenced conduct that is unbecoming to you and unbecoming to this institution. One more problem was some chattering birds who told false stories to the BBC about conditions in our facility. Three months ago, I asked for your help with these problems, and there has been no trouble since."

He smiles, showing beige teeth not much larger than the kernels of young corn.

"You have all cooperated in the suppression of bad elements, and we are now in a mellow time. And so I call you my friends."

A young man named Ter translates this information for Ron Tolenaar. "Yeah, a mellow time," brays Ron, Ter's patron and house boss of Dorm 23, Zone A. "Five men out the ghost door last month. Keep doing like this, the Moob will be a nice, quiet place. You won't hear a fucking sound but the waves and the birds going 'tweet.'"

Ron is 6'7", wears a size fourteen shoe. His lips, nose, and eyes bulge from his large crimson head, which looks like an infected thing that wants to be lanced. Ron is serving his first year of a forty-year sentence for exporting prostitutes stuffed with narcotics to Holland, his fatherland. Ter, his cellmate, is small and mantis thin. He is seventeen years old and serving no sentence at all. Before his death, Ter's uncle—Ter's last living relative—was a warder here, and he and Ter lived in an apartment off the seaside gun gallery. Pancreatitis killed the uncle in December of last year. In deference to the uncle's memory, the assistant warden has arranged for Ter to stay on in Thep Moob.

"Not five, I think," says Ter, his voice lowered to a whisper he wishes Ron would match.

"Yeah, five: three ODs, plus one AIDS, plus my man Julio, the Mexican faggot the yellow boys whipped," Ron intones at bullhorn volume, drawing the scrutiny of three yellow boys, high-ranking trusties kitted out with yellow shirts and white clubs. He meets their gaze sneeringly. The pineapple hooch Ron has been drinking since daybreak has put him in an heroic bent of mind. "They bashed his face to marmalade. I guess he is pretty mellow now."

"Would you be quiet, please," murmurs Declan Weyde, one of Ron's on-and-off roommates in A-23. "The Captain's not talking in terms of reality. He's talking in terms of, 'Yeah, this summer was a mess, but no one said shit about it.' He's happy. It's a good thing. Shut up."

Declan has been in Thep Moob six years. When people ask him, he says, not very credibly, that he is serving an indefinite sentence for stealing a coffeepot. Declan's actual crime is a mystery of not much interest to other inmates, necessarily obsessed with their own survival. Ron's jabbering, he worries, will draw the yellow boys' attention to the elderly bronchial case who lies beside him, unconscious. Those caught napping during assembly are often made to run laps in the concrete courtyard on naked knees. This might kill the frail man, who is, after a fashion, Declan's friend.

"None of you people here has any balls," Ron says. "I really liked that faggot. Okay, he was a short-eyes—so what? People dig what they dig. He was a funny guy, the Mexican. Somebody give me a computer. I'll say shit to the whole world."

"Man, there aren't two people within a thousand miles who want to hear you talk," mutters Declan. The old man, who is suffering through the early stages of Pontiac fever, makes a sound in his throat like rock salt being flung against a chalkboard. He spits feebly. Rusty sputum darkens his moth-colored beard. The man is large and sickly pale, with a belly like a raw pork bun, rubbed to gleaming hairlessness by seventy years of textile friction. His only garments are a pair of maroon BVDs whose elastic is scalloped due to tensile breakdown. The leg welts swag away from the man's skinny thighs, displaying a crepey poundage of urological tackle. He is, in Declan's eyes, a man past all caring, and Declan worries that he will die very soon.

The old man himself is not frightened by the prospect of death. He is the Ralph D. Hepplewhite Distinguished Professor of Economics at Conant

University, and he believes himself to be a rational person. By his own measure, he has lived a full and venturesome life, and it seems to him fitting that it should come to an end in a foreign land on a warm autumn day by the sea. The man is an American, and he is my father.

His name is Osmund Tower. The letter we will receive about his days in death's mudroom is not, as my mother puts it, "a masterpiece of earthly reflection." It will contain nothing much in the way of a farewell, and no specific mention of us, his family. This will appall my mother and my brother, who will hear a passive cruelty in the blitheness of my father's tone. Let it go, I will tell them. Let us think the best of him.

At the assembly, Ron Tolenaar goes on voicing his drunken complaints about the death of Mexican Julio. A yellow boy waggles a truncheon at him. Ter pats Ron on the arm. "Yeah, maybe good shut the fuck up, Mister Ron," says Ter. "You stink like a party. You don't want they come to the dorm and take the fruit and jars and tubes."

Ron sees the wisdom in this. For the time being, he closes his mouth.

My father's mouth is open. Declan puts a hand to Osmund's face so that the yellow boys do not hear his moist, dragging snores.

Captain Surongporn turns his sallow, minuscule face to the gun-gallery wall on whose far side lies the sea. Mines bob in the near harbor against abettors of a marine escape. Farther out in the gulf, trawlers and pleasurecraft putter and glide. Today, a lucky wind from the south bears dim sounds of merriment from a yacht party miles out on the green deeps. Music is playing. Captain Surongporn can just make out "Dancing in the Moonlight" by King Harvest, a song he knows well. The windborne tune confers a felicity on the announcement the man is here to make.

"We have heard a wish for more recreation, by means of which to improve one's health and self-esteem," says the Captain. "Because you have respected my wishes and concerns, I will repay you with respect for yours. I am pleased to say that today we will grant this wish."

A roar goes up. The inmates want for much in Thep Moob, but more recreation is high on no one's list. They want a less repulsive daily meal, instead of their present ration—a ladleful of weevil-ridden rice topped with a few fish ribs to which crumbs of flesh rarely cling. They want improvements to the visitors' hall, whose telephones are so decrepit it sounds as though your loved one is speaking through a kazoo. They bawl for the lifting of the ban against intramural boxing, long forbidden as too generous a boon to the prison's bookies, who grow rich as it is. A spotted old man rises and roars for a ration of ice with which to soothe his gouty feet. "You pig fuckers won't give me medicine, you can give me ice, at least!" he says. A nearby warder takes issue with "pig fuckers." He knocks the gouty man square on the skull with the pommel of his steel baton. The man collapses neatly into a sitting position. The long truncheons of the trusties drub the concrete.

The thunder quiets the shouting. Captain Surongporn's high, flutelike voice can again be heard. "What I am happy to tell you is this," he says. The Captain pauses, uncurtains his tiny teeth, pans the hard hump of his belly from right to left. "We will have a dance contest here in Thep Moob. Every dorm will participate. Every man will dance. We will have transparency in the competition. The performances will be videoed, and these videos will be placed onto the internet. The winner will be determined by public vote. This is a wonderful opportunity to display your talent, and to show the world that our facility is a facility where fun and creative expression drive our process of reform."

"A wonderful opportunity for the Captain to fuck himself," growls Ron Tolenaar. "Go ahead and shoot me. Put me in the Suitcase before I'll jump up and be a monkey."

This sentiment is general in the courtyard. The Captain looks out at fourteen hundred stone-faced men. Then he announces that an electrical outlet and a color television will be installed in the dorm that takes first prize. Second prize is a ceiling fan and an electrical outlet. Third prize is an electrical outlet.

"Piss in your outlet," Ron calls out, as a minor gleeful bedlam breaks out among the few dancers in the crowd. "Me and my men, we like to live in the dark."

"Sorry, but I would not piss on a little more splendor in our house," says Henri Permeuil, twenty-eight, a Frenchman strung with yoga sinew, Ron's best friend in A-23. "We could have music. A teapot. A thing for soups and stews. We could boil the beer and drink something very nice. And we could make some money, charging people's devices."

A contemplative suction draws the purple welt of Ron's lower lip into his mouth for an instant. He glances at the twin celebrations occurring among a crew of Nigerian smugglers and the transgendered prostitutes who run a brothel in Zone C. "Okay, an outlet would be nice, but we are still fucked," he says. Most dorms in Thep Moob house no fewer than fifty men. A-23 is a luxury cell, its six residents (save Ter) all Westerners who pay a high monthly bribe to hold the population to a comfortable half-dozen. They would make for a paltry choreographic spectacle.

"And who do we have who knows how to shake his ass? You can dance, Henri?"

Henri flutters a sophisticated hand at his temple, as though to say that dancing may be one of his undiscovered gifts.

"Declan?"

"Well, I guess I'm pretty aware of my body," Declan muses. "I've got pretty strong legs and my balance is pretty good. I don't often trip for no reason."

"And then this guy," says Ron, nodding at my father. "Professor Hippopotamus. Maybe we push him in a wagon. No, we totally are screwed."

The Captain has surrendered the microphone to the Director of Programs for a discussion of the contest's logistical details. The Director of Programs states once more that participation is mandatory. Each dorm will be randomly assigned, via bucket drawing, one of three songs around which to craft a routine. These are "Gonna Make You Sweat," by C+C Music Factory; "Ice Ice Baby," by Vanilla Ice; and "All My Rowdy Friends Are Coming Over Tonight," by Hank Williams, Jr. These will be played over the public address system twice each during the daily recreation period. A line forms for the song draw, and the assembly is adjourned.

"If we get Bocephus, maybe we have a chance," says Ron. "I know a little bit the Texas Two-Step from my wife. If we pull Vanilla Ice, it will piss me off completely." He watches Declan Weyde cross the yard, burlesquing a little waltz across the broken concrete.

Through large and womanly plastic shades, Captain Surongporn, roving with his lieutenants, has an eye on Declan, too. The two have never met, but Surongporn pauses to say hello. "Mister Weyde," he says in English.

A flush rises in Declan's face. To be singled out by the Captain makes him feel dizzy and ill. He grins. "Yes, sir."

The Captain grins back. "Mister Coffee. The coffeepot man. You like dancing?"

"Yes, sir! I love it! Good for the body, good for the soul."

The Captain's smile goes even broader, showing a spot of beige gum where a molar fell out. "Good for the body, good for the soul," repeats the Captain, turning into the crowd of shirtless men stumbling rearward from his path. His heart drumming, Declan takes his turn at the bucket. He reaches into the dry, rustling salad of small paper strips. "Ice Ice Baby" is the song he draws for the men of Dorm A-23.

A LITTLE SIDE ACTION

When the syndicates draw up the odds, the famous transsexuals of C-5 Dormitory blow out the field. Not only are they Thep Moob's fanciest steppers, they own many small outfits to hurt a man's heart. Also, they have drawn for their number "Gonna Make You Sweat," an ideal match for their gifts. The bookies are nettled. No one will bet against C-5 for first prize. The bookies pay a visit to the Director of Programs; for a bribe of 3,000 baht, five pounds of dried fish, and two cartons of cigarettes, the Director agrees to ban women's clothing from the competition. The bookies pay this gladly.

In light of this dispensation, gamblers are now willing to look at the Nigerians of A-14 for first at eight-to-five. A good-size squad, three dozen men, share A-14, all of them convicted of muling heroin for the same Lagos importer, most of them living out death sentences that Thailand's capricious Justice Ministry rarely insists on carrying out. The Nigerians are Christians. Their Sunday vespers service is a beloved spectacle in Thep Moob. At the conclusion of the liturgy, it is their custom to strike up a song, lay hands on one another's shoulders, and shuffle and sway in a graceful, hunkering

ring. Among the general population, rare is the man so dead in spirit that his soul does not rise when the Nigerians dance. But can this power be harnessed to "All My Rowdy Friends Are Coming Over Tonight"?

The real excitement on the card is third place. Forty-eight teams will be vying for number three, all of them dark horses. One team that is not a dark horse is A-23, where my father and the others make their home. In the eyes of the gambling syndicate, A-23 is no horse at all.

Osmund Tower's illness is not helping the team's chances. Two days after the assembly, his fever has risen to 104. A colony of *Legionella pneumophila*, which started in his lungs, is franchising ambitiously throughout his body. Hundreds of bacterial lesions have sprung up on his palms and the soles of his feet. The lesions are tiny; the largest is smaller than an oat. Despite their modest size, each of these lesions is an open circuit to an arresting voltage of pain. This makes it impossible for my father to walk, or to wield a pencil or an eating utensil. His illness, dangerous only to the elderly and infirm, is easily curable. But a powerful gang of older Chinese inmates—also stricken with Pontiac flu—has bought up the infirmary's store of antibiotics, leaving nothing stronger than aspirin for the rest of the population until the next fiscal quarter. So my father lies on his mat, slipping calmly, pointlessly into death. Yet he is not in despair. The stupefying languor of his fever is pleasant in its way, a powerful narcotic. His roommates do not molest him. Their dorm's design recalls a '50s-style Holiday Inn, with a fourth, barred wall open to the air, allowing access along an exterior promenade; warm sea winds sough into the cell, drying my father's sweat without leaving him chilled.

My father is not the only dying man in A-23. On the far side of the dorm lies Oliver Fehar, twenty-eight, of Johannesburg. Last year, larking in Phuket, Oliver got drunk and drove a dune buggy over a pregnant bather, killing her. The baby survived, and will outlive Mr. Fehar. Oliver is dying of a systemic staph infection that entered his body through an ingrown toenail. His skin is the color of grape sherbet.

The two invalids do hold some interest for the prison's gambling community. The bookies of Thep Moob will offer action on which raindrop will first reach the bottom of a windowpane. They offer action on how many times Captain Surongporn will use the word *mellow* in his weekly addresses. And now there is lively action on whether my father or Oliver Fehar will be the first to die. Because of his age, and his visible speckling of sores, Osmund is the favorite in this contest, at three-to-two over the South African.

My father has been in Thep Moob awaiting trial for five weeks. Prior to his illness, he had gotten along well with his roommates; he is a natural follower of rules, and his fellows have yet to hear him utter a word of complaint. If Professor Tower had the dorm to himself, the area around his sleeping mat would resemble the detonation site of a bomb containing Kleenex, blood-pinkened frowses of dental floss kept for reuse, dirty laundry, coins, leaky pens, peanut shells, cockeyed reading glasses from the dollar store, magazine subscription cards, and splayed books. But here, out of respect for the commons, my father has kept his effects stacked and folded, neat as a pin.

As sick as he is, he is not wholly unresponsive. Late in the afternoon, when Ron and the others begin to complain that the sick men have dashed all hope of a good showing in the dance contest, Osmund is returned to the searing shame of a Boy Scout hiking trip fifty-some years before, when he fell in a creek and ruined his cargo of hamburger buns for the troop. "This is just terrible. I really do apologize," he murmurs now, rubbing phantom creek mud from his knees.

The dorms are unlocked between the hours of 5 a.m. and 8 p.m. Toward dusk, Declan Weyde shoulders past a knot of gamblers and Death Race spectators and into A-23. Declan is carrying a crock of lime yogurt purchased at the black-market grocery in Zone B. When the gamblers learn of Declan's plan for it, they say, in a babel of tongues, "Hey, get away from him, you rotten bastard!" and "Don't fuck me, Coffeepot, I've got money on that boy." Declan intends to feed Osmund the yogurt, queering the odds.

Whether spooning yogurt into my father will prolong the man's life is unclear, but Declan does not have much else to work with. To facilitate the feeding, he cradles Osmund's damp and fragrant head in the crook of his knee. My father is not a man to refuse a meal; he is a lifelong licker of plates and a meticulous herder of tabletop crumbs. Now, though, as he loiters in death's lobby, angular cheilitis, a painful, scabrous breakage of the joint of the lips, prevents Professor Tower from opening his mouth wide enough to garage the laden spoon. So the yogurt's entry is a two-phase process: first my father slurps the mounded yogurt from the utensil, taking in about a two-thirds portion; then his gray tongue eels forth to polish off the unslurpable remnant. After each intake, a sensuous little air-brake sound of satiety—*auh!*—bursts from his lips. "Mm. Thank you, Declan! Man alive, this is just excellent," he murmurs.

"Take her easy, Professor," says the coffeepot thief. "You don't gotta *hoover it*. I'm not going anywhere."

My father does not hear this. He cranes avidly for the spoon, greedy as a newborn.

"Jesus, hey, cool it, man. Just let that settle for a second. This shit wasn't an easy score. If you puke it up all over the place, I'll be seriously pissed."

This rough talk is a show for the others. Declan has some skin in the Tower-Fehar Death Race game: in exchange for Declan's services as a fixer, my father has, since his arrival, been paying Declan's share of bribe-rent in the luxury dorm. This assistance has come at a time when Declan's finances are in some disarray. But even if Osmund's death did not mean Declan's eviction, I think Declan would be spooning the yogurt all the same.

At this moment Declan is fifty-five, a native of Vancouver, British Columbia. He has a kindly, squinting face, fringed by hay-colored hair through which a freckled pink scalp gleams. Many women have loved Declan Weyde, but he has no children. He wishes he'd had children. A physical expression of this desire is the fawn-colored, dime-size dimple on his forearm where an Amazonian botfly once laid an egg in his skin. Out of a sense of maternal duty, Declan attempted to carry the creature to term. When the boil finally split and the light of day broke upon a still-born larva, Declan grieved. Emotionally twinned to the botfly scar is a tiny white line above the knuckle of his left thumb; this he received while driving across Mauritania with his then-girlfriend. Over her protests, he stopped to take on a pair of hitchhikers, teenage sisters, the elder extremely pregnant. The pregnant girl went into labor in the Fiat. Defying his girlfriend's hysterical objections, Declan delivered the baby. The umbilical cord he severed with his Leatherman tool, also lacerating his thumb. The wound caused Declan's girlfriend to worry that he had contracted a serious bloodborne illness (the young mother's blood had been everywhere), and the incident marked the end of their sexual relationship. This is all to say Declan is a man rich in a kind of patience and charity I'm not sure my own heart contains.

Why is it that water comes into my eyes, when I ponder this stranger's efforts to keep my father alive? Perhaps it is that the easy decency of Declan's yogurt kindness throws my own brokenness and selfishness into hard relief. I do love my father, but I am sorry to know that were I in Declan's place, the sight of the man, of the fat blind muscle of his tongue flexing and swanning for yogurt, would offend me. The impulse to rap the bridge of his nose with the spoon would be a low temptation I might lack the goodness to resist.

Ron Tolenaar has nothing against either man, but he wants both Professor Tower and Oliver Fehar to hurry up and die. The dance contest is only a month away. Perhaps a pair of ringers can be recruited to take the place of the dead men, and A-23 could make a viable bid for third place. Or perhaps it is time to make nice with the Portuguese book artists who toil in the prison glassworks. A book artist is a counterfeiter of passports. In the glassworks, ladders could be built and saw blades stolen. Then, some night, Ron and his accomplices could make for the dark stretch of fence in the citrus grove. The Cambodian border is only fifteen miles past the fence. Ron's loving wife and children are waiting for him in Breukelen.

The yogurt has no effect on the Legionella bacteria, which go on building grand cities in my father's lungs. But this spot of light grubbing ushers strength into his feeble frame, and Osmund's soul brightens, drawing vigor from the knowledge that Declan's promise to look after him was not the swindle he suspected it might be.

My father's first nights in Thep Moob were not pleasant. He'd been thrown into a sixty-man dorm whose only spot of unclaimed floor space was a small crescent of territory alongside the toilet hole, which was in constant use throughout the night. In the more crowded dorms, three square linoleum tiles (twenty inches on an edge) constitute one's allotted sleeping area, making the fetal position mandatory. No one clarified this code to my large father, who, to his terror and bewilderment, was anonymously cursed, kicked, punched, and, at least once, bitten in the black of the night. Declan had been enduring these barbarities for six months, since losing the last of his savings on a failed appeal. When he approached my father with the proposition of buying into A-23, Osmund, in his misery, did not hesitate to accept.

In addition to his own expenses, my father is paying two hundred and fifty dollars a month for Declan's protective companionship, which covers the younger man's dorm rent and canteen account. The thought has nagged at him that $250 per month for Declan's services is above fair market rate. Now, with his head in Declan's lap, he feels he has at last gotten some real value for his money, which unties a little knot of unease inside him.

The others in A-23 are not so pleased about the yogurt feed. Ron Tolenaar scowls at my ulcer-spangled father, sprawled like the pietà in Declan's lap. "You guys are really cute like this, but Declan, man, come on. This is stupid shit," the big man snarls from his hammock. "The Professor wants to die, give him respect and let him die."

"Except he obviously wants to live," says Declan. "Look at his appetite. He's practically eating the spoon."

"This yogurt is truly excellent," Osmund mutters through a cough.

Ron gestures at the dying men with the magazine he's reading, a publication called *Maximum Combat Aeronautics*. "I will turn him over to the hospital, both of these guys." Thep Moob's hospital is an ironical place, an amoeba zoo and diarrhea museum whose undisguised function is to hasten patients into death.

"You want to throw Oliver on the shitheap, go ahead. He's mostly furniture already," says Declan. "But nobody's going to fuck over my man here. Osmund is in my personal care."

"You care about your rent," says Ron, scowling now at Declan. "I care about electrification. I care about having tunes and stew and nice beer in the house. How we will do something competitive to your shitty 'Ice Ice

Baby' is a hard thing, Declan. To do it with these guys is not possible. The team of two dead fuckers is not a winning team. I am making a new rule. In this house, if you can't feed yourself, no other man can feed you."

Henri Permeuil speaks up against this. So do Declan and Ter. The limits of Ron's authority strain against the far-reaching rules he has already put into place. These include prohibitions against chewing tobacco, harmonicas, durian, and masturbating while others are present. The residents of A-23 tolerate these restrictions, but to effectively ban a man from saving his cellie's life is a bridge too far.

"Okay, okay, but I don't give a shit if you are puking sick—you pull your weight in here. Hear me, guys?" says Ron. "A week. Oliver? Professor? Any man who is not on his toes next week, we send you to the hospital."

"The big man's bouncing back. He'll be shaking his ass in no time," Declan replies, plying Osmund with another mouthful. By way of testimony, my father sucks the yogurt down with a loud, vehement slurp. Ron glowers over his magazine, which is open to a photo essay of bikini women posed alongside combat drones.

"Tower, if you don't eat more quiet I'm going to tear off your head and pee in it. You hear me, man?"

"I heard 'peanut,'" says Professor Tower, who is slightly (and selectively) deaf. He owns a hearing aid, but it was so expensive he has been afraid to take it out of the box. He did not bring it to Thailand.

"Don't try to talk," says Declan. "It makes your mouth bleed."

"You heard me, man," says Ron. "You play dumb, but you hear me. I'm trying to look at my book, and some guy going *sluccch* isn't a very super thing to hear when I'm looking at bitches. You're making me really fucking nuts. I think maybe I'm going to have to smash you so I don't hear this *slurrch sluurch* anymore."

"I heard 'nuts.' I'm quite fond of nuts," my father murmurs. "And I expect I'll be able to manage nuts in a day or two, Ron. But for now, best to play it safe and stick to this delicious goop here. Declan, if you could fix me up with another bite, that would be great. Boy, the old head is really throbbing. There are some just extraordinarily vivid lights swirling and swooshing around behind my eyes right now."

Through all of this, Oliver Fehar says nothing. The five gamblers at the bars, all of whom have backed my father in the Death Race, are sick at heart. With rehearsal hour approaching, they make for the prison's citrus orchard, where a rapist from C-building with famously nimble feet is drilling a squad for the dance contest.

The familiar sixteenth-note overture pilfered from Bowie and Queen crackles over the PA system first. Henri Permeuil, who has taken on the role of A-23's choreographer, showcases for Ron, Declan, and Ter the latest revision of his routine. The cycle consists of jogging in place and madly gnashing one's teeth while slapping an invisible wall. Hostile confusion is the audience response.

"The dance is chewing?" says Declan. "Some kind of chewing fit?"

"It is very frightening," says Ter.

"This dance is garbage," says Ron. "I don't understand it at all."

Henri's miming palms wilt to his sides. "Hey, piss off, yeah? This is only concept number one," he says. "For your information, what I am doing, I am trapped in a freezer. Shivering in a freezer. What we do should have meaning. Not just be stupid, just hopping around like idiots. The world will see us. My idea is the world will see men who are dying, trapped in this place."

"The world will see some assholes biting around and slapping and looking pretty weird," says Ron.

"This is one idea. I have many ideas. We can win," says Henri, his chin tucked sullenly to his sunburned throat.

"Ah, motherfucker," says Ron, climbing back into his groaning hammock. "We all stay in the dark."

THE ANGEL OF THE GHOST DOOR

These, in ascending order of expense and preciousness, are the goods and services available on Thep Moob's healthy black market: laundry and housekeeping services, sexual services, haircuts, books and magazines (non-pornographic), rice, fresh-caught fish, dried fish, coffee, fruit, yogurt and hot menu items, clothes, loose tobacco, parasols, playing cards, prerolled cigarettes, knives, aspirin, books and magazines (pornographic), knifeproof vests and cod protectors, batteries, cannabis, opium, heroin, antibiotic ointment, hypodermic needles, narrow-spectrum antibiotics, anti-retroviral medication, anti-anxiety medication, cellular phones, broad-spectrum antibiotics—specifically, azithromycin, which is used to treat Pontiac flu—and laptop computers.

As I have mentioned, the Chinese clique has commandeered the prison dispensary's entire store of azithromycin. Declan Weyde understands that Professor Tower's life, and his own standard of living, can be saved only by appealing to a fat, walleyed warder named Sudrit Nut—the fickle angel of Thep Moob.

Sudrit's good works are diverse. When your letters are waylaid by Chokdee Boonma, the wicked guard whose industry it is to ransom inmates' mail, Sudrit can be petitioned to intercede in your favor. If you are an addict consigned to a term in the Suitcase—the refrigerator-size steel crate that stands in the wildflower meadow behind the glass factory—you pray to Sudrit as you broil. If you are lucky, Sudrit's hand will dim the air vent, and a life-giving cellophane bolus of brown heroin will parachute down.

Illiterates have successfully enlisted Sudrit's help in crafting applications for a King's pardon. Victims of rape, extortion, or secret slavery can make a case for relief to Sudrit. He does not hear every plea, and he does not side with even one of ten plaintiffs he hears, but once he determines to take your side, his aid is expeditious.

In his forty-three-year career at Thep Moob, Sudrit has saved the lives of an uncounted number of inmates, and he has killed forty-two. In the days when the condemned died by beheading, Sudrit decapitated eleven men. In the days when the condemned died by gunfire, Sudrit's victims numbered nineteen. And in 2003, when the Thai penal authorities bowed to international pressure and decreed that men should die from a dose of potassium chloride injected by a licensed physician, Thep Moob's warden and the inmates were of an equal mind that in partial disobedience of the order, the job should be given to Sudrit Nut.

Since learning the art of the needle, Sudrit has put down twelve men. His touch is gentle and his observance of the last rites is scrupulous and performed in a soothing tone. He chants the sutra. He whispers the names of the Buddha. He anoints the forehead of the condemned with a cloth moistened in eucalyptus water, murmuring *ci*, *ce*, *ru*, *ni*—which means "heart," "form," "mental concepts," and *Nibbana*, letting go. Then he depresses the plunger with a heedful thumb. Only insane or unreasonable men curse Sudrit Nut as he stops their hearts.

The execution chamber is a block bunker down a white shell path from the glass factory. Beyond the bunker, the path winds to a gate of rusted iron plate. This gate is called *Pratuphi*, which means "the ghost door." It is only opened to admit a corpse. Through the ghost door, between the third and second walls of the prison, lies a cemetery for men whose bodies no one comes to claim. Marking each grave is an oblong of teak engraved with the inmate's number but not his name. Within a decade of each new burial, the Gulf's salt air will efface the wood to illegibility, and the useless marker can be uprooted and thrown out.

Executions are not announced in advance in Thep Moob. A condemned man is kept ignorant of his fate until, having been summoned from his cell on some false pretext, he finds himself being led down the shell path. The other inmates would not know with any certainty that one of their own had been executed if the prison administration did not believe in ghosts. Not long after a prisoner has been ushered through the ghost door, the hoarse and soothing tenor of Sudrit Nut is heard over the intercom. Softly, the prisoner's name is intoned, followed by these words: "We invite your spirit to leave us now."

You treat with Sudrit Nut in the Zone B yard on weekend afternoons. Sudrit owns a white plastic patio set stippled with green mildew. There he sits, under a ruined yellow parasol, playing checkers terribly. A goldfish could give Sudrit a run for his money in a checkers game; it is the petitioner's job to architect courses of triple jumps for Sudrit's pieces while you tell him of your troubles. His cocked eyes never meet yours, and there is no way of telling whether your story is working on him. "Hello," "Move, please," and "Thank you" are the only words he tends to utter. At the end of the game he bids you farewell, and in a few days, your problem will be taken care of or else it will not.

Sudrit does not often help inmates with an aegis of money from home. Westerners regard his chaotic mercies with apprehension, bewilderment, and contempt. To the Euro-American mind, the obscure moral logic of Sudrit's interventions is something wanton and unholy. By what perverse divinity does this beady-eyed angel disdain, for example, to procure insulin for a falsely imprisoned diabetic, only to take up the case of a pederast whose cat has been abducted? And how could it be worth the humiliation to lay out your agony and helplessness before a grunting stranger who will likely do nothing for your cause—and, furthermore, to stage a credible loss to a man who, checkerswise, is nearly retarded?

The morning after Declan's administration of yogurt, my father's fever is nearing 105 degrees. Declan appears at Sudrit's patio set. He *wais* and winces and grins. He minces and murmurs in his Tarzan Thai, *I don't to disturb; I don't to annoy; yes, some minute of his time?* Sudrit, blinking froglike in the bright yellow shade of his parasol, invites Declan to sit. What is said? This isn't known; only that Declan defies suppliant protocol by thrashing Sudrit in eight straight games, and that both men laugh after each walloping. The day after Declan's visit to Sudrit, the executioner's errand boy appears at A-23 with a fourteen-day course of azithromycin. Twenty-four hours later, my father awakens, slick as a newborn, his fever broken.

RECREATION

For forty-eight hours after his fever's retreat, Osmund Tower lies on his mat, trying to will a revival of the lung infection. His is the futility of the sleeper who fights to remain in a dream as the white sunlight of morning and the concerns of the day haul him, like a whaler's spear, inexorably into consciousness. The matter of his disgrace is one of the larger buoys in the harpoon's cord. His name has not yet appeared in the international press, but it surely will when his case goes to trial weeks or months from now. He is being prosecuted for extreme foolishness. The American embassy in Bangkok assures us that a guilty verdict is a foregone conclusion.

The promise of romantic fulfillment pulled my father to Thailand. His aim was to meet a relatively beautiful Australian woman he had gotten to know over the internet. In the course of a three-month correspondence consisting of email and video chats, a credible facsimile of human connection developed between them. Concupiscence held only a minor share of Osmund's interest in the woman. Age, and a long bout with leukemia five years ago, have diminished his sexual appetites. To pass entire hours untroubled by seizures of sexual desire, he has told me often in recent years, is a wondrous form of liberty.

The woman, who gave her name as Emily Hughes, had struck my father as kind and playful and undesperately lonesome. She said she was a travel agent in her early forties with a broken womb. The prospect of a romantic friendship, more than an unlikely coupling, had been thrilling to Osmund. And so, over Conant U's fall break, expecting nothing, he flew to meet Ms. Hughes in a resort town on Thailand's gulf coast.

She failed to appear. An intermediary with a face like an old-style ice bag appeared instead. She claimed to be Emily's older sister, Camilla. Camilla bore news that Emily, laid low with food poisoning, had been compelled to stay in Melbourne, but that she was keen to see him all the same. Camilla presented my father with a ticket to Australia and a pink suitcase containing bolts of Thai silk. At the airport, the police discovered in the case a false bottom that would have been obvious to anyone less abstracted than a Distinguished Professor of Economics. The false bottom held three kilos of opium, which, when unwrapped by the policemen, let a wonderful smell into the room.

After his arrest, Camilla came to visit Osmund in his holding cell. She told him that for $100,000, all would be put right with the authorities, and he would be on a plane home that evening. This upset him. By way of declining the proposition, he told her, "I feel very twitchy about entering into arrangements in which there are such obvious asymmetries of information. One hundred thousand dollars is a lot of money, and, I have to say, Camilla, where you're concerned, there ain't a real surplus of trust."

She departed, and the offer was not renewed.

The horror of the situation troubled my father less when he believed he was dying. Now he frets. He has always cut an eccentric figure among Conant University's economics faculty. He does not own a single tweed jacket, but instead layers Oxford shirts, as many as four on chilly days. He wears purple, iridescent Skechers sneakers, purchased because they were on sale at Walmart. He drives a twenty-five-year-old Toyota Tercel which he brush-painted shamrock green because that shade was on sale at Walmart. But neither his character nor his intellectual capacities have ever been in doubt. Now both of these things are in doubt. His department chair, who had already been gunning for Osmund's retirement, intends to strip my father of his salary, his tenure, and his pension plan. I have gone to plead with this son-of-a-bitch, unavailingly. An attorney friend of mine says we have grounds for a lawsuit against the university, but my father—my guileless, daft, loyal father—wrote in a recent letter that he "couldn't bring [him]self to muck things up for the department."

Osmund does not garden or turn wood on a lathe or read novels or cook. He teaches and produces scholarly articles. Without his work, life holds nothing for him. What of his Great Books in Macroeconomics class—has a substitute lecturer been found? If not, what damage has this inflicted on his students' academic careers? What of Marko Klyodz? He is Osmund's very promising Bulgarian thesis student, whose face is broken out in a half-dozen brownish cutaneous horns. My father believes the cutaneous horns, the longest of which is one-and-three-eighths inches, will be an obstacle to Marko's career. Marko lacks the money to have these removed, so before he left for his ill-fated vacation, my father offered to pay for the surgery. What has now become of Marko? Does he think my father made generous promises only to renege? And why does the possibility of a life sentence seem less frightening than excarceration from this cell, which seems a right and proper container for an unusually stupid man?

On the third day of his recovery, a small, slippered foot lightly kicking his ribs stirs my father from his sleep. A trusty stands over Osmund, jabbering in an unfriendly way.

"He says you stink, Tower. He's on solid ground there," Ron says from his hammock. Oliver is the only other man in the dorm. Declan is attending to a matter at the Activities Office. "He says you have to go have a wash."

The trusty leads my father to the bathhouse at the rear of the Zone A courtyard. He takes his place at the back of a queue of soot-blackened men, fresh from a day's work shoveling charcoal into the glass factory's kilns. At the far end of the line is a basin of water and a ladle, presided over by a trusty armed with a bamboo cane. Each man is afforded fifteen seconds of ablutions, which the trusty counts off. At "sixteen," if the inmate has not replaced the ladle, the trusty clouts his neck with the cane.

My father enjoys any game with such clear and easy rules. Even in his depressive languor, he washes lightning-quick. The ladle rings against the basin before the trusty gets to nine. Proud of this achievement, my father stands at attention for a moment, as though expecting a salute. With the bamboo cane, the trusty gently goads him toward the side door.

The door opens onto a small paved yard, where, to dry themselves, wet bathers promenade in a ring, holding their shorts in their hands. Osmund's wet skin thrills to the coolness of the air. The sensation so captivates his consciousness that he fails to notice a small, withered man making his way toward him against the current. In this man's hand is a parody of a knife made from a peanut-oil can. With a shrill cry, he flails for Osmund's throat. In a reflex of terror, my father swipes at the knife fortuitously, if unthinkingly, with the hand that holds his underpants. His parry bends the feeble blade.

The scrawny assassin does not give up. The man is a gambler in serious debt. His bookie—heavily leveraged in the Tower-Fehar ghost-door wager—has offered him amnesty in exchange for Osmund's murder. The debtor jumps onto my father's back, tugging at his head, attempting a bit of Hollywood business in which a deft jerk of the hands breaks a man's neck. He lacks the know-how for this feat, however, and the effect is mostly comic: my father howling and stumbling, the little gambler grappling and fumbling at Osmund's large, egglike head before a crowd of laughing men. The two are still conjoined when Declan Weyde rushes in upon the scene. Declan takes two fistfuls of the assassin's hair and pulls him from my father's back. He knees him several times in the face and stomach and balls. The miserable little man flees in a stumbling lope.

Declan hustles my father, still naked, down an opposite path toward the main yard. One of the assassin's bicuspids is lodged in the bone of Declan's knee. Grasping the tooth with the hem of his shirt, he works it free and puts it into his pocket.

"Ouch," says Declan, taking a seat on a concrete bench.

The surgery escapes my father's notice. He coughs, sniffs, blinks back tears of shock. "It isn't clear to me what that guy was so pissed off about," he says.

To Osmund's professional fascination, Declan spells out the statistical havoc the azithromycin played with the handicappers' forms. "So maybe the guy had money on you. Or maybe someone put him up to it. Fucking Ron, man. I can't believe he let you out of the dorm. You don't leave the dorm alone until this thing's sorted out."

"I'm not sure I understand how this industry functions. How can they calculate anything resembling a reliable market of probabilities if folks are just going to interfere and manipulate the outcome? Why would anyone pay out on an obviously crooked result?"

"The whole thing would have been a forfeit. Nobody would have to pay. People would have been pissed, but the guys covering your marker would have saved a shitwack of baht."

"Cripes. I haven't been in a fight since grade school, and I got the worst of that one. I'm extremely grateful for that guy's incompetence. You're fairly certain he isn't coming back?"

"I think he'll be under the weather for a while. You can put on your shorts now."

"Righty-o," says Osmund. A trio of heavily tattooed inmates, laboring at a garden plot, pause to grin at the sight of my father stepping into his underwear.

Punctured knee notwithstanding, the afternoon has been kind to Declan Weyde. While my father was en route to nearly being killed, Declan was in the office of the Director of Activities, receiving the glad news that his fishing license has come through.

Thep Moob is an aged prison. In the days when running water was considered too grand an amenity for felons, inmates bathed at a saltwater pool fed by a sluiceway running beneath the gulfward gun-gallery wall. The pool is now a recreational luxury. One cannot swim in it; to discourage escape attempts, two grids of one-inch rebar, stacked three feet apart, imprison the remaining water. The voids formed by the intersecting bars are approximately six inches by six inches. In an inadvertent mercy to fishermen, the voids of the two grids lie in alignment, allowing small fish to be hauled from the violet depths.

Fishing licenses are granted to fewer than thirty men a month, and Declan has been on the waitlist for five and a half years. He is eager to run his lines immediately to catch dinner for the dorm. My father wants to return to his mat.

"No one's going to get at you, Ozzie," Declan assures him. "We'll be right underneath the gun tower. It's safer than the dorm."

"I think I'd just as soon go lie down for a while," says Osmund. The bathhouse violence has renewed his melancholy.

"Is that a joke? All you do is lie down."

"Yeah, I'm just not feeling a tremendous surplus of energy at the moment."

"I don't give a shit," says Declan. "I can't carry you forever, Ozzie. You need to pull your fucking weight. I need help running lines. Getting those meds was a pain in the ass. I wouldn't have fooled with it if I'd known you were going to be such a waste of resources."

Here is proof of Declan's subtle wisdom. Of all the wrongs to detest in Thep Moob, Declan has heard my father lament nothing so vehemently as the fruit left daily to rot at the Buddha's knees in the Zone A yard. His acquaintance with my father spans only thirty-three days, yet he understands that above all things "a waste of resources" is what Osmund Tower most deplores. The phrase has a magical effect.

"I'd be delighted to fish with you, though skin cancer is an issue with me," my father says. "I'll need to go and get my hat."

Beside the sea pool stands a ramshackle structure made of salvaged plumbing pipe and minor lumber, clad in a patchwork of torn sheet plastic and canvas waterproofed with cooking grease. This is the prison restaurant. Guards and wealthy prisoners eat here. The restaurant's proprietor is a *kathoey* named Meena, an unpreened, square-skulled beauty in the Valerie Bertinelli mode. She does business under the sanction of Sam Wunon, a much-feared warder who has been Meena's faithful spouse for over a decade. They supply bait and loan tackle for a 50 percent tax of each fisherman's catch.

Declan knocks at the restaurant's window and displays his license. Meena, her face gridded with rope lines from a hammock siesta, passes him hooks, lines, a baggie of chicken skins, and, after some pleading, a fistful of old chopsticks.

At the sea wall, my father saws up the chicken skins, which behave under his plastic knife like a sort of durable mucus. Declan readies the tackle. Other inmates fish with the line wrapped around their fists, or else tied to the rebar, but Declan has a more cunning method in mind. From his pack, he takes a dozen or so of the wooden paddle-spoons that come free with an ice cream purchase at the prison canteen; using a knife made of sharpened bottle glass, he bores a hole through the center of each spoon's handle. He spits a chopstick through each hole, forming a little pile of crosses. In the spoons' paddles, he cuts a notch, to which he ties the lines.

These are tip-up rigs. The chopsticks sit on the rebar members of the sea pool's enclosure; when a fish takes the bait, a spoon will tip up, alerting the anglers that dinner is on the line.

"It's an old ice-fishing deal," Declan says. "I don't know if it'll work here, but I thought it would sit on the cage okay. I haven't done this since I was a kid. My father used to take me out on Dilworth Lake with him. He had a little trailer-cabin. I fucking hated it. He'd just sit in there getting plastered, which is basically what ice fishing is all about."

"You say it's about plaster," my father says. The assassin's forearm has left a raw place under his jaw. He rubs the spot with a palmful of seawater.

"Getting shitfaced drunk."

"Drunk."

"Yeah, you know—you pass a frozen lake and see all those little sheds out there, it's basically a freakin' cirrhosis colony. Half of them probably don't even have a line in the water, but a hundred percent of the guys in there are blitzed out of their minds, just out there getting away from their wives. With me and my dad, it was kind of this unspoken thing that I'd handle the fishing stuff, and he'd handle the cabin—get the little coal fire going, get it staked into the ice and everything. And I'd spud out the holes and keep them skimmed and bait the hooks and do pretty much everything else, while he sat in a little camp chair pounding Molsons.

"One day we're in there—I'm maybe fifteen, sixteen, and suddenly the wind blows up and all hell breaks loose. Turns out, my dad didn't stake the fucking cabin, and the whole shack blows over onto its side. Of course it's the side with the door in it. So we're stuck, and not only that, the coal stove is spilling these fucking embers everywhere and the dog is going apeshit, and my dad's being totally useless, just kind of yelling. So I break out the window, which is now in the ceiling, haul myself up, and I'm going 'Dad, hand me Poxie, boost Poxie up to me,' but he doesn't know what the fuck he's doing, so he decides to just make a break for it. Climbs out the window and kind of falls on me, knocks me down on the ice. I'm just about to go back in to get the dog when another gust blows up and the cabin goes skittering off until it runs up against this island about a quarter of a mile away. 'Oh, jeez, oh jeez, oh jeez,' is all my father's saying. So I get in the truck.

"I just leave him standing there, freezing his ass off. I didn't care. I can see all this fire coming out the window of the cabin, so I know my dog's gotta be dead. But I drive after it anyway and I take the tire tool and I get a sheet of the plywood loose. A big wad of smoke comes billowing out, and then the damn dog trots through it like a little magician. She's coughing and her fur's burned in a few places, but otherwise, she's basically okay. Kind of a miracle. She was such a great little dog. So we drive back to where my dad's standing, watching the cabin burn. No apology, no nothing. Not even a, 'Hey, thanks for handling that there, fifteen-year-old kid.' I couldn't believe it. And usually I'm a pretty passive person. Or I was. I'm working on it. But I also have this real well of anger I can draw on, that sometimes gets me into trouble. I had to consciously put down the pry bar so I wouldn't hit him. I was that mad. And I was really lighting into him, verbally I mean. You know, just 'You're supposed to my father? You almost got us killed, just because you were so hot to get drunk you didn't anchor the fucking cabin? You're pathetic. If I ever have a kid and I do something like that, I hope I get locked up. I'd deserve it. Look at Poxie, you fucking asshole. You burnt up my dog!'"

Declan's story moves my father greatly. A tear comes to Osmund's eye, on a tide of feeling for fathers and sons. He thinks of me, and of my brother, and he feels that the guilt must be partly his that we have not grown into better men.

"Oh, Jesus, we do fuck them up, our children. Don't we, Declan?"

The tear falls. He clears his throat to make this confession.

"My boys couldn't have been older than six and eight when our cat had kittens. I told them to find homes for them, and when they didn't, I filled up a trash barrel with hose water and drowned the kittens while the boys watched. They cried and cried, which I didn't understand because I'd seen both my father and my grandfather do the same thing. But now I see how cruel this was, and perhaps this explains why my boys are furtive, solitary men incapable of forming meaningful human connections or even holding decent jobs." He closed his eyes. "My sons, I love you. I have failed you so."

Actually, I'm making this up. Not the part about the kittens. That really happened, but Osmund isn't thinking about that right now. It's good to be acknowledged for one's achievements, is the lesson my father takes from Declan's tale.

"It is important, isn't it? This sense that one is appreciated," my father says. "I remember very early on in my career, I just happened to be reading an article by George Stigler, who maybe you know, won the Nobel Prize in 1982, and there in the footnote it said, 'For a pellucid investigation of symmetrical inflation targets, please read such-and-such,' and holy mackerel! There was a reference to the *first article I published* out of graduate school. I had to look up 'pellucid,' but boy, for a guy like that to just reach out and show that kind of appreciation for somebody just getting his start..."

"Must have been a real headfuck," Declan says.

"I still get warm fuzzies when I think of it. These things are important, to be recognized when we do something useful."

"Yeah, I guess on some level, everybody's kind of a fame hound," Declan says. "Which reminds me—you want to know something weird? With this stupid fucking dance thing, yeah, it'd be great to have a TV or whatever in the dorm. But more and more, I'm thinking it'll be kind of cool to have it on the Web—to know people out there are seeing me. Which makes no sense. We're going to look like a bunch of retards. Anyone who knows me and sees it, they'll either laugh or it'll depress the shit out of them."

He glances at his spoons. "When I first got in here, I just wanted to disappear. I'd have gone in the Suitcase before I'd have gone along with this Mickey Mouse bullshit. But you'll see, Ozzie. Or I hope you don't. Once people stop writing, stop making the trip to see you, you start to feel like a ghost." Declan frees a length of line snagged on a scab of rust. "I dunno. What the fuck."

The sudden bucking and hopping of Declan's rigs halts this gloomy line of talk. The men go into a panic of delight, hauling in their tackle. Bucking on the hooks are small, oblong fish with aristocratic, underslung jaws. A shifting aurora of yellow and blue plays over the fishes' flanks, colors that quench to dull dun the instant Declan dashes their brains against the wall of the sea pool. The two of them haul fish and bait lines as fast as they can. It is like a dream in which you keep finding money. They catch fifteen fish in eight minutes, but before ten minutes are up, the school has moved on.

As though to announce the end of the jubilee, a voice comes over the intercom. It utters a phlegmatic incantation in Thai that, uncharacteristically for public addresses here, does not suggest the imperative mood. My father fails to discern the name of Oliver Fehar in the stream of foreign jabber.

"Thank Christ," says Declan Weyde. "Oliver bailed."

"You say Oliver left," says Osmund.

"Sailed through the ghost door," Declan says. "He's out of here, man."

My father draws in a hungry lungful of wharf-scented air. His gaze registers the arrangement of salmon and slate hanging in the western sky.

"Boy," he says. "Being alive sure beats being dead."

THE ARIZONA DEAD ARM

Who is the new man grooving alone in the Zone C yard? A blindfold hides his eyes. His body is lean and chiseled. His groove device is a hula-hoop made from half-inch Pex plumbing conduit. He seems never to touch the hula hoop. No muscle in his body concerns itself explicitly with the revolving plastic O. The hoop, rather, wanders over him—his arms, his torso, his legs—taking the measure of some deep and powerful rotaryness, some strong orbital electron play within the gentleman. His feet seem to glide above the earth on a film of slick air. There are Balinese fancinesses of hand. No fooling: this man can get down.

Declan and Osmund encounter him on their way back from the sea pool. Declan says, "Hey, man, you're pretty good with that thing," and "Hey, excuse me?" and "Speak English, bro?" before the man pauses in his hoop work and lifts his blindfold. His name, he says, is Johnny Francis. Austin, Texas is his home. By way of friendly chitchat, my father describes Austin as "neat" and also "funky."

"No offense," Johnny replies, "but I'm trying to get through a workout here." He tugs the blindfold down. The hoop resumes its tour of the Texan's perfect frame. His routine is idle and meditative, the dance of a sleepwalker, the finning of a sleeping fish. Should Johnny Francis be persuaded to invest a little energy, it will be a motherfucker, dancingwise.

Declan fetches Ron Tolenaar. Ron sees what is at stake and attempts to recruit Johnny Francis to take Oliver's place in A-23. Nothing doing, says Johnny. He's already got a spot in a Westerners' dorm in Zone B. Say Ron covers three months of Johnny's rent in exchange for his directorship of the A-23 dance team? But Johnny's dorm drew "Gonna Make You Sweat." It would be a creative concession to have to craft a routine for "Ice Ice Baby." Five months' free rent plus laundry service? Ron has himself a deal. Johnny moves in the following day. Rehearsals begin that afternoon.

The autumn rains begin as well, and between midnight and dawn, the prison is a place my father does not want to leave. The susurrus of water on the lead roof is deafening, absolving. It drowns out all sounds of men crying in their sleep, of voices raised in fury, of the yard guard who, just to be obnoxious, bawlingly croons "New York, New York" at his audience of captives trying to sleep. The view from my father's mat is of the seaward rifle tower. Through the curtains of rain, the tower is a distant glow, an emblem of watchfulness as wholesome as a lit belvedere in a village church.

The choreography Johnny designs is complex and challenging. It calls for much lively ankling and swift pivot work. With only two daily broadcasts of "Ice Ice Baby," the lessons take place under a generous pressure. Declan, Ter, Ron, and Henri (despite his boasts) are not natural dancers, but after a few days' instruction, they have grasped the rudiments of the pivot step. My father has not. When the others shuffle left, he lumbers right, squandering precious rehearsal time.

"Fuckin', come on, dude, left!" Johnny roars at Osmund. Their common nationality makes him no gentler toward my father. "How hard is the concept of left?"

"Left, left, left, got it. Sorry," my father says.

"*Shuffle*, dude! Don't—I don't even know what to call what you're doing. Plant the right foot, T-step with the left. T-step. *T-step*! Are you shitting me, man? Jesus, this is really blowing my mind."

"I'm sorry," says my father. "But the tendons in my feet aren't in great shape. My ankles tend to swell, so the pirouettes are hard for me."

"*Pivot*, not pirouette, like this," says Declan Weyde, whirling slowly on the ball of one foot.

"How about you just stay the fuck out of everyone's way," says Johnny Francis. "Make that your priority."

"Stay the fuck out of the way," my father murmurs. "Got it."

At night, with the sound of the rain as a cover, Johnny Francis revolts against house rules by whacking off in the dark. This puts Ron Tolenaar in a bind: Johnny's gifts as a dancer and choreographer have raised his status in Ron's eyes, and so Ron feels not wholly entitled to rebuke Johnny over the violation. His wan wish is that Johnny will get it out of his system and desist on his own.

This does not come to pass. On the fifth night, Ron's tolerance reaches its limit. Shortly after Johnny starts up, Ron turns on the light and storms over to the other man's mat. With his foot he nudges the blinking Texan, who still clutches a stiff prick in his hand.

"I told you, Johnny. You don't do it when other people are in the house. Now get your penis out of here, man. You do this some more, I'm gonna tear off your head and crap on it."

Johnny drags his waistband north of his erection. He grinds the palm of his hand against an eyesocket. "Look, Ron, I gotta tell you, man, the way you're running this house ain't sitting so cool with me."

"What? It is the rules. You need to get off, you come and do it before we get back from chow."

"Yeah, see, that doesn't really work with my deal," says Johnny Francis. "I'm an insomniac, which I've got ways of dealing with, one being I need to get empty before I can fall asleep. Plus, I work an Arizona Dead Arm, so it takes a while to get my hand to where I can do my thing."

"You Arizona what?" Ron asks.

Johnny Francis explains the Arizona Dead Arm, a practice of which he is surprised the others aren't aware. The notion is this: you lie for a time on your back in a self-administered "hammerlock" hold, in which the arm is wrenched upward toward the scapula. When the nerves have "gone to sleep," one can masturbate under the neural illusion that the hand on one's private parts belongs to a second party. This idea so intrigues Ron Tolenaar that the masturbation ban in A-23 is eased for a provisional, exploratory period.

Within a couple of nights, A-23's residents conclude that the benefits of the Arizona Dead Arm do not justify its procedural complexity. Neither my father nor Ron Tolenaar can compel his arm to fall asleep. Declan and Henri successfully clear that hurdle, but both find the benumbed arm too maladroit to deliver any satisfactions. Whether Ter has any luck with it is unknown; during the Dead Arm research, Ron remands Ter to the small areaway behind the toilet enclosure so as not to subject the young man to perversion.

Even after the experiment has been deemed a nonstarter the formidable yearning at the heart of the Dead Arm episode continues to suffuse the dorm. One evening, Ron Tolenaar can bear it no more. He seizes the hand of Henri Permeuil and puts it to his crotch. Ron will not return the favor, but under a quid pro quo agreement, Henri is able to persuade Johnny Francis to masturbate him in turn. By bedtime, Henri's forearms are sore.

Now, of an evening, the darkened cell is alive with the sounds of briskness and cooperation. *Schwitt-schwitt-schwitt.* A blind eavesdropper would believe he is overhearing the scrimmage of a lint-removal team.

So what of my father? He does not join in. Since being serially whittled by surgeons, his prostate is a sliver of its former self, reduced in size and shape to a lozenge of hotel soap in its last day of use. The lozenge is still technically operable, just as the old Bolens weedeater in his garage—with much priming and white-knuckled pull-cord jerkage—can sometimes be persuaded to start, but the reward rarely justifies the effort. The textile chorus inspires in him a complicated sort of envy akin to watching others gleefully gorge themselves on food for which you lack the appetite.

Tonight, he lies in the dark, manipulating a partial stoutness with no real clasmic ambition. Just showing his support for the spirit of teamwork and tenderness that has come into A-23, just tapping his foot at the edge of the dance floor. Beside him, Declan achieves manumission with what strikes my father as fearsome efficiency and dispatch. It is after the sounds of Declan toweling himself off desist that my father feels Declan's hand on his abdomen.

My father has not been touched by another person in this way in over a decade. The sensation he experiences is the equal and opposite of jumping into a freezing pool. His lungs bind up. Every cell in his body goes silent and hearkens to Declan's hand. His penis does stiffen, though perhaps less in venereal salute than sensual shock. Also connoisseurial curiosity. It is not necessarily that Osmund wishes to be masturbated by a man, but he does expect that a handjob administered by a fellow owner-operator of male anatomy will be first-rate.

But as the procedure wears on, my father is able to assess more clearly the quality of the experience. Declan's hand is clawlike, his motions jolting and importunate. Osmund is bewildered that another man should manage this familiar operation so clumsily; the vision of his father-stuff spilling onto Declan's cracked and calloused fingers is homely and impossible. My father's penis begins to wilt, which causes Declan to palp and wring it with renewed intensity. Not only is this awkward, it is quite painful. When he can stand it no longer, Osmund clears his throat.

"I don't know that this strikes me as being particularly effective," he says.

Declan's hand retracts. The men lie side by side on their mats, listening to the coursing rain.

A MORNING OF REFLECTION

The next day Osmund Tower rises and dresses at 5:35, shortly after the trusty unlocks the dorm. The morning is one of surpassing gentleness. The sunrise has not dispelled the rain-washed courtyard's atmosphere of predawn lavender. My father pauses on the catwalk and flares his nostrils for a maximum intake of fresh air. Far to the south, a merchant marine vessel creeps across the sea's Scope-colored breadth. The boat cheers Osmund as a happy augury. He considers the young man's fantasy of viewing the world from the decks of a container ship, and he is able to muster a warming delusion that his arrival at Thep Moob constitutes a fulfillment (though a denatured fulfillment) of a noble and swashbuckling dream. This delusion quickly abandons him. "Ree-diculous," my father says, smirking and shaking his head.

Behind him, he hears the tread of bare feet. Ter steps onto the walkway, delicately currying the sleep from his eye with a pinky nail.

"Good morning, Ter. You're up early."

"Johnny, man, he snore like a pig."

Ter and Osmund head down to the courtyard, where Meena is readying the coffeeshop for the day's trade. Osmund is her first customer. A slender hand parts the cloudy Visqueen that covers the service window. Meena's face is damp from her morning ablutions; even without her makeup, she is lovely, her beauty no trick of cosmetic art.

"Mm," my father says. "Your cheekbones are just extraordinary."

Amid the quick exchange of Thai between the warder's wife and Ter my father hears what sounds like "melon branding." Meena laughs, then vanishes behind the Visqueen to concoct a pair of coffees.

"What's this about melons?" my father asks Ter.

"Marlon Brando. Movie star. She think you look like him."

My father chortles his way into a bout of prodigious phlegm haulage. "I'm extremely flattered."

"Not young Marlon. Not *Streetcar* Marlon. *Superman* Marlon. The big guy."

The smile dims but does not vanish. "Fair enough. I suppose there is a resemblance there."

"No, you Peter Boyle. *Young Frankenstein?* Peter Boyle. He dead."

"How do you know so much about American movies, Ter?"

Ter's late uncle and guardian, it is explained, kept up a sizable video library, and he let Ter show films in the refectory on Saturday evenings. After his uncle's death, the library was plundered by the other guards, putting an end to movie night.

"Do Thai universities offer degrees in film, Ter?"

A lit cigarette falling from the rifle tower seizes the young man's interest. It strikes the pavement in a bloom of sparks. Ter has snatched it up before the second bounce.

Osmund persists. "You're a very good dancer, you know. Very artful and athletic. Maybe you'd like to study dance, or physical education of some kind. Your English is quite good. You could be an English teacher."

Behind a plume of dense blue lung smoke, my father's cellmate squints and shrugs.

"Let me ask you this: picture yourself in ten years, doing exactly what brings you the most pleasure. What would that be?"

With a moistened pinky, Ter smooths a rent in the rolling paper. "I don't know. Maybe I drive the bus."

"Okay, good. Bus driver is a fine profession. A city bus, or tours and things?"

"The prison bus. The bus take you to the court."

"Come on, man, you don't want to stay here. Talk about a waste of human capital. You're a bright guy. You ought to be out having adventures and enriching the world."

Ter pinches out the cigarette and puts it away for later. "My friends are here," he says.

The boy's complacency inspires in my father something close to anger. Mercifully, the coffees arrive and cut Osmund's line of questioning short. With Meena's miserly stub of a pencil, he signs for both coffees to be debited from his canteen account. Ter declines to drink his coffee, but instead thanks my father and carries it upstairs to Ron. Alone at the counter, Osmund downs his drink with many wet decibels, feeling curiously spurned.

But the morning air is sweet, and the coffee is, he tells Meena, "religious—just spectacular." He orders a second cup and a breakfast of eggs which he drowns with pepper vinegar and chili sauce. The meal is so delicious that Meena's disgusted scowl does not prevent my father's licking the plate. The bounty restores his mood. Osmund takes from his pocket a blank aerogramme and writes his weekly letter home.

My father has just sealed up the aerogramme when Declan comes ambling into the yard. He is making purposefully toward the bathhouse. When his eyes meet Osmund's, they exchange a humiliated greeting: partial wave, shallow nod. The trusty at the bathhouse door stands in Declan's way; he has arrived too late for bath call. Declan pleads with the trusty, to no success. He is desperate not for a bath, but to be spared the discomfort of passing Osmund at the coffee counter. For an agonized moment, he loiters, shamming interest in the graffiti on the bathhouse wall. The men's shared unease thickens over the courtyard like smoke. The sole means of relieving it is for Declan to go and bid my father good morning.

"Hiya."

"Morning, Declan. Let me fix you up with a cup of this excellent coffee."

"All set, thanks."

"You sure? It's truly exceptional."

"I'm cool."

Osmund: *glurp, mm, gah!* "Man alive, you're missing out." At the northern end of the courtyard, a troupe of shirtless teenagers covered in bright tattoos cycle through some break-dance moves to razzing and flatulent human-beat-box accompaniment.

"So, uh, yeah, I guess the scene in the dorm got a little too groovy last night," says Declan, through a forced grin. "Just for the record, that type of thing is really not my vibe. I was just, uh…"

Osmund is not looking at Declan, but at the dancing boys. Under the strain of his mortification, Declan's explanation of what is or is not his vibe peters painfully out.

"Boy, those guys have a lot of energy. And their tattoos are marvelously colorful," my father muses, apparently to himself. "I imagine the pleasure of having a colorful tattoo is somewhat akin to the joy of publishing an elegantly written paper. It's about distinguishing oneself in an artistic way."

"Yeah, I guess. But I mean, just to clear the air: I don't know where your head's at this morning, but as far as that deal last night—"

"I feel good, I feel good," says my father, gazing off across the courtyard. "The lungs are operating properly, and the pain I'd been feeling in my ankle has diminished."

"Because, look, just so you know, I wasn't like, wanting, necessarily to—"

Osmund cuts him off: "Boy, being locked up ain't ideal, but it is nice to be around youthfulness and energy and this wonderful sea air. I don't think I'd last too long in an old folks' home."

Declan supposes Osmund is disgusted with him. With this fusillade of platitudes the professor seemingly wishes to silence, to annihilate the man who wrongly palped his cock. A helpless outrage mounts. Declan had only been following the mode of the moment. No big deal. But rather than discuss and void this minor mishap, my father has fled into abstraction. Declan begins to feel like Osmund's cranky wife, gassed up with unacknowledged feelings.

Osmund summons Meena for a third cup of coffee, which he drinks with noise and relish equal to the first. "I don't know what sort of coffee-maker it was that you stole, Declan, but if it made coffee half this good, I'd say the temptation was justifiable."

Declan's jaw distends to rake a patch of dry skin from his upper lip. "Are you fucking with me?"

"In what sense would I be fucking with you?"

"What, Henri told you?"

"Henri hasn't told me anything."

The tale is one from which Declan, until now, had striven to protect Osmund. But in his present state of mind, he is glad to have language that might do my father harm. The light of morning hardens in the yard, and Declan Weyde tells Osmund Tower the story of the coffeepot.

THE KETTLE THIEF

Sometime in his late forties, Declan Weyde became invisible to the women of North America. His descent into invisibility was not unforeseen—Declan's vision of a fulfilled life was one of constant travel, of knowing the world and its people and languages and lands, of fleeing the rat race for sporadic work as a handyman and spreader of mulch. What this life would cost him in comfort and respectability, it would repay him in illuminating experiences.

His voyaging had carried him to all of the planet's continents, Antarctica included. The only home he owned was an inherited hunting cabin that lacked indoor plumbing. In his twenties and thirties, women had seen past his penury and lack of ambition and beheld a kind and decent man who'd had many unusual experiences and who could talk about them amusingly. When Declan reached his middle years, though, women started to perceive him as an immature misfit or a potential dependent. In time, they seemed to perceive him not at all. When he was at home at his cabin, which was miles from the nearest village, he could pass many months without so much as being looked at by a fellow member of the human race.

In his late fifties, Declan applied for work as an English teacher in Thailand. It had been his hope that his colleagues would be a campfire team of European backpack women with unshaven bodies and thick hair kerchiefed in bandanas. They would be the sort of women who would have an appreciation for a man who had traveled widely. They would not scruple over Declan's age or his composting commode.

He did not find these sorts of women. His posting was in the northern city of Chiang Rai. He taught not at a school, but at an experimental call center dedicated to the trading of latex futures with Western commodities markets. For the first time in his life, he had a job where he was expected to wear a necktie. The students in his classes were professionals with advanced degrees. Behind their politeness, Declan could sense their bewilderment at how a *farang* of his age should be working so lowly a job. On days off, he would journey to Bangkok or to the beach towns in the south. These he found too expensive, too young, too reverberant with confusing music. After a while, on the advice of a fellow traveler, Declan went to Ngop Na, which is where he got into trouble.

He found Ngop Na to be a town populated chiefly by prostitutes and their patrons. Declan was lonely, but not so lonely as to overcome a lifelong resolution never to hire a woman to sleep with him. He did not drink, so bars were out too. But he had paid ahead of time for a nonrefundable three-day hotel stay. He was stuck in Ngop Na with nothing to do.

"So I pretty much walked around and got massages. There was this one place on the corner near my hotel, with this one woman who gave me these great fucking massages—I got a three-hour massage from her every day. Feet, body, head. It was incredible. By the third day, we'd sort of gotten to know each other. Her name was Miaow. She had a couple of kids in Bangkok. She hated Ngop Na, but she got paid more there than she did in the city. So anyway, my last night, I took her out to dinner. We took a walk on the beach. And I guess we kissed a little bit, but nothing too heavy.

"I went down a few weeks later and saw her again, and it was really nice—we kind of got into a romance, that time, and it went from there. I met her kids, I met her mom. And I was really starting to think about setting up a life for myself in Thailand. The fucked-up thing was, right about then, my visa expired. I could have renewed it if I kept working, but Miaow didn't want to move her kids up to Chiang Rai, and I couldn't get anyone to hire me in Ngop Na. It's not a real education hub. So I told her, 'Look, I'll go back to B.C. I'll see if I can sell my cabin, and then I'll come back and we'll get married.' So that's what I did. I went home and I sold my place for sixty thousand bucks. I could live a long time on that in Thailand. In the meantime, I'd been talking to Miaow when I could, but she didn't have a computer, so she'd Skype me from the internet café a couple of times a week. Anyway, right after the closing, I head back to Thailand, and I go straight to Ngop Na, but Miaow's not at work. The other ladies at the massage place are saying, 'Oh, she stay home, she stay home. She sick.' I think,

'This is weird. I just heard from her. She knows I'm coming.'

"So I go to her apartment. She's not there, and I'm wondering what the hell is going on. I mean, I just sold my house, everything, to come and be with this girl. So that night, I'm walking past the bus station, and I see Miaow getting on a bus with this guy. I run over. I'm like, 'Hey, Miaow, what's going on?' She's with this weird-looking Thai dude. He's older than me, mid-sixties. Dressed like he's got a lot of dough, but in a Vegas sort of way. Shiny purple shirt and a bunch of gold chains.

"Miaow's all, 'Oh, Deck, Deck. Hi, hi, I'm so sorry.' She tells me her sister's been sick and that this guy here is her brother-in-law. They're going off to see the sister somewhere, and they'll be back in a few days. I say, 'Well, why don't I come along?' And she's like, No, no, her sister's a very private person, blah blah. Meanwhile the guy's on the bus, sort of huffing around, throwing their shit in the overhead thing, and looking daggers at me. For a second, I actually buy the story. That's how fucking stupid and gullible I am. I'm like, 'Fuck it, I'm coming with you,' just to see what happens. She's kind of pleading with me. 'No, no, no.'

"Anyway, I get on the bus with them. Turns out they're heading to this little string of resorts down the coast. The guy keeps turning around in his seat, looking at me, getting pissed off, and she's trying to calm him down. Was I upset? I mean, kind of. Though I guess I was also just kind of blown away that I'd been so dumb. Of course someone like Miaow's going to have a few guys on the side, and this guy definitely looked like a better bet than me, at least financially. But so now, I'm just like, you know what, fuck it. I came all this way and this asshole has wrecked my scene, fuck it, I'll wreck his. So I do this sort of crazy thing. I follow them to the resort. I book a little cabana just down the beach from theirs. It's like a hundred fifty bucks a night, more money than I've ever spent on a hotel anywhere, let alone in Thailand. But, shit, I've got the cash, at least for now. And then I make it my daily thing to just sort of fuck with them.

"I'd get up early and tail them to breakfast. Like, 'Hey, guys, what're we doing today? Want to rent some jet skis? Want to go snorkeling?' I'd send them drinks and stuff at dinner. I'm actually having a blast. I'm sort of proud of myself for, like, letting this thing that could have really knocked my whole self-concept out of joint just turn into a kind of a joke. And I can tell it's working, the number I'm doing on their little deal. Like, they're not really talking. I can see them bitching at each other. She wants to just get the hell out of there to get away from me, but the guy's gotten territorial. Like, 'That *farang* asshole's not gonna run me off!' It was really pretty funny. She begged me to leave a few times, but when she saw I wasn't going to, she just started trying to ignore me.

"One thing I did: on one end of the beach, there was a kind of a hip little sunset cliff thing you could take a path to. The second night, after she sort of had it out with me, telling me she wouldn't see me anymore, she and that guy go off up the path. I'm actually a pretty good rock climber, so I do this thing where I go around to the other side of the little hill and scale up there really quick. I bust my ass doing it, so when they get to the top, I'm already there—like, 'Hey, guys, glad you could join me. Killer view!'

"By the third day, though, I was just about over it. I was going to head back to Ngop Na, and maybe go see if they'd take me on in Chiang Rai again, figure out how to get on with my life. I'm chilling on the beach in one of those chairs they have set up, checking on the train schedule. And Miaow and the guy are down the beach in their own little chairs, just carping at each other, having a fucking miserable time. I'm not even really paying them any attention by then. I've literally got my face in a train timetable, about to get the fuck out of their hair, when suddenly I'm out of the chair, in the sand, on my back. The guy must have been a black belt or something. I didn't see him coming. He just flipped me out of the chair, rabbit-punched me in the nose, and then he like grabbed me by the hinges of my jaw and hocks a fucking loogie into my mouth. I don't know where he learned that one, but man, it's a pretty good way to humiliate somebody. I could taste the cigar he'd been smoking. And before I even know what the hell happened, he's on his way back up the beach.

"So I go back to my little cabana. I'm realizing the guy messed me up pretty good—I know it's bad, because when I get in there, there's this plumber in the bathroom. He takes one look at me, sort of goes pale, and he just hauls ass. My nose is totally broken and I'm coughing like I've been poisoned, trying to get this dude's lunger out of my throat.

"And you know, I'm really not a very angry guy. I'm not. I don't ever get so pissed off that I can't control it. Once or twice with my folks, but really, I've got a good handle on it. But something just kind of broke that day. And I don't know how I thought to do this, but do you know how they seal a joint in a cast-iron pipe? They tamp this stuff, this fiber stuff, oakum, down into the joint. Then they pour lead into it, which seals it off. That's what the plumber guy had been doing in my cabana, sealing a cast-iron pipe. And he'd left his little kettle there. I'd laid a little pipe before, so I knew what it was. This was a funny little third-world rig, not electric, but it had some, I dunno, sterno or magnesium in a little heating element in the base to keep the lead liquid.

"Anyway. Mr. Kung Fu had snuck up on me pretty good, but I got him even better. He was just lying on a chair, eyes closed. Miaow wasn't anywhere around. By then, she was probably thinking, 'Fuck both these guys. I'm done.' So I sneak up behind the dude, and when my shadow crosses his face, he opens his eyes. That's when I let him have it with the kettle. Probably there was a good pint of liquid lead in there. Man, what a freaky thing to see. His eye just sort went *fffff!* like a marshmallow in a campfire."

My father is not sure how to take this. The temperature of his bowels suddenly drops several degrees. "It killed him, I assume."

Declan coughs into his fist. The raconteur's brio that had briefly brightened the younger man's mood has departed. "He lived for a few months. It wasn't good. He couldn't really eat. The lead went through his sinus cavity. It messed up his tongue and his throat."

A sheeny black bird alights on the wall of the sea pool and makes a computer sound. Declan squints at it. A solid minute of silence passes.

Declan's story poses a challenge to Osmund's conscience. How does one respond to such a confession? What would his ex-wife, my mother, do? Perhaps she would condemn the man as evil and sever all contact with him. Or she would play at being the murderer's therapist. She would buy Declan a journal and instruct him to chronicle his feelings and childhood hurts.

Osmund suffers an onset of spiritual exhaustion. For a time he is quiet. Then he says, "Funny, funny, this desire to transgress. When I was seven I became very preoccupied with trying to commit the perfect crime. One night, my parents had a party. I knew they would sleep in the following morning. So I got up very early. Downstairs, in a corner behind the radiator, were three nesting stools we rarely used. The smallest one was never used at all, so it struck me as an ideal victim. I took it outside, the dwarf stool, and got my father's hatchet from the toolshed. I loved that hatchet. Its size seemed to imply that I, as a child, was somehow sanctioned to destroy things. Anyway, I chopped up the stool with the hatchet, and I buried the broken parts under the pear tree in the backyard. The fruit of the tree was bitter. No one ever gathered the pears, so there was a sort of a haze of yellow jackets buzzing around its roots during summer and fall. The earth there seemed somehow evil and also off-limits. A good place to dump a body.

"As it turned out, it *was* the perfect crime. No one ever noticed that the stool was missing. About thirty years later, we stopped at my mother's on the way up to Maine. The pear tree had died and been cut down a long time before, but before we left in the morning, my mother asked me to dig out the stump. We were in a hurry and it infuriated Marian that I would delay our departure to truckle for my mother's favor by doing this menial chore. She always accused me of being tied to my mother's apron strings. Well, when I was rooting up the stump, I found the remains of that stool. I wanted to mention it to Marian, as evidence of my, I don't know, resistance to my mother's will. But I figured my wife would have a way of turning it on me, so I kept mum. Funny, funny."

Declan has nothing to say about my father's dismemberment of the dwarf stool. Already, his motives for making Osmund his confessor for the lead-kettle tale are obscure to him. A mild nausea of regret thickens his gullet. He watches the computer bird strut madly along the bars of the sea pool. Declan notices now that this bird is living with a serious injury. It has swallowed a fishhook. From its black beak curls a length of monofilament that takes an apricot hue in the day's young light.

THE DANCE CONTEST

It is the first Sunday in November, contest day. Thep Moob's general population waits outside the refectory, where the prisoners will dance for the video camera. To say that the inmates are stricken with dance fever would not be accurate. Most faces are leaden or asmolder with quiet rage. They are sacrificing a Sunday, a day of leisure in Thep Moob, to forced participation in disgraceful minstrelsy. The men are not even afforded the diversion of watching their fellow prisoners perform. Fearing that competitive passions might turn violent, Captain Surongporn has decreed that the teams will perform one-by-one, behind the closed doors of the refectory. The last team in the lineup will dance after a nine-hour wait in the yard.

The six men of A-23 slouch against the wall of the refectory, absorbing the bricks' banked heat against an unseasonable morning chill. "You hanging in there, Ozzie?" Declan asks my father. "We should have brought you a blanket or something."

My father is dressed only in a diaper, or rather, a towel swaddled around his midsection to resemble a diaper. He sniffs. "A little cold," he says. "If I'd been more organized I would have put on shorts or underpants so that I could have used the towel as a shawl. But there we are. It isn't unbearable."

Minutes before noon, A-23 is summoned to perform. "So, Johnny," my father is saying to Johnny Francis, as they pass through the refectory doors. "Just to be clear, I'm basically to stand there—"

"Don't just *stand there*. Move and shit. Do some baby shit."

"Sort of say, 'goo goo,' and things."

Johnny's eleventh-hour solution to the problem of Osmund's unfitness as a dancer has been to turn his liabilities—his unnimbleness and obesity—into, Johnny hopes, a winning gimmick. My diapered father is to portray a giant baby in A-23's now famous "Ice Ice Baby" video.

"I don't give a fuck what you say," says Johnny. "No one will be able to hear you. Just make sure you turn in the chorus."

"And the chorus is which?"

"When he says, 'Check out the hook while my DJ revolves it,' you just start turning around in a circle."

"And you'll say this?"

Johnny slaps his own temples. "The *fucking record, man!* Where the fuck have you been for the past month?"

"I'm very sorry, but my hearing—"

"Just listen for 'revolve,'" says Declan. "I'll tap you if you miss it."

"I'll stomp you on your prick," says Ron Tolenaar.

"Goo-goo, goo-goo, revolve," says Osmund. "Got it, got it."

Perhaps you are one of the four million online viewers of the "Ice Ice Baby" clip. I sometimes wonder if any of you four million has failed to ask me whether the video of my incarcerated father dancing in a diaper causes me pain. Yes, his imprisonment has been an agonizing ordeal for us, and yes, the first time I saw the video, I thought I would swoon and barf with shame. But beyond his letters (and the odd note from Ter, with whom I've struck up a correspondence), the video affords my only real glimpse of the old man's life in Thep Moob. Having now watched it dozens of times, I can honestly say that I'm grateful for it—it is a documentary testament to much of what I love and admire about my father. With the family resources under strain, I can't justify the time and expense of a trip to Thailand merely to speak with him through a Plexiglas window for twenty minutes once a week. So this brief film is what I have.

Even on the umpteenth viewing, the look of worry in his face in the opening moments makes my pulse hammer. He stands in the center of the shot, a pace or two in front of the other men. His nose and upper lip quaver, threatening a sneeze or a sobbing jag. His eyes swivel in their sockets, trying to glimpse his teammates, who crouch behind him, pumping haunchily in sprinters-at-the-starting-blocks attitudes. Naked terror distends his features, as though he expects the men to claw him to pieces. When they rise and boil out around him, his fear does not subside.

But a wise friend pointed out something remarkable about my father's performance here: he looks only at his fellow dancers. My father is the only member of his dance team with an entry in *Who's Who*, yet he is also the only dancer who glances not a single time at the camera, the eye of the world. His anxiety is not for himself, or for the certain harm the video will inflict on his reputation. His only worry is that he will be a bad baby and let down his team. No one can tell me that this is not a kind of valor.

The fellows move with a coherence and discipline that obviously took scores of hours to refine. It's hard to spot a false step. No one loses the beat. But despite each man's near-military commitment to the choreography, some impression of six particular spirits comes through. It stirs me to imagine how hard it must have been for this arbitrary association of variously damaged personalities to pull a routine together.

Ron Tolenaar seems to stand about seven feet tall—my father's letters have, if anything, understated his monstrousness. He looks like an enormous rubber pop-eye squeeze toy made in the likeness of that actor from the *Hellboy* movies. Ron's dance is sort of Mick Jaggerish, a fantail-pigeon strut. He jacks his neck, bugs his eyes, and works his lips in a burlesque that somehow transforms his grotesquerie into a kind of proud plumage. It's a weirdly sexy, mesmerizing sight. It identifies him beyond doubt as the leader of the dorm.

From what little I'd known about Ter up to my first viewing of the video, I'd expected his performative presence to be one of cautious near-invisibility. But he's a frenetic, hectic dancer, fiercely teenage in the viciousness with which he kicks his feet and swings the shaggy black blur of his hair. "Ice Ice Baby" vanished from the airwaves years before he was born, but he pumps his fists and mouths the lyrics with an arrogant, proprietary intensity. Watching him glide in and out of the chorus line, materializing and vanishing at his own whim, I feel reassured that Ter will make his own way in the world.

And there's Henri Permeuil, dogging the heels of Johnny Francis. He's sort of dancing *at* Johnny, moving with a vaguely vengeful fervency, desperate to upstage the Texan ringer. The glossy black do-rag knotted over his skull says, "I am the real artist here." During the breakdown, when the guys stridingly mill about before resuming their sprinters' squats, note Henri's two-second rendition of his stuck-in-the-freezer concept. Even if it does not transmit the suffering fullness of a captive soul, it doesn't look too bad.

Declan Weyde is confounding to watch. Nothing about him suggests a man capable of doing what he did. He's a shyly pretty man with strawberry blond hair and sturdy, Norwegian features. Hard muscle wraps his arms and legs. But where the other men violently buck and jerk—especially in the "arm-worm" and "give-me-elbow-room" sequences—watch the fluid, feminine economy of Declan's movements. He doesn't want to accidentally bash somebody, doesn't want even to bruise the air around him.

I love the choruses, especially the first one. You see Declan moonwalk past and touch my father's elbow to cue his revolving. Osmund begins to turn, one hand on his diaper knot, the other crooked over his head. He looks like a jewelry-box ballerina. I love it how he giggles while the other dancers steeple their arms about him, showering my father in handfuls of shredded toilet paper, a simulation of snow, of Ice-Ice. It's wonderful how he sort of gets lost in this moment, keeps revolving into the second verse until Declan touches him again. Watch his lips at 1:15, my favorite instant in the video. Declan touches him, and my father says, "Got it, thanks," and comes out of the turn. "Got it, thanks." All business. You can detect a new dignity in his manner here, a prideful awareness that he is the star of this show. The decency of Declan's vigilance and my father's obvious gratitude at being looked after—this does something to me. Also, other than that "Got it, thanks," I find it somehow winning that my father doesn't stop soundlessly murmuring "goo-goo" from the moment the action starts until he is led out of the frame.

PUBLIC RELATIONS

The contest ruins dozens of Thep Moob's gamblers and makes the bookies rich. The Nigerians do not place. The transgendered prostitutes of Zone C do not place. First prize goes to members of the Hard Snakes, a homicidal youth gang whose dancing talents no one suspected. Second prize goes to a team of heroin addicts whom the jackpot roused to a frenzy of choreographic dedication. The addicts swap the ceiling fan and the outlet to a drug dealer for a substantial amount of heroin. In the week after the dance contest, three members of their team die tranquilly of overdoses, which may be construed as compounding their triumph, or not.

An unqualified winner of the dance contest is Captain Surongporn. The outpouring of media comment on the contest establishes Surongporn as an inspired, liberal innovator in the science of rehabilitation, and blunts, somewhat, international outcries over abuses and overcrowding in Thai correctional facilities.

A-23's third-place victory is a double bounty for Ron Tolenaar, who, after recruiting Johnny Francis, laid a heavy bet on his own team's success. The purchase of a two-gallon slow cooker, a television, and a hot plate and kettle for the boiling of pineapple wort do not put a dent in his winnings.

The press attention begets mixed fortunes for the men of A-23. Neither the *New York Times* article about my father's performance, nor the video's endless rebroadcast on CNN, helps Professor Tower's case with the Economics department. Though my father's guilt has yet to be determined in court, after reviewing the diaper footage, the provost agrees with the chair that my father is insane and possibly a deviant. Over the protests of a few loyal students and members of an internet fan site sympathetic to the straitened diaper man, Osmund's salary is halted and his tenure rescinded. I have initiated a lawsuit on his behalf, but the odds of success, I'm told, are small.

A reporter for the *Bangkok Post* uncovers Ter's astonishing story and, several weeks after the contest, publishes an article about the guiltless boy's lost youth behind the walls of Thep Moob. He is evicted and given a garret in Ngop Na, where he is employed, not all that happily, on a municipal landscaping crew. He makes the ninety-minute bus trip to Thep Moob on visiting days, once a week, ferrying to my father books, medications, fresh produce, and whatever other necessities can't be obtained inside. Six months after Ter's eviction, he impregnates a widow twice his age who lives in the neighboring apartment. They marry. Ter's visits to the prison taper off.

A-23 has lost another inmate by then, as well. Three days after the votes are tallied, a trusty escorts an electrician into the dorm to install the electrical outlet. While the installation is taking place, a second trusty comes to the cell to summon Declan Weyde. He is told that a man from the Canadian embassy awaits him in the visitors' area. Declan leaves the dorm at 9:45 a.m. By late afternoon, he has not returned. The men wonder what has become of him. Shortly after 7, the voice of Sudrit Nut comes over the public address system, inviting Declan's ghost to leave the prison grounds.

Declan Weyde's death by lethal injection is Thep Moob's first execution in two years, and the only execution of a Western prisoner in recent memory. Word in the prison is that the brother of the man Declan murdered is the politician Pechawat Phititommuphruak, lately appointed Minister of the Interior. Among conspiracy-minded inmates like Henri Permeuil, the timing of Declan's execution is grist for speculation.

"Do not be ignorant," says Henri. "The contest, the whole thing was a trick. The minister, this big man, he says to the Captain, 'Okay, that guy killed my brother. You have to kill him for me.' But a white guy? A Canadian? It's not so easy with the press. With the diplomats, with the tourist industry. You need some cover, doing this in The Land of a Thousand Smiles. So we were the cover. 'Everybody, look at the dancing monkeys while we put this poor bastard down.'"

Ron Tolenaar dismisses this theory, pointing out that Surpongporn couldn't have possibly known that the dance contest would develop the viral momentum that it did. "And be serious, if really, they are so worried, they'd have the Snakes hit Declan. They would hang him in the lime trees."

"Yes," says Henri. "And it was two little airplanes that brought the towers down. You don't like information you can't handle, so you put your hands over your eyes. Stay sleeping, Ron. I am awake."

BRUTAL BEANS

The loss of Declan Weyde sends my father into a confused depression. During the weeks following his friend's death, the distant grin into which Osmund's features lapse during moments of pain or bewilderment never leaves his face. My father's lifelong armor—his ebullience—thins, and his emissions of gnomic wisdom intensify. When Ter expresses his condolences over Declan's execution, my father's eyes go vacant and his grin stretches to the back molars.

"Yes, well, it is interesting, the importance of good judgment," my father says with musical elocution. "I'd say Declan demonstrated a pattern of extraordinarily poor judgment, both in his choice of a lover and in allowing his anger to get the better of him, so the outcome isn't terribly surprising.

Ah, Ter, let us be grateful for our ability to suppress craziness and keep one's demons at bay."

But during insomniac hours before dawn, my father lies awake on his mat, plagued by two species of disquiet concerning his dead friend. The first lies in the purity of his affection for Declan's memory. In his secret heart, Osmund cares not at all that Declan killed a man. This seems proof of a kind of decline. Second, my father is haunted by a formless shadow-thought that he might have prevented Declan from killing the man, but out of laziness or cowardice chose not to. This thought is nonsensical and seems proof of another kind of decline.

His letters home make no mention of Declan's death, but dwell merrily on the quotidian details of his life in Thep Moob.

> There is a real satisfaction in attaining fluency with the system here. For example, during my first weeks, I was paying 70 thb for haircuts, which it turns out is outrageous. I now go to a fellow who does a reasonable job for 10 thb. I usually give him 11 or 12, and it's wonderful to see how much this little generosity delights him.

Or:

> This week's big news is that in place of the unsanitary toilet hole which is standard, we've had installed in our cell a proper commode, to which is attached a hose for squirting one's butt. The butt-squirter is a great device. I don't know why American politicians are universally unwilling to propose anything in this line of innovation. The Thai save on paper and waste processing, and it turns out, there are really quite a number of nerve endings down there, so there is a good bit of pleasure to be derived from use of the butt-squirter. I would give my vote to any presidential candidate unafraid to say, *I am resolutely for saving resources and for stimulating nerves that don't otherwise get stimulated.*

In addition to the toilet fixture, mealtimes in A-23 mark an improvement in living standards. The men pool their money for groceries, and Ter prepares stews in the slow cooker that are the high point of the men's days. After Ter is sent out of Thep Moob, it is Ron Tolenaar who volunteers to cook the first meal, a dish he calls "Ron's Brutal Beans." This consists of kidney beans slow-cooked to paste and seasoned with ketchup, molasses, and whole chilies.

The dinnertime mood that night is somber. In their conscious hearts, the men of A-23 do not set much store by the fellowship of their dorm mates. Yet, with Declan and Ter gone, the unacknowledged tribal comfort of the dance-troupe days has gone, leaving a vacancy that cannot be discussed.

The men ladle out the beans in silence, and they would eat the beans in silence. But, as a queer mercy, Ron's stew is so revolting that the men have no choice but to talk about it.

"I've ate assholes that tasted better than this," says Johnny Francis. "Way better."

"Give me the knife," says Henri Permeuil. "Right now I will cut out my tongue."

"Fuck yourselves," says Ron. He takes a huge spoonful into his mouth but does not swallow it. For a moment, he goes still, panting through flared nostrils like a bull. Then he retches the beans back into his bowl. "Unspeakable," he says. The three men laugh.

Osmund does not, though he, too, finds the stew disgusting. Around a hot mouthful, he says, "I don't know what you guys are complaining about." His voice trills with a jolliness that is a form of fury. "I think these beans are very nicely spiced."

POSTSCRIPT

The personal letter is nearly extinct, and I think this is a loss. Digital communications are, I believe, subconsciously composed with a mass audience in mind. Even the direst, privatest sorts of emails professing love or requesting divorce betray the flavor of an interoffice bulletin or an entry for the Toastmasters prize. If one is lucky enough to get a personal letter these days, it's a thing to hold dear and keep confidential from the general public. That said, my father's recent messages have been somewhat stinting on intimate revelation, working mostly in the plumbing-and-haircuts line. When I am feeling hopeless about his situation, there is an earlier dispatch I reread for strange comfort. The letter is eccentric and probably more candid than a father should be with his son. Yet, if my father survives this ordeal, it will be his pliant nature and appetite for exploration (to which the letter testifies) that will guide him through. What follows is a transcription of the aerogramme Osmund wrote the morning after his confused episode with Declan Weyde, which confusion was never wholly resolved. I wish his friend had gotten a chance to read this letter before he was killed.

Dear Wells:

It is truly ridiculous to think back on how much psychological energy I expended over the years, worrying about the possibility that I might be a homosexual.

This wastage of energy began as early as sixth grade, and probably a good while before. There was a glade behind the school which my friend Miles Yoder and I would use to conduct these little experiments in preparation for the temptations and challenges awaiting us the following year, in junior high school. One of these researches involved smoking cigarettes stolen from Miles's mother. The thinking here was that we ought to familiarize ourselves with the experience of smoking, so that when older boys pressured us into using cigarettes we could do so without the risk of becoming nicotine addicts. (Totally absurd!) We also engaged in experimental "What if?" conversations about homosexual acts: "Hey, Miles, imagine me doing blank to you!" I would describe various deeds, and he would make retching sounds to prove that these things didn't appeal to him, and I would do the same when he described these things for me. At one point, we did put our tongues into one another's mouths to prepare ourselves for our first opportunities to French kiss a girl. (In my case, this would be nearly a decade in coming.) It was my assumption that Miles and I would ultimately perform oral sex on each other. When this failed to come about, I did feel some disappointment and this terrified me.

In graduate school, I fell under the influence of Keynes, whose homosexuality was, for me, another source of confusion. I was just fanatical about his writing. I would walk around the Harvard campus reciting lines from his marvelous treatise *The Inflation of Currency as a Method of Taxation,* which, man, I thought was just wonderful. The limberness of thought and generosity of spirit with which Keynes accomplished his work seemed of a piece with the man's erotic fluidity. Yet, I worried that my fanaticism for Keynes's writing might be indicative of my own homosexuality, which, I know, sounds completely outrageous and idiotic. The other side of the coin was that perhaps I was *not* a homosexual, so therefore I constitutionally lacked the deep wellspring of creativity from which Keynes's intellectual genius flowed. Either possibility was agonizing to me. I went to see a therapist. I can't remember what he said.

At the time, there was a beer and hamburger joint in Cambridge called The Beef Station. Homosexual adventures were known to be available in the toilets of The Beef Station. When I was having difficulty getting going on my thesis, I had a cuckoo notion that it might help if I were to pay a visit there. Totally bananas. I never did it. Anyway, I was married to your mother at the time. All of this madness may in some way explain why I did not ultimately become a Keynesian, though his observation about the downward inflexibility of wages continues to inform my thinking on monetary policy.

My homosexuality was one of your mother's pet conversational baits. I remember one night, we were driving to a dinner party at the Kerners' house in Durham. I thought it would be faster to take Erwin Road and she thought it would be faster to take the bypass. I took Erwin Road, and this enraged her. "If Bill Larsh were with us, and he'd said 'Take the bypass,' you'd have taken the bypass. But anything I say, it's just so much white noise, isn't it, Ed? You don't hear a thing women say." My choice of Erwin Road, according to your mother, demonstrated a covert interest in sodomy. We did not enjoy ourselves at the Kerners'.

This argument, specifically as it pertains to Bill, got another airing more recently. You may remember Verla, the woman from USAID

I was seeing during your freshman year of college. I was very much in love with her. She had an incisive mind, and she wrote a working paper on Sri Lankan rubber tariffs that was absolutely extraordinary. She had a tuneful laugh, and her calf muscles were extremely well formed. We took a vacation to Scotland one summer, and Bill, who was teaching in Paris at the time, came to visit us. He was absolutely gross with Verla. Constantly touching her and making very ugly and childish innuendos. We ate dinner one night at an Indian restaurant. He persuaded her to get up and dance with him there in the crowded dining room, though no music was playing. Bill, as you know, is phenomenally attractive and has slept with an astounding number of beautiful women. As much as I was disgusted by his behavior, I recall also feeling a little flattered that a sexual conquistador of Bill's high rank should be so taken with my girlfriend.

The following morning, I awoke to find myself alone in my bed. Verla had gone. At about half-past ten, Bill came and knocked. He said, "I had a visitor last night."

"Ah, did you?" I said.

"I did. Boy, oh boy. She's extraordinary, Osmund. Listen, I'm going skiing in Lucerne this weekend. I invited her to join me and she's accepted. Would you like to come along?"

Crushing is how this felt. Yet, I couldn't see how it would have helped to have discussed my feelings with Bill and Verla. (I never saw her again. At her request, Bill gathered her things from my room. She couldn't bear to face me.) So they went to Lucerne that day, and I climbed Arthur's Seat. I remember the air being very pure there. I remember wondering whether I might be the sort of nonessential person who would be wise to kill himself. You and I were not speaking at the time and I was at odds with your brother and suicide seemed like a possibility with general benefits. But I knew that this was a silly and self-pitying line of thought, and anyway, I couldn't find a good precipice, only very steep grades which would probably have left me badly contused but alive.

According to your mother, my failure to be violent with Bill or

Verla was further proof of my homosexuality, specifically, of my hidden desire to make love with Bill. But it is not the case that I had erotic feelings for him. I haven't thought about the Verla stuff in years, and now that it occurs to me, I am appalled. I suppose the lesson is that one ought to be grateful that one is not phenomenally attractive, seeing as being phenomenally attractive, in Bill's case, appears to have assisted his belief that he can behave like a crook. It's some comfort that he is a third-rate scholar and I know he gets paid less than I do. A petty comfort.

But all this is to say that I am sorry for the time I hit you with the belt when you were seven. If you don't remember this, your friend Brendan was over at the house. I didn't like his shrill, nelly voice. On the afternoon in question, the two of you had taken a bag of cashews with you and climbed into the "way back" area of the old Datsun. I found you both there without pants. I believe you'd been inserting the cashews into your bottoms and playing some sort of snacktime roulette with the tainted nuts. I striped you with a belt, thinking it might discourage you from turning queer. This now strikes me as cruel and shameful. Maybe it is telling you too much to say that I have just recently, at the age of seventy, sampled gay sex (a mild, risk-free variety) for the first time in my life and I found it unappealing. It was with a man named Declan Weyde, a Canadian serving a very long sentence for the theft of a coffeemaker, which should give you some sense of the jurisprudential craziness I'm up against here. At any rate, Declan is a man I like and trust very much, and he is not physically unattractive. I mention this only to say that if I were inclined toward men, I think it's safe to say that I would have had a satisfying experience with Declan. Yet, I did not, which, I think, certifies me as a man of mainstream appetites.

What a lot of my life I've wasted on this issue. If I had it to do over again, I would have encouraged you and Brendan to do all you pleased with the cashews or whatever else. You could have learned a great deal. It is never a good or useful thing to diminish the scope of one's awareness or to restrict the flow of information.

At any rate, I am sorry for any harm I have done to you over these years, and though you were an unexpected addition to my life, you are a vital one. My love for you and your brother sustains me here. Know that I am safe and having good conversations with people. Ah, the absurdity of it all.

Love,
Dad

PS Months ago, I told my student Marko that I would reimburse him for a medical expense. I would be grateful if you could handle this for me. The procedure was to remove several prominent, hornlike growths from his cheeks and forehead. Please examine the bill from the doctor before paying, and if possible, do try to give him the check in person so that we can be sure he's had the surgery. Trust, but verify. If he still has the growths, do not give him the check.

BIRTHDAY GIRL

by TOM BARBASH

A young girl lies on a snowy country road. Her head has fallen to the side as though she's sleeping, and her hair fans out across the snow. She is clothed in a blue parka with a white fringed hood, a red knit scarf, frayed jeans, and dark blue snow boots. She's alive, thank God (her breath warm enough to melt snow), though unmoving.

I never saw her, you tell yourself. She'd been running in the cold night with her dog, who sprints up and down the road, barking. You were rushing a little, to score some Advil before the market at the gas station closed, but really, the girl came from nowhere. You are banged up yourself, a cut on the inside of your lip, and shaking, and the scene emerges before you in pieces: dog/girl/car/snow/scarf. You can't wait for it to settle; for now there is getting the girl to a hospital. You don't own a cell phone to call for an ambulance. You will take the girl yourself.

But loading the girl into a compact car isn't easy as you are five foot three, and in your doctor's words, *small boned*. Straining, and chanting profanities under your breath, you manage to drag and then slide the girl—who looks to be around fourteen, but weighs as much as you—positioning her with legs bent and head ducked down, so that the door can close without hurting anything. You recall too late the rule about not moving someone when they're injured.

The dog, you think then, because you can't just leave him out on the road like this. He has stopped running and stands a few feet away, staring at your car and the girl. You yell *Here boy. Come here boy*, to no avail. You grab a slice of chicken from the plastic container of your dinner leftovers and hold it out in your palm. He walks over, dragging his leash, and eats from your hand. *Thatta boy*, you say, and then wrestle him into the passenger seat of your car. He has a blue bandana around his neck, same shade as the girl's jacket, and tan-colored fur. You try to calm yourself down.

In ten minutes or so you reach the emergency room entrance of the hospital, which lies at the eastern border of what they poignantly call downtown. You run inside and shout, "Can someone please help me? There's a girl in very bad shape. She's been hit." An attendant with greasy blonde hair tied back in a rubber band follows you back out with a metal gurney. He braces the girl's neck, places her carefully on the gurney, and rushes her inside.

You follow with the dog. There is dried blood on your hand, which you rinse off at a water fountain. A few people smile over at you when you sit down in the waiting room. They think it's *your* dog.

Eventually a young man in faded green scrubs with a chart in his hand emerges. His sentences come forth in disconnected sounds: The police dropping by... a report.

You give him the sequence of events. A flash of something in your headlights. Brakes. A skid. A crashing sound. It doesn't feel like you're slurring your words.

"So the dog was running ahead of the girl," he says.

"I guess. I didn't see either of them." If only you'd hit the dog, you think. But it's good you didn't hit the dog.

"Where were you coming from?" he asks.

You consider telling him the truth, that you were in a bar, but because you ate at a restaurant called Howell's on Montgomery Street earlier you decide to simply say "Howell's." You were there with two friends, talking about your week of housesitting for your boss, who is on vacation in the Florida Keys. You like staying in a place with leather couches, a nice sound system, and shelves of clever movies. Even now you're wearing her stylish red wool coat.

"Did you have anything to drink?" he asks.

"A glass of wine," you say, and surprisingly enough that seems to satisfy him.

"One," he says, writing this down, and you say, "Yes."

People are still coming in, one woman crying in pain and others with small or invisible bruises and limps. A TV plays Fox News, a story about a man donating his kidney to his brother. Beneath the television, a waist-high plastic Santa stands behind a pack of small plastic reindeers. There are other Christmas decorations still up, and a small, fake tree adorned with little red ribbons. A young boy asks if he can pet your dog, and you say yes.

"What's his name?" the boy asks.

"Max," you say, the name of a hamster your father gave you when you were six.

You consider calling one of the friends you'd been to dinner with, but it's late now, and they are likely both asleep. There was a lawyer you dated a few times last year, but you lost his number, and that had ended awkwardly.

As you wait for the doctors to evaluate the girl, you are waiting too for the blood levels in your brain to shift, though you can't tell if it's alcohol that's causing the dull ache in the front of your head or if it's an aftereffect of the collision. There is a formula that has to do with your weight, what you've eaten, and how many hours have passed; you recall seeing a chart about this a few years ago on a bulletin board at college, with the message

A GOOD TIME TO MISPLACE YOUR KEYS. Your mouth feels dry. It's hard to swallow. You drink a cup of weak coffee from the dispenser in the waiting room, and take several long sips of cold water from the hallway water fountain.

It's no big deal to drive with a few drinks in you, not in a town without traffic, where you can down a few shots of Patrón at a place like Finnegan's or The Orchard and still make it home—people do. You've had far wilder nights and been fine, although once after a party you did scrape a curb, and after another you pulled into the wrong driveway. Still, you have no record of unsafe driving, not even a speeding ticket.

On a dare when you were thirteen, you once told four separate store managers it was your birthday—though it was still months away—and that no one in your family had remembered. You were so convincing in your disappointment (your eyes were disturbingly red) that you walked home that night with a compact disc, two T-shirts, a poster, and a beautiful silver necklace with a locket, which you are wearing now. It was alarmingly easy to do. The key was tricking yourself into believing it. You think of this as you try to decide what you'll say to the police.

At the sink in the women's room you splash cold water on your cheeks, then pat dry your face with a paper towel. You look like you always look. An image through the windshield flashes in your mind. The girl's eyes are less scared than bewildered, as though she'd seen not a car coming at her but a UFO.

"You all right?" There's a woman at the next sink; you don't remember her walking in.

"Fine," you say. "I thought I lost a contact."

After a second coffee you feel more jittery than sleepy, and nervous, though this doesn't distinguish you from anyone else in the waiting room.

You can be whatever you need to be here, which is something you've always been good at. You have an inborn empathy, your drama teacher said. You starred in three plays in high school and another in college. You earned a fawning write-up in a regional newspaper.

For now you focus on your role here. You locate a plastic soup bowl and fill it with water for the dog. It isn't much, but it feels good to watch him drink.

A couple in their mid-forties wearing heavy coats and scarves arrive and run to the desk. They have kind faces, you think; you recognize them from when you worked as a cashier at the Price Chopper. You realize you've seen their brown-haired daughter before, and vaguely remember slipping her a packet of gum her mother had denied her. The girl was eight or nine. Her mother had been fumbling through her purse and didn't see the exchange, but the girl's face opened into a smile. At that thought a chill crosses your skin. You consider slipping away, but the nurse is already pointing over at you, and you rise from your chair.

"Thank you so much," the mother says, and then glances at the dog. "And look, you brought Lemon here too."

They are so appreciative you realize that they think you might have saved their daughter's life.

You tell them how you worked at the hospital as a candy striper in high school, mostly in the pediatric ward. And then you report what little you've heard about the condition of the girl, whose name is Eden.

At some point in the conversation you tell them—because you *have* to, and because you figure you are as sober-sounding as you are likely to be— "I'm the one who hit your daughter."

Your declaration confuses them.

"I'm so sorry. She came out of nowhere. I never saw her."

"It was *you?*" the father says.

"I'm so sorry."

"Dear God," the mother says, and she sits down.

"It was all ice out there. I wasn't going very fast."

"You were going fast enough," the mother says. "How long have you had your license?"

"I'm twenty-three," you say.

"Then there's no excuse."

"No, you're right. There isn't," you say. "I wish more than anything in the world that I could do something. I wish I could go back wherever she is and do something." You feel yourself growing upset. "I really don't want to bother you. But I'd like to stay here until Eden wakes up."

The father studies your face, then looks over at his wife. They are registering the fact that you look quite a bit like their daughter.

"I want to make sure she's all right," you say.

He purses his lips and nods.

"I'm just so *very, very, very, very* sorry this happened," you say, close to tears.

His expression softens. "I believe you," he says.

A doctor emerges. The good news, he says, is that the CAT scan showed no skull fracture and no evidence of internal bleeding.

"She isn't awake yet," he says, "but her pupils are reactive, which suggests she might simply have a small concussion."

"So she's going to be all right," the father says. He's trying to read the doctor's face, which reveals only an affable competence.

"We'll have to wait and see. There could be some things the CAT scan didn't catch," the man says, and adds that they may need to take her to another hospital for an MRI. They'll have to keep watching her closely.

Eden's left kneecap is shattered, he adds, probably from the impact of the car. Her left shoulder is dislocated. "We did a pretty good job of putting it back in place," he says.

The father nods. "We appreciate everything you're doing," he says, and from your seat you nod too in thanks.

It is a record night for accidents, someone at the nurse's station says. Already there have been three other serious ones in and around town, including a fatal, which is why the police are so slow in getting here. If enough terrible things happen out on the roads they may forget about you, though you know it's wrong to hope for this, and really, all you want is for everyone to be fine and healthy and sleeping in a bed, which is where you should be right now. Your headache has eased and your buzz feels weaker, almost not even there at all.

*   *   *

Over the next hour and a half there is a heart attack and a bar fight. More people being wheeled in and more waiting. You talk with the girl's parents about Eden, who they tell you is an accomplished gymnast, swimmer, and amateur comedienne. She performed stand-up at a school talent competition. "She'll have some good material about this," her father says.

He is a short sandy-haired man with the build of a wrestling coach. His eyes pucker at the corners with appealing little wrinkles. You think of your unnervingly handsome father who left when you were eight, and who'd stop in on the odd year to take you out to dinner, then ask you to pay half, or for all of it, explaining in a fatherly voice that he would make it up to you next time.

"She goes out every night with that dog, for an hour or so," Eden's father says. "She likes to get on the back roads past the edge of town and let Lemon find their way back. One time they were away until midnight. A force of nature, that one. She's going to need some rehab, I guess. Maybe a lot, but she'll be better than ever after that. One of our others I'd worry about, but not her."

It would be nice to have someone worry about you, you think.

"I'll bet you're a great father," you say. It feels as though you're auditioning.

"Not always," he says. "But it's kind of you to say that."

By two-thirty they still haven't heard anything, which the father says is a good sign. If it was bad news, they would have already heard by now.

"Do you think that's true?" the mother asks you, as though you know about these things.

"I think so, yes," you say, because there's no reason not to believe it. You kneel down and rub Lemon's belly, and he makes high-pitched happy sounds in response.

It is the sweetest family moment you've had in a long while.

*   *   *

At around three a.m. the mother says that you should go home and get some sleep. You can come back later in the day when Eden is awake, she says, if you would like. The mood is hopeful, though no one has come out to offer an update. The police arrive, finally, and ask you questions about the accident. Their faces show the strain of a difficult night. Perhaps it is because you were talking warmly with the girl's parents when they walked in, or because the dog is resting his head on your lap, but it's all quite casual. They take down your phone number and address, and they leave. Nine out of ten times, you are sure, they would have administered a Breathalyzer. This is the tenth time. When they're gone you almost feel disappointed.

You ask the father where Eden wants to go to college.

"She's only a sophomore," he says, "but she has her sights on Tufts. She's got the marks to get in—or maybe she'll go to Holy Cross like her big brother."

The fact that she has a big brother seems like a good sign. You picture him talking to her on the phone the morning after a miserable date, the way your brother used to do for you. And now he'll hear all about the girl in town who ran into his sister.

But she drove me to the hospital, Eden might tell him.

If he's at all like your brother he'll answer, "I still don't like her."

There is a room somewhere where the girl is lying with IVs connected to her, her body fighting heroically, or struggling, and this is your doing. You want to find her now and tell her that you're sorry. You imagine the scene as it would be in a TV drama, with you as a flawed but sympathetic character, pretty in an unmemorable way.

You go to the lunchroom and buy a packet of Lorna Doones from a vending machine. You eat one under the droning of the fluorescent lights and throw the rest away.

At close to four you volunteer to take Lemon for a walk. The streets are silent until a snowplow makes a wake of slush on its path across town. Has it gotten warmer? You think of heading home. But what would you do? It's too early to call anyone. As the dog bounds up the street you imagine the heady privacy of Eden's nighttime walks. You did this in high school studying for parts, lost yourself in a stranger's life—not only in rehearsals, but for whole weekends. There was a magic to it. Method acting, your teacher called it, but it wasn't acting. It was another way of being, a better path. You can guess where the girl would go, and what she thought about in the hours spent out of her parents' house. You used to believe this place would kill you if you never left. You came back to take care of your mother when she was sick, and with her dead now you will leave again soon. If people ask about your father you say he's dead too.

You walk a mile or so in the white with the dog bounding ahead and the moonlight glinting off the snow, then halt abruptly when a car heads at you from the opposite direction. A block away the car turns, and when it's gone from sight you think: *I need to get back there.* The wind loosens a clump of ice from a nearby tree branch and it hits the ground like a box of dropped dishes.

You jog and then run the mile back. When you round the corner by the hospital Lemon tugs at his leash.

Inside, at the nurse's station, you ask for news about Eden. You hear the pleasing sound of a child laughing, and then realize it's the television.

"Oh dear," says the nurse, who began her shift when you left on your walk. Her accent is from the islands, someplace like Barbados. She says compassionately, "Nobody went to *find* you?"

"Beautiful *girl*," the nurse says, and clucks her tongue. "Was it a hit and run?"

"Yes," you say.

"Well, I pray to God they get him."

In the waiting room Eden's parents are conferring with one of the doctors. Your brain shuts off and there's a tingling in your arms and hands.

Years from now, on vacation with your husband and six-year-old son in Hawaii, you will make friends with a psychologist and find yourself more comfortable with her than you are with anyone in your everyday life. The psychologist will be traveling from Canada with her own family, staying in a bungalow a few hundred yards down the beach. Things will have turned

out well for you on many fronts. You will be having drinks with her at dinner one sultry night and you'll slip and say that there are things no one
will ever know about you. The psychologist, on her third mai tai, will joke
and say, "You mean the sweet little child you killed once." It will be a terrible coincidence—a macabre line put out for no reason other than that she
hadn't felt like doing her job on vacation. She will read your face and then
switch the subject. She will slip you her card the next day and say she works
by phone if need be. You will want to tell your husband that night, but
then you'll wonder how he would feel about the fact that you kept it from
him this long. You will ask him to drive for the rest of the vacation. You
will fall asleep in your son's bed twice that week, with the boy in your arms.
You will try and forgive yourself. Home from Hawaii you will pull an old
man back from the curb, though in truth no car was speeding toward him,
only a slow-moving cab a few hundred yards away.

Bless your soul, he will say.

The doctor in the emergency room catches your eye now, and purses his
lips, the way you've seen in hospital shows, and once in a dream about your
mother.

"Go and be with your parents," the nurse says.

It's as though she's asked you to leap from a plane in flight.

"Go on in there, dear," the nurse says.

They gaze up at you with unreasonable kindness. You plummet toward
them, into the purity of their grief.

YOU HAVE TO SEE THIS

PORTRAITS OF
LAWRENCE WESCHLER

INTRODUCTION

by RACHEL COHEN

A LITTLE WHILE ago, the filmmaker Michael Benson wrote to a group of friends and colleagues expressing his frustration that the wonderful work of Lawrence Weschler, a man who has written about seemingly everybody and everything, is not itself often written about. As the letter circulated, it became clear that many people had been waiting for a chance to talk about Weschler, and about the effect of his work on them. Dave Eggers offered space in the pages of *McSweeney's*, I was asked to be the guest editor, and the company whose writings and portraits fill the following pages was assembled.

One of our hopes in forming this symposium has been to try to present together something of the astonishing variety of Weschler's work, the facets of which can seem to exist in separate realms. Readers of *McSweeney's* will be familiar with his Convergences series, and with the resulting book *Everything That Rises: A Book of Convergences*, in which Weschler finds startling and revealing lines of association as he ranges among Baroque paintings, diagrams of trees, war photographs, brain scans, and hieroglyphs. Some will know his work as a political correspondent in books such as *The Passion of Poland* and *A Miracle, A Universe*, or will have read his brilliant meditation on David Wilson's Museum of Jurassic Technology, *Mr. Wilson's Cabinet of Wonder*. Some may have come upon his literary essays for journals like *The Threepenny Review*; Weschler's long relationship with *Threepenny* is chronicled here by editor Wendy Lesser. Others will have encountered the wide-ranging profiles—often first written for the *New Yorker*, an environment evoked here by Bill McKibben—that figure in *Shapinsky's Karma, Boggs's Bill, and Other True-Life Tales, A Wanderer in the Perfect City, Vermeer in Bosnia*, and also as book-length considerations of artists Robert Irwin and David Hockney. And then some readers will be familiar with Lawrence Weschler's life as a cultural impresario, as the artistic director of the Chicago Humanities Festival, and as the man in charge of the New York Institute for the Humanities, at New York University, a tenure now regrettably come to its close. We hoped here to celebrate, and to introduce to those who have yet to encounter his work, some of the myriad elements that go into making up the World as Weschler Sees It.

Lawrence Weschler, known as Ren in his great network of friendship and acquaintance, is a proponent of conversation where others see cultural and political life breaking up into isolated fragments. In fourteenth-century English, the word conversation meant "living together, having dealings with others," and this derived from Latin roots, where "to live with, keep company with," was based, literally, in *con-* and *vers-*: "to turn about with." In all these senses, and maybe especially the last, Ren, as a person and a writer, is a conversationalist. He keeps company with what turns about. And, in keeping company, with poets and crocheters and war correspondents and film editors and nuclear physicists and installation artists and magicians, he has, as Riva Lehrer put it, become a sort of "P.T. Barnum of the Mind." People whose lives and work Ren first discovered as subjects for his writing have become his steady companions and the regular participants in his imaginative public events.

Who else would have had the inspired idea of inviting Jonathan Lethem and Geoff Dyer, both contributors here, together with professors and judges and DJ Spooky, to be part of a symposium on copyright called "Comedies of Fair U$e: A Search for Comity in the Intellectual Property Wars"? Could any other public intellectual have gotten people in Greenwich Village to line up around the block at seven in the morning for the chance to watch a day-long battle royale among physicists and artists and art historians over the optical theories of David Hockney?

Everyone who has written tributes here has wanted to honor at least two Rens—the public figure, his pockets overflowing with gifts, and the writer whose breadth has been astonishing his readers for decades. William Finnegan has been learning from Ren about their shared Los Angeles since he and Ren were in college together. Andrei Codrescu has been working on parallel, and sometimes intersecting, explorations of virtual reality for nearly twenty years. Film editor Walter Murch felt that it was somehow inevitable that he and his projects on the music of the spheres and on translating Curzio Malaparte would find their way to Ren, and so did Belgian political scientist Peter Vermeersch, who has written here on Weschler's *The Passion of Poland*. They, like many of us, have found in Weschler's books, and in his conferences and events, new realms—and, perhaps just as important, in knowing Ren they have found a home for their own concerns.

Throughout his career, Weschler has relied on visual artists as guides to interpretation and understanding. We are fortunate to have a significant presence of artists here, and I want to express gratitude to David Hockney, Ben Katchor, Riva Lehrer, Bill Morrison, and Lauren Redniss for allowing us to reproduce their portraits of Ren in this issue, and to Ricky Jay and Coco Shinomiya-Gorodetsky, for their playbill of the Weschler cabinet of characters. We wouldn't have been able to offer a picture of Ren in the round without them.

*   *   *

I would like now to say something of my own particular debt of gratitude to Ren and to his writing. The first Weschler essay that I remember reading was the one that came to be called "Vermeer in Bosnia," which appeared in the *New Yorker* in the fall of 1995 as "Inventing Peace." For me, the piece came as a shock, as it was meant to. Not because of the gruesome war crimes that were described in its second paragraph, although these were so skillfully conveyed that I have never forgotten the details. Nor did the shock lie in the exquisite evocation of Vermeer's "Girl with a Pearl Earring," although this description was not only breathtaking, but self-consciously about breathtakingness, about the shock of contact, for there follows a beautiful analysis, leaning in part on the work of art historian Edward Snow, of just how Vermeer gives his viewer the sense that the girl in the painting has just looked *at us*. Nor, really, was the shock of the essay due to the fact that there turns out to be an important relationship between the serenity of Vermeer and the horrific crimes that people perpetrate on one another, although it is true that I shivered that first time, and have every other time I've read the essay, when Weschler points out that "when Vermeer was painting... *all Europe was Bosnia*." (It is characteristic of Weschler to be able to draw into relation the most beautiful and appalling deeds of which people are capable without trivializing tragedy or banalizing art.) No, for me the shock of the essay belonged to none of these things, except insofar as it was founded on all of them. The shock of the essay was *that it was an essay*.

The force and coherence of an essay may derive from many combinations of narrative, image, argument, tone, syntax, and personality, and a Weschler essay is certainly at work in all of these dimensions. But the really unusual formal elegance of the Weschler essay at its finest has to do, I think, with his ability to keep consistently present the whole range of his preoccupations. This is true both of the sentences (the parentheticals, the ellipses, the em-dashes, the jagged subordinate clauses) and of the overall structures. You could not simply take a Vermeer and plonk it down in Bosnia and insist on their mutual relevance—if they are to converse, there has to be, in all the language about Vermeer, a consciousness that this is the same world in which the massacres of Bosnia happened, as it must be understood in every line discussing the war crimes tribunal that this is the same world from which Vermeer painted. In Weschler's essays, achieving this integration is both a matter of great structural ingenuity and a stance of moral integrity: it matters that all of this is part of one world.

When I read "Vermeer in Bosnia," I had formed an ambition to become an essayist, and for a few years had been trying to fathom what that might mean. I was attempting to hold essays together by whatever means came to hand, including pretty much everything from rivers of gerunds to wood glue. I was also hanging around New York's used bookstores, and, after that piece in the *New Yorker*, I read all the Weschler I could find—*Shapinsky's Karma, Mr. Wilson's Cabinet of Wonder, Seeing is Forgetting the Name of the Thing One Sees*. Weschler's work was for me a kind of extended hand, and, as I've since taught overlappingly with him, at Sarah Lawrence and at NYU, I've seen it have a similar effect on many writers starting out. As Baynard Woods, who took the bus up from DC every week to sit in on Weschler's writing seminar, The Fiction of Nonfiction, writes here, Weschler's work offers fellowship, and it shows a way forward.

A year or so after my initial encounters with his writings, I had the chance to send some writing to Ren, and, with the generosity that defines him, he began reading the pieces I was working on and saw how they could be essays. I think there are probably hundreds of writers, not to mention furniture builders and paper folders and documentary film-makers, going about their daily lives encouraged by the fact that Ren Weschler saw some significance in what they were after. Ren senses the clouds of potentiality around ideas and artworks and acts and people in the way I imagine migratory birds pick up the magnetic currents that guide their voyages.

I remember once, sitting at lunch with Ren, as he was readying for publication, or re-publication, *Seeing Is Forgetting the Name of the Thing One Sees*, which now represents more than thirty years of conversations with the artist Robert Irwin, and *True to Life*, with its twenty-five years of conversations with David Hockney. Ren was saying that his ongoing discussion with these two artists was like the double helix of his career. I think he also pointed out that he had begun writing about Irwin and about the Solidarity movement in Poland at roughly the same time. He said something like, "some people plant different crops in succession, but I planted all my seeds at once, and I've been tending them all ever since." I know that whatever he said left an impression in my mind of tilling, and also of him hurrying from one plant to another to see how each was doing.

This symposium makes a partial record of Ren's long loyalties, of his indefatigable and supportive curiosity, and of how that curiosity has affected his companions and his readers and audiences. Just as writing about art is for Ren inseparable from writing about politics, so writing as a whole should not really to be distinguished from presenting; it all follows from the same Weschlerian imperative: "You have to *see* this." Our section opens with an interview that Lawrence Weschler and Errol Morris conducted for this issue, loosely on the topic of "Ren Weschler: The Most Annoying Public Intellectual in America," which explores many of the themes and efforts and delights of Ren's career to date. There is a moment in the interview that brought home to me something about Ren's relationship to politics and to art; in it, I hear his indignation that people are suffering and making beautiful things and *no one is noticing*. "In each of these cases," he says, referring to the subjects that draw him,

> there is the pleasure of being confounded, and of not taking things for granted, of waking us up to how we all sleepwalk. And, by the way, that's not only a delight, but, in some cases, it seems to me—and I think you'd agree with this—it's an imperative that we wake people up to how they're sleepwalking. You have to find ways of doing it. In some cases, I think you can make an argument that we're sleepwalking to our doom, and you want to wake people up. But if you do it head on, it doesn't tend to work. It's almost better if you can insinuate yourself into the dream and from within the dream wake people up...

It is an honor and a pleasure to be part of offering this tribute to Lawrence Weschler, whose work has contributed to so many awakenings and nourished so many dreamers.

Cambridge, Massachusetts
June 2013

THE MOST ANNOYING PUBLIC INTELLECTUAL IN AMERICA

A CONVERSATION
WITH LAWRENCE WESCHLER

by ERROL MORRIS

ERROL MORRIS: [*by phone from Cambridge*] How can we start up from where we left off? It was such an auspicious start, and then I wrecked it all.

REN WESCHLER: [*at home in Westchester*] We were talking about LA, and I said, "Do you know Brecht on this subject?" And I went over to my bookshelves, because I'm here with all my books, and I read to you a passage from Brecht on LA. But since then, I found an even better passage from Brecht on the subject.

MORRIS: Well, you should read me the prior passage.

WESCHLER: I'll read you that, too. But here's one that really applies to you, called "Hollywood." "Every day, to earn my daily bread / I go to the market where the lies are bought / Hopefully / I take up my place among the sellers."[1] Which, as you know, is the correct use of the word *hopefully*, by the way.

MORRIS: Are you sure I know this?

WESCHLER: For years Roger Angell of the *New Yorker* was trying to get people to use the word *hopefully* correctly. He would have these various pieces, and one of them was a "Talk of the Town" piece that went, "Today in my efforts to get you to understand the correct use of this word, I will present a play consisting of three characters: Self, Wife, and Child. It takes place in the morning; Self is shaving."

> *Self*: Ouch.
> *Wife*: What happened, dear?
> *Self*: I cut my nose.
> *Child*: [*hopefully*] Off?

So. "Hopefully I take up my place among the sellers." Hopefully. Hopefully people will someday know how to use the word *hopefully*— that is not a correct use of the word *hopefully*.

MORRIS: Brecht interests me, because I've always been interested in—

WESCHLER: Sourness as a way of life?

MORRIS: Emotionless despair. For example, the end of my movie *Standard Operating Procedure*,[2] where Lynndie England is talking in this completely de-emotionalized way, and you see her as a product of her environment and see the choices open to her—that is, no choices at all. And there's a kind of matter-of-fact bleakness to it. It's not bleakness

---

[1] Bertolt Brecht, *Poems 1913-1956*, Methuen (1976), "Hollywood" tr. Michael Hamburger.

[2] About Abu Ghraib. Lynndie England is one of the people who was convicted of abusing prisoners.

underlined. It's just simply stated in a kind of dispassionate way that I think of as Brechtian.

WESCHLER: Or another way of putting it is kind of simultaneously flat and upending.

MORRIS: Upending?

WESCHLER: It turns your world upside down, but in a very flat way—and all the more shattering, or shuddering, for its flatness.

MORRIS: Okay. I told you my idea for this interview: "Ren Weschler, the Most Annoying Public Intellectual in America." It occurs to me that a lot of the people that you have profiled, interviewed, et cetera—I, perhaps presumptuously, include myself—are really, truly annoying people.

WESCHLER: You think that because I wrote about annoying people, I'm annoying?

MORRIS: I'm not saying that. I think you are annoying, but I don't think that's *why* you're annoying.

WESCHLER: Why do you think I'm annoying?

MORRIS: I'll get to that. I wanted to talk first about why you write about annoying people. Why you picked certain subjects, particularly the subjects that I find the most interesting, e.g., Boggs. Boggs is clearly annoying. Why Boggs? Why'd you pick Boggs?

WESCHLER: I don't like addressing issues head on. For instance, when I would cover Bosnia—talk about an annoying place!—I didn't want to be the hundredth person describing conditions head on there. I tried to come at it at an angle. Hence, eventually, *Vermeer in Bosnia*. I often spend a lot of time—I'm talking decades—thinking about a subject and waiting for a vehicle to approach it with.

What I used to love in the *New Yorker*, was the way that you would pick up a piece of writing—and not all of them worked this way, but many of them did—and you had no idea what it was about. You would just read it because of the narrative energy, and for the first five thousand words you might not have any idea of what it was about, and only about halfway through the piece would you realize that it was about the most important thing in the world. It seems to me that's a much more interesting way to get at something.

So, in the case of Boggs, for years I'd wanted to engage the history of art and the history of money, the comedy of art and money, but I didn't want to write a treatise on the subject. Now, as regards Boggs and for that matter several of the ones that you have in mind of my annoying subjects, they strike me as Socratic figures.

MORRIS: Well, one important point here, of course, when you call these people Socratic figures, is that—and this is a point that cannot be made often enough—Socrates himself was intolerable.

WESCHLER: He was, absolutely.

MORRIS: He was annoying; he was insufferable. It's very easy for me to understand why they gave him the hemlock. They just couldn't stand it anymore.

WESCHLER: I often think about you, in that context.

MORRIS: "Well, I could call myself the most virtuous man in the world, but if I *did* call myself the most virtuous man in the world, that, in itself, wouldn't be terribly virtuous now, would it? So, I'm in a quandary." If it was me listening to that, I'd say, "Could you please get the hemlock now? I think we've had just about enough."

WESCHLER: I agree with you completely.

MORRIS: Socrates—the Most Annoying Man in the Ancient World.

WESCHLER: This reminds me of a wonderful, wonderful moment in my own education, in my freshman class at Santa Cruz, the first week we were reading *The Republic*. And it was a little seminar led by Harry Berger, the great literary critic and theorist, and I was just mouthing off, and I said, "Well, of course Socrates always wins these arguments. I mean, look at these idiots who he's talking to, you know? 'Yes, Socrates, that is true.' 'Yes, Socrates, that is also true.' They're all a bunch of doofuses. No wonder he was—This is totally a rigged—" I was going on and on. And Berger looks at me sagely and says, "But the thing of it is, Ren, Plato was a genius and you're a freshman." Two beats. "He's playing you like a piano. Why don't you shut up for a second and listen to the music?"

And the point he was constantly making was that Plato/Socrates was someone who was never able to find an interlocutor in his own world, and that the function of the dialogues is an ongoing search for someone to have a dialogue with. And that that annoyingness is of the essence of that dialogue. I love annoyers, actually, so I don't take any offense that you call me annoying.

MORRIS: In fact, Boggs has made a career out of annoying people, existing on an edge between the legal and the subjects that I find the most interesting: the illegal. The most interesting stuff in the Boggs book is to actually see Boggs's interactions with people, which you record. So, here is this guy who has this cockamamie idea, which of course is, like many cockamamie ideas, a deeply profound and interesting idea. Do you want to explain it?

WESCHLER: The way it happens is that Boggs will take you out to dinner, let's say, and at the end of the dinner he'll take out one of his drawings. [Boggs's drawings are meticulous, but slightly altered, re-creations of real banknotes. —*Ed.*] And the waiter, or whoever, will always say, "God, that's a great drawing." And he'll say, "I'm glad you like it, because I intend to use it to pay for this meal, this record, this pen," whatever it is that he's trying to buy. And he then makes it even more confounding—maybe *confounding* is a better word than *annoying*, don't you think?—

MORRIS: I like *annoying* more than *confounding*, but go on.

WESCHLER: Well, I'm sure you do. But he then takes out a regular one-hundred-dollar bill, let's say, or a regular twenty-dollar bill, and he says, "If you want, you can have this one. I don't know what this drawing is worth. It must be worth something. But if you take it, you have to give me my change in real money." And that usually is what really drives people crazy, they can't handle that, and usually it doesn't work. But that's a big mistake, because, in fact, the drawing is worth more than the real bill—more than its face value.

MORRIS: Well, it turns out to be worth a lot more. But they don't know that.

WESCHLER: Of course not. That's the Socratic test.

MORRIS: Picasso routinely did this kind of thing.

WESCHLER: Sure. He would write a check—there are car dealerships in the South of France, where he would buy a Rolls-Royce, and on the back of the check he would do a substantial drawing, and the checks would never be cashed.

MORRIS: Yes.

WESCHLER: But Boggs is no Picasso. He's just a guy who you'd encounter on the street. The phenomenology of what happens in those two situations is different. In the case of Picasso, you don't cash it because he's a famous artist. In the case of Boggs, it becomes a test of virtue in some sense. It's a fairy tale. Most people will refuse it. But the ones who accept it will be rewarded tenfold, a hundredfold. Because there are many people who want to buy the drawings, and he won't sell them, he'll only spend them, but the next day Boggs will call one of those people and say, "I spent a drawing at such and such a restaurant yesterday, and if you want to procure that drawing I have the receipt,

I have the original bill that I used as the model for the drawing—in other words, it has the same serial number—and I have the change. And I'll sell you, Collector, all of that for ten thousand dollars." And the collector will happily pay ten thousand dollars to Boggs, because he knows he can then go back to the restaurant, because the receipt tells him where it was, and offer the waiter, for that one-hundred-dollar drawing, one thousand dollars, or five thousand dollars. And he'll do that because he knows that if he puts all those things together and puts them under a frame and takes it to Sotheby's—in those days it was going for fifty thousand dollars.

MORRIS: Really?

WESCHLER: Yes, and the comedy was, what's going on here? Why is that happening? And then, of course, one of the things that would happen is that the Secret Service and so forth would get pissed off, and they would try to arrest Boggs. He was regularly getting arrested or harassed. But the minute it was taken to a jury, he could make a very strong case. And every jury of his peers found him innocent. He argued for one thing—"How can it be counterfeit if it's worth more than its face value?"

MORRIS: But that's not the definition of *counterfeit*.

WESCHLER: There you go. You, as a serious judge—and I know you are someone who has thought about the law, and, frankly, a good deal more than you should have for the last few years, given your most recent work and how much it has confounded you... But absolutely. By the letter of the law, he is completely engaging in something weird. But juries always use their common sense and find him not guilty, which is all the more confounding.

MORRIS: And yet he is also annoying. Just what is it that he's doing?

WESCHLER: He is playing with authority. In the same way that

Socrates did, he is playing with things that are fundamental, and that people don't like played with. In fact, it's a little bit like Wile E. Coyote going off the cliff. He just points and says, "Look underneath here. There's nothing supporting this. It's all a series of conventions and unsaid, unspoken agreements and so forth and so on. And if you tug on it at all, it begins to come unraveled."

MORRIS: We like to think of ourselves as being, on some level, shrewd, so that if someone gives you a counterfeit one-hundred-dollar bill, and you take it, you've been conned. You've been tricked.

WESCHLER: You've been *had*.

MORRIS: You've been had.

WESCHLER: And to be had means that somebody else owns you, which you hate.

MORRIS: And so, we like to think, when presented with a counterfeit one-hundred-dollar bill, we either have that strange felt-tip marking pen—

WESCHLER: That's right, whatever that is.

MORRIS: And it turns the wrong color, and so we say, "You no-good blackguard. You tried to pass off a fake one-hundred-dollar bill, but I'm too smart for you." Here, it's—

WESCHLER: He does the opposite. He offers you something and you, in your shrewdness, refuse it, and hence make a mistake. But he is completely transparent in everything he does. You pull one over on yourself by being so goddamned shrewd.

MORRIS: But one second. See, what I find puzzling is, go back to the Picasso example.

WESCHLER: Okay, very good.

MORRIS: Okay, so Picasso is Picasso. World famous.

WESCHLER: Famous for being an artist and a womanizer.

MORRIS: Famous for being an artist and a womanizer, and for painting flounder-like portrait profiles where you see clearly two eyes on one side of the head.

WESCHLER: Right, exactly. Though let's stop for a second. David Hockney is very good on that. David Hockney points out that Picasso is, in fact, a consummate realist. When you want to portray the woman you love, say, when you're right up close to them in bed and looking quite carefully at them, your eyes begin to swim, and you do get two eyes out of the same side of her profile.

MORRIS: Well, Hockney, we will get to this, but Hockney as a person, who is a consummate—you know what my son used to call himself?

WESCHLER: What?

MORRIS: He would explain to us very carefully, he said, "But don't you see: I'm an annoyifier."

WESCHLER: There you go. That's good.

MORRIS: Yeah, "I'm an annoyifier." And indeed he was, and still is.

WESCHLER: Bless the annoyifiers, for they shall find calmness in the end.

MORRIS: But let's just go back to—

WESCHLER: To Boggs.

MORRIS: Because this does interest me. With Boggs, say they accept the drawing.

WESCHLER: They are being given the occasion where they can. And even when they don't, they often give great answers as to why they don't accept, very sensible answers.

MORRIS: No, that's the best part of the essay.

WESCHLER: Right, right. And you know what else they're given? *A story*. They get to go home that night and tell the wife, "You wouldn't believe what I was offered today," dah-dah-dah. And then the wife and the husband have a story, or the boyfriend or the girlfriend, or brother and sister.

This reminds me—*this* reminds me—of something which I *have* to read you. That poem of Szymborska's, do you know that poem?

MORRIS: No.

WESCHLER: Okay, I've got to find it, it'll take me a second. Okay, okay, here: "An Opinion on the Question of Pornography."

And the poem goes,

> There's nothing more debauched than thinking.
> This sort of wantonness runs wild like a wind-borne weed
> on a plot laid out for daisies.
>
> Nothing's sacred for those who think.
> Calling things brazenly by name,
> risqué analyses, salacious syntheses,
> frenzied, rakish chases after the bare facts,
> the filthy fingering of touchy subjects,
> discussion in heat—it's music to their ears.

In broad daylight or under cover of night
they form circles, triangles, or pairs.
The partners' age and sex are unimportant.
Their eyes glitter, their cheeks are flushed.
Friend leads friend astray.
Degenerate daughters corrupt their fathers.
A brother pimps for his little sister.

They prefer the fruits
from the forbidden tree of knowledge
to the pink buttocks found in glossy magazines—
all the ultimately simple-hearted smut.
The books they relish have no pictures.
What variety they have lies in certain phrases
marked with a thumbnail or a crayon.

It's shocking, the positions,
the unchecked simplicity with which
one mind contrives to fertilize another!
Such positions the Kama Sutra itself doesn't know.

During these trysts of theirs, the only thing that's steamy
  is the tea.
People sit on their chairs and move their lips.
Everyone crosses only his own legs
so that one foot is resting on the floor,
while the other dangles freely in midair.
Only now and then does somebody get up,
go to the window
and through a crack in curtains
take a peep out at the street.[3]

---

[3] Wislawa Szymborska, *Poems New and Collected (1957–1997)*, Harcourt Brace, 1998, "An Opinion on the Question of Pornography," tr. Stanislaw Baranczak & Clare Cavanagh.

Which, of course, that last phrase is great in terms of martial law, but it's also an inversion of the Peeping Tom.

MORRIS: Yes.

WESCHLER: Isn't that a great poem?

MORRIS: It is, indeed.

WESCHLER: And isn't it pertinent to what we're talking about?

MORRIS: I believe it is.

WESCHLER: I guess, by the way, that another word, what you're calling *annoying*, I call *delightful*. I take delight in annoying people.

MORRIS: Here's what puzzles me about Boggs, which is one of the things that I find really interesting about your work. If you've done something really, really well, you've set up a kind of conundrum, you've set up an unanswered question, which leaves people uneasy. Uneasy in many ways. Uneasy because they don't know, ultimately, what this piece was about. And can I tell you what that feeling is? When you don't know what something is about?

WESCHLER: What is it?

MORRIS: It's a feeling of enormous annoyance.

WESCHLER: No, it's a feeling of enormous pleasure. James Baldwin says that the function of art is to reveal the questions that have been occluded by the answers.

MORRIS: That's a great line.

WESCHLER: Let me see: Where did I get that from? I can't remember.

But it's a great line. And there's this other passage where Freeman Dyson—let me see if I can find you that passage—at one point Dyson says that people have the wrong understanding of what science is. They think it is—I'm paraphrasing—a compilation of facts, whereas, in fact, it's an ongoing investigation of mysteries. Isn't that good? But anyway, we got distracted here. We were having an argument about whether this is annoying or whether this is a pleasure.

MORRIS: Yes.

WESCHLER: And I guess, for me, and this comes back to why I like these people—and let's rack up who some of these people are: I mean, it's Robert Irwin, who ends up doing what seems to be empty rooms and calling them art; it's David Hockney with all these cockamamie ideas that he has about whether old masters were using optical devices; it's definitely David Wilson.

MORRIS: David Wilson is of course a classic example.

WESCHLER: In each of these cases, there is the pleasure of being confounded, and of not taking things for granted, of waking us up to how we all sleepwalk. And, by the way, that's not only a delight, but, in some cases, it seems to me—and I think you'd agree with this—it's an imperative that we wake people up to how they're sleepwalking. You have to find ways of doing it. In some cases, I think you can make an argument that we're sleepwalking to our doom, and you want to wake people up. But if you do it head on, it doesn't tend to work. It's almost better if you can insinuate yourself into the dream and from within the dream wake people up, rather than just shake them and hit them.

This is kind of what I enjoyed doing for the last twelve years, as I was running the New York Institute for the Humanities was to find ways to come at things at a slant. For example, when Abu Ghraib happened, we did an event called "Shocked! Shocked!! Just How Many Times Can a Country Lose Its Innocence?" Which ended up focusing on of all things Norman Rockwell.

MORRIS: Right. I remember.

WESCHLER: There was this wonderful lit professor from Johns Hopkins named Richard Halpern, who'd argued that far from being one of the main protagonists of the innocence industry in America, Rockwell was one of its greatest critics, and that he understood that far from marking the transition from innocence to experience, "being shocked" is more usually a way of disguising from ourselves the fact that we knew all along.

Then, later, at the time of what was happening with the tenth anniversary of 9/11 and the kind of pornographic exploitation of that event, where every single magazine had to have a "Tenth Anniversary of 9/11" cover—that relentless lashing of "You will remember, you *will* remember," with its grotesque and pretty unseemly instrumentalization of memory—we had an all-day event called "Second Thoughts on the Memory Industry." To be able to be part of it, you had to have had first thoughts on the memory industry. You had to be people who had thought, like I did for a long time, that the most important thing you can have is memory, how you have to never forget this that or the other. But when you see what happens in the name of that spirit, the vulgarization of it—Holocaust tourism, genocide Olympics, "my genocide is worse than yours" et cetera, you can't help but have second thoughts.

MORRIS: How do you put these events together?

WESCHLER: One of my last Wonder Cabinets, as I've been calling them, was this past Saturday. This one was called "Should You Ever Happen to Find Yourself in Solitary."[4] And it began with a whole slew of playwrights and artists and mosaicists and monologists and insect people and scientists talking about how they imagine they might be able to keep from going crazy if they were ever in solitary.

The whole thing was my attempt to figure out some way to do an

---

[4] Indexed video of the event is at nyihumanities.org/journal/video-of-solitary-symposium.

event to highlight the fact that the United States currently has something on the order of eighty thousand—eight, zero, thousand—people in solitary confinement. Which is arguably more than any other place in the world has ever had at any previous time in history. By comparison Canada has three hundred. It is a truly, truly horrendous thing. But the thing is you can never get people to come to a conversation about that if you just do it head on. So as usual I was trying to approach things, as I always do, at a slant. It's a way of ensorcelling people into the room who might otherwise not come. And it turned out to be quite terrific, very interesting, and maybe even moved things forward a little bit.

Haven't you had that fantasy of what you would do if you ever found yourself by yourself?

MORRIS: Not really. I have this ongoing terror that someday I will discover that other people actually exist!

WESCHLER: So you're *already* in solitary. You know that E. M. Forster story?

MORRIS: Which one?

WESCHLER: There's this E. M. Forster story that he wrote in 1909 or something, called "The Machine Stops." And basically he is anticipating today—a world where everybody lives in little monads, in cells by themselves, and they have all kinds of Gchats with each other. They basically Skype each other. This is all written in 1909. And nobody ever actually sees anybody else in the flesh. An entirely web-based reality. And the whole story is about a guy who kind of breaks free and tries to go to make his way to the world on the surface. It's an amazing story. It's so, so prescient.[5]

MORRIS: Prescient?

---

[5] E. M. Forster, "The Machine Stops," archive.ncsa.illinois.edu/prajlich/forster.html.

WESCHLER: Just because it seems to me that we are increasingly finding ourselves like that. Except that in terms of this solitary event, it turns out that any fantasy you have—including your fantasy that you're the only person who's real—none of it would be of any use to you. We had Breyten Breytenbach, the exiled Afrikaner poet and painter who returned incognito to pursue the anti-apartheid struggle and got captured. He spent the next seven years in prison, the first two in solitary on death row. He'd spent years studying and practicing Zen, he was a virtual master, but in the crunch none of it was of any use: he fell apart almost completely. We heard from Robert Hillary King of the Angola Three, who spent twenty-eight years in solitary for a crime from which he was eventually exonerated! And Shane Bauer, who was one of the three people who were arrested by the Iranians for hiking and were held for two years—four months of that in solitary. And when he came out he was commissioned by *Mother Jones* to go look at Pelican Bay, the supermax in California, and he talked about how he basically considers the conditions at Pelican Bay much worse than anything he was subjected to by the Iranians. But the point is, when you get testimony from people who've actually spent time in solitary, it's just completely shredding. The bottom line is, even phenomenologically, even a misanthrope like you—your reality is formed on the basis of other people looking at you and responding to your misanthropy, and if that were taken away from you, the possibility of that sort of interaction, it would be horrible.

MORRIS: Okay. I give up. Solitary would be the worst fear of someone whose raison d'être is frustrating others because in solitary, there is no one left to frustrate beside yourself.

WESCHLER: There is this part of me that really does enjoy this particular thing of, not only bringing things before an audience, but bringing people together who wouldn't otherwise meet each other. Introducing people who have set out to pull the rug out from under the rest of us. So Boggs is an example, but for that matter, David Wilson is a good example.

MORRIS: It reminds me of the Duchess's poem in Lewis Carroll's *Through the Looking Glass*.

> Speak roughly to your little boy,
> And beat him when he sneezes:
> He only does it to annoy,
> Because he knows it teases.

WESCHLER: [*Laughs*] That's not exactly the first thing I would think of, thinking of David Wilson—and you call *me* the most annoying person in America! David Wilson is an absolutely extraordinary and completely lovely man.

MORRIS: We should talk about Wilson. And solitary confinement. Given a world to populate, why populate it in the same way as everyone else? Why not figure out a new way to repopulate it? Inherently, we all live in a form of solitary confinement. Some of us use that opportunity to sort of reimagine the world; others, I suppose, repeat the world in all of its boring exactitude. I don't claim to understand the Museum of Jurassic Technology, and in fact I think I have no understanding of it at all, even though I adore it. It's incomprehensible and that's one of its great virtues.

WESCHLER: It doesn't demand comprehension.

MORRIS: Well, it's an essay, even, on the stupidity of explanation.

WESCHLER: Uh-huh.

MORRIS: Where all imagined explanations backfire on you. It's this weird combination of Dada, surrealism, and existential hopelessness, coupled with a desire to annoy, perhaps the highest art form there is.

WESCHLER: And coupled with a capacity for marvel, for wonder—the splendors of things that can't be known for sure.

MORRIS: Why is the world constituted the way it is? Why do we accept the world as constituted the way it is?

WESCHLER: When I first went to the museum, one of the first things I saw was this display called "Protective Auditory Mimicry," and it had an iridescent beetle and an iridescent stone on little stands inside of a glass vitrine. You picked up the phone over to the side, which had the voice of institutional authority, and it explained, "This beetle has learned to make exactly the same sound when threatened that this pebble makes at rest." The voice has absolute authority when it says this, and you look at it, and there's this kind of slippage, and you go, "Uh-huh." At first you begin to think that it's all some kind of postmodern spoof—that it's one of these elaborate send-ups of institutional authority. But the more time you spend there, it is pitch perfect—somewhere between parody and reverence.

MORRIS: A great way to describe it.

WESCHLER: It's funny, but it's also deeply profound. And in fact it's not at all postmodern, it's premodern. It's a throwback to a time before everything became certain, before the Scientific Revolution. David just loves the undertow. That is something in a lot of the pieces I write, and for that matter in many of the seminars and the Wonder Cabinet extravaganzas I put on as an impresario. I love that moment where you're on the beach, the wave came in, and then the water's rushing back out, and you *feel* the rush at your toes. Are you going backward or are you going forward? That undertow—it's just a great feeling. It can be an intellectual feeling. And I think Boggs is one of the people who is like that. David is like that. You know he's just an extraordinary character. A deeply profound and at the same time wonderfully antic human being.

MORRIS: A modern form of Dada?

WESCHLER: The Museum of Jurassic Technology? I don't think of it that way. I have the sense of Dada as being a profound response to World War I, to the despair of World War I. Meanwhile, there are people who think the Museum of Jurassic Technology is a deeply spiritual place—a reliquary where the relic of the saint would be a funny bone.

MORRIS: What's really interesting about many of these characters— it's certainly true about Boggs, because Boggs was incarcerated, so that you know through that fact alone that he irritated the authorities. What is the greatest sign that you have irritated the authorities? It's incarceration. That's *proof* that you've irritated somebody.

WESCHLER: Which reminds me of Ryszard Kapuscinski, the Polish foreign correspondent who lived this incredibly insane life. He'd been... he'd been present at thirty-seven civil wars, some ungodly number of coups d'état, constantly getting himself arrested, subject to twelve death sentences, all of which he somehow survived and when he was subsequently asked how he had evaded execution or murder at all the various checkpoints—these terribly scary situations he'd kept putting himself into—he said, "I always tried to make myself *unworthy* of the bullet." And he was! As a person, he was the mildest, most self-effacing, seemingly bumbling and harmless presence. Why would anyone want to waste a bullet on such a person?

MORRIS: But Kapuscinski's annoying, too, because he called himself a journalist, but then ultimately you have to ask yourself the question of whether any of it's true. I don't think of him as a journalist, per se. More as a writer, an artist. I would never ask Franz Kafka whether Gregor Samsa literally turned into a dung beetle. It seems irrelevant. He is trying to capture a state of mind, not a literal reality.

WESCHLER: We once talked about the way various people have pointed out that the only place where you can be absolutely sure that things happened the way they are alleged to have happened is in fiction. In any work of nonfiction, or at any rate any work of nonfiction that's any good—any work of biography, autobiography, reportage, and so forth—the question arises, "Was it actually like that?" And it has to.

MORRIS: Let's get back to the annoyers. You have David Hockney, who is an immensely successful artist, one of the premier establishment artists of the twentieth century, who actually infuriated curators, really pissed everybody off. Which is fantastic. You may have artists thumbing their nose at the establishment in one way or another. But he wasn't just thumbing his nose at the art establishment. He was also taking on the entire art-history establishment. You throw out the bait—you draw the counterfeit money—and then you see what happens. And what happens is that many people go batshit crazy because they just can't deal with it.

WESCHLER: You're referring, in the case of Hockney, to when he basically claimed to have discovered that Old Masters, long, long before anybody thought they were, were using lenses and all kinds of curved mirrors to make their marks and to establish a certain kind of look—the "optical look," he called it—which lasted from 1430 to 1839. You can see it happen out of nowhere, and you can see it fall away at the end.

MORRIS: It was as if he had accused the Old Masters of painting by numbers.

WESCHLER: Oh, he wasn't saying that! But what he was saying was deeply, deeply disconcerting. He claimed to have found that artists—certainly Caravaggio, but presently even all the way back to Van Eyck—were using these instruments. And you're right: the assertion just drove art historians crazy. At first they claimed that there was no evidence. First it was, "No, no, that can't be true" and then, "Oh, we knew that all along." And I think Hockney will basically be proven right, not on any particular painting but on the fact that very early on, projection, camera obscura, camera lucida, curved lenses came into the world and established the standard for a certain kind of visual reality which then held hegemony over the art world for four hundred years. And whether or not any particular work was done that way, I think he's right. But it was hilarious to watch the reaction of the art world. I do love the sociology of response to these sorts of things.

MORRIS: Have I told you about my "Fuck-You" theory of art?

WESCHLER: No. What's that?

MORRIS: That the greatest works of art are thinly disguised forms of "fuck you." Take Bach's *St. Matthew Passion*. Perhaps the greatest work in the Western canon. When Bach took his new job, he was required to sign a codicil to his contract, which stipulated three things: no overly dramatic music, no overly complicated music, no overly long music.[6]

WESCHLER: I see.

MORRIS: Bach agreed. And subsequently produced the *St. Matthew Passion*. I imagine the church elders arriving for the mass and asking, "What's with the two orchestras? And the *two* choirs? And there's also a boys' choir?"

WESCHLER: And he said—?

MORRIS: "And why is this work almost three hours long? And why is it so incredibly dramatic?" There's a very simple answer. It's because Bach was replying to the elders of the church by saying, "Fuck you."

WESCHLER: So that explains your work. What about mine?

MORRIS: I believe it explains your work, as well.

---

[6] Denis Laborde, "The Strange Career of Musicoclashes,"*Iconoclash*, Latour, B., and P. Weibel, eds., Cambridge: MIT Press, 254–280. The language from the contract asked Bach to promise that "to contribute to the maintenance of good order in the churches, I will arrange the music in such a way that it shall not last too long, that it shall be of such a nature as not to seem to belong to a theater (*opernhaftig*), but that it shall rather inspire its listeners to piety" (264).

WESCHLER: I suppose so!

MORRIS: Or take Beethoven's *Diabelli Variations*. Diabelli had given a rotten theme to some twenty different composers, and asked each of them to write one variation on his rotten theme. Beethoven was one of them. At first he refused. Absolutely refused. For many reasons: his total contempt for Diabelli, his contempt in particular for the rotten theme that Diabelli had written, and that he didn't want to do Diabelli or anybody else's bidding. He was *Beethoven*. And then he thought, at least as I imagine it, "Why, this would be a perfect opportunity to say, 'Fuck you!'" And proceeded to create one of the great immortal works of art. Thirty-three inspired variations on an insipid theme. A supreme work of art based on Beethoven's contempt for something utterly worthless.

WESCHLER: Once again, I hear you talking about yourself. I assume you're not talking about me! [*Laughs.*]

MORRIS: Let me read to you this passage from this essay by Denis Laborde. Laborde's description is drawing on the writing of a man named Christian Gerber, who wrote about the first performance of Bach's *St. Matthew Passion*.

"In the clamor of the two orchestras playing at both ends of the nave, in the chaos of the two choirs responding to each other in waves of dissonances, while in the center the congregation struck up their Lutheran chorales, one believer was becoming irate. Christian Gerber saw her stand up suddenly and leave the church, crying out: '*Behüte Gott ihr Kinder! Ist es doch, als ob man in einer Opera oder Comödie wäre.*'" ["May God protect your children! It is as though one were at an opera or a comedy!"]

Laborde goes on to say that, "Under the pretense of composing a musical piece for the Passion, he let effusion, that is, confusion, take hold of the believers' hearts…"

WESCHLER: So you are talking about yourself.

MORRIS: It's still Boggs, in a simplified form; it's a version of "Fuck you."

WESCHLER: Socrates, too.

MORRIS: I haven't really read recently I. F. Stone's argument for why Socrates should have been killed.

WESCHLER: Well, according to the letter of the law, he really was corrupting the youth of Athens, is his argument, basically.

MORRIS: He was *annoying* the youth of Athens, properly considered. So there is something really strange about the real need, ultimately, to tell people that they have it all wrong.

WESCHLER: I don't think it's so much that they have it all wrong, but that they're taking it all for granted. I think it's rather—it more has to do with the way in which, "You're sleepwalking, you people. Wake up!"

MORRIS: *Wachet auf!*

WESCHLER: [*Laughs.*] As said by the great annoyer, J. S. B.

For further conversation between Lawrence Weschler and Errol Morris, see publicbooks. org/interviews/errol-morris-forensic-epistemologist. For further glimpses of the world of Weschler, see lawrenceweschler.com.

REMINISCENCES

by WILLIAM FINNEGAN, LAUREN REDNISS,
BILL McKIBBEN, BEN KATCHOR,
WENDY LESSER, GEOFF DYER,
BILL MORRISON, AND RIVA LEHRER

Ren Weschler has taught me a lot about, among other things, my hometown. We both grew up in Los Angeles, but when we first met, as undergraduates at the University of California, Santa Cruz, I thought Ren, while he might be from LA, technically, was not *of* it. He was both too worldly and too open, too febrile, too urban in a good sense. He lacked the half-assed carapace of Southern California cool—in conversation, the brief, wary, laidback pause. He had none of the early-onset world-weariness of our site-specific desolation. There are and always were many LAs, of course, but this was 1970, and a certain shared generational experience seemed particularly intense and inescapable; and yet, I thought, Ren and I had not crossed paths at any rock festival or hitchhiking spot or Topanga Canyon acid test. Maybe at a peace march. It wasn't important—I wasn't hoping to meet in college the same folks I might have found at some hippie hot springs while ditching high school. But it was a resonant first misunderstanding and underestimation of this bright-eyed, exceptionally well-read enthusiast from (was it possible?) Van Nuys.

We studied with some of the same professors. Then, after graduation, Ren did something inspired: he moved back to LA.

I don't think I can describe (Ren would disagree, in any case) how poorly an education at the hands of teachers like Norman O. Brown, the classicist turned counterculture oracle, or Maurice Natanson, the phenomenologist, prepared one for journalism, but Ren boldly started freelancing for the *LA Weekly* and the *LA Reader* nevertheless, doing his trade apprenticeship, while working a day job at something called the Oral History Program at UCLA, which led him to interview, among others, Robert Irwin, the Southern California artist. It's tempting to say that the rest is history, oral and otherwise, as if the meeting of Irwin and Weschler just naturally produced something remarkable, but the truth is that only Ren's hard work and polymorphous originality could have turned those Irwin interviews into anything like his extraordinary first book, *Seeing Is Forgetting the Name of the Thing One Sees*.

Through that book, I for one saw many things I hadn't seen before, not least of them a new Los Angeles. Irwin was such a strange, splendid native, his work and his sensibility inseparable from the city's streets and buildings, its racetracks and drive-in restaurants. He had gone from abstract expressionism and a conventional studio in the '50s and '60s to installations of extreme simplicity and subtlety, and Ren managed to trace his career and the evolution of his thinking in a way that opened up both local art history and a provocative set of aesthetic conundra through narrative. I wasn't the only astonished reader. William Shawn, then the editor of the *New Yorker*, ran a two-part excerpt from the book. Shawn had already published some of Ren's early reporting from Poland, and Ren soon moved to New York, became a staff writer at the magazine, and began taking on the great range of subjects, political and artistic, that fire his voracious curiosity to this day.

Unlike some of us prodigals, however, he never forgot LA. He kept up with Irwin, who went on to create and design the spectacular Central Garden at the Getty Center, and he wrote more about other LA artists, notably Edward Kienholz, from the seminal scene that had once coalesced around the Ferus Gallery. He wrote about David Hockney, who had famously moved to LA. He found, in "a small nondescript storefront operation located along the main commercial drag of downtown Culver City," the Museum of Jurassic Technology, a mysterious only-in-LA establishment that became the main topic and takeoff point for *Mr. Wilson's Cabinet of Wonder*, possibly Ren's best-known book. It's a dizzying, nimble tour de force—a narrative meditation, if that's possible, on art, science, authenticity, and the imagination.

Then, in 1998, Ren wrote a piece about the unusual quality of the light in Los Angeles that made my scalp prickle repeatedly. He consulted Hockney, Irwin, astronomers, cinematographers, poets, architects. Their eloquence and quasi-theological debates about shadows and shadowlessness were enchanting and, to this long-displaced child of the San Fernando Valley, not at all arcane. Ren found a scientist of smog who broke down the visual effects of different-sized particles in the air, including a particle with the same diameter as the natural wavelength of sunlight, which causes even nearby mountain ranges to vanish on a sunny day. He described his grandfather, the Austrian émigré composer Ernst Toch, and his relationship to the gorgeousness of his patch of Southern California. He even called Vin Scully, the legendary radio announcer for the LA Dodgers, and got a long, phenomenal quote about the evening light in Chavez Ravine.

Now this was my LA, my hometown, but it was also a wholly new place, brought into being, brought into focus, by a playful, determined, passionate native son with a panoply of unusual gifts. It may seem trifling, a sidebar, to zero in exclusively on Ren's writing about LA. He has, after all, written widely about major world issues and history as it was being made, in Eastern Europe, the Balkans, South America, South Africa. He has organized and curated so many shows and conferences, brought together so many talented people, and encouraged so many struggling artists and writers, very much including myself. In fact, thinking of his teaching, his editing, his long and distinguished directing stints at the Chicago Humanities Festival and the New York Institute for the Humanities at NYU, it seems that his personal and intellectual generosity have probably had more impact on our cultural life than can ever be properly measured. But for me his patient, tender, inventive, multifaceted take on LA is the prototype for the delight he takes in the people and ideas he finds everywhere.

—*William Finnegan*

"Prepare to have your mind blown," Ren Weschler might tell you on your way over to his office. You will not be disappointed. He might have new magic dice or a film about outer space. There could be a poet visiting from a sparsely populated island in the Pacific or a physicist who has designed heart stents based on origami folding techniques. Last time I went to see Ren, the art historian Benjamin Binstock was there, presenting his theory that many paintings credited to Vermeer were in fact painted by Vermeer's daughter. A number of the drawings reproduced here, on pages 216 to 219, were done that day.

—*Lauren Redniss*

I joined the staff of the *New Yorker* in 1982, when I graduated from college. I was by quite a good stretch the youngest staff writer, and even though I had no experience of any other professional workplace, it was immediately apparent that it was both a grand and a slightly odd place to be at work. Grand because: turn a corner and you'd run into Pauline Kael or Jonathan Schell or Calvin Trillin or Ian Frazier or Jamaica Kincaid or John McPhee or George Trow or any one of the greatest essayists and reporters that ever there were. Odd because: well, where to begin. Mr. Shawn was the finest magazine editor America has ever produced, but he had his quirks, which over time seemed to have transmitted themselves to much of the rest of the staff.

One was that no one was ever to ask another writer what they were working on. This was held, somehow, to stifle the creative muse; that it might, like the groundhog seeing its shadow, scuttle back into the mental hole from which it had begun tentatively to emerge. And given the time scale on which *New Yorker* writers in those days tended to work, never mind six weeks: it might be six years, or maybe sixty, before the piece ever saw the light of day.

Having come straight from a college newspaper, and being the sort of person who had more than enough ideas and liked to try them out, this seemed to me insane. So I was very glad to find at least a few people who liked to talk. One, in fact, liked to talk at least as much as I did. That would be Ren. And what's more, he liked to talk about cool things other people were doing. He had an ego, I suppose, but what he really loved was to describe what great artists or writers or scientists he had come across were up to. He hadn't yet become the cultural impresario charged with organizing great festivals of ideas, but he was already a finder, an enthusiast, a backer, a booster. He had—and I have never observed this in quite so literal a way before or since—a gleam in his eye when he described something that, say, Robert Irwin had done or said. He was a buttonholer—he clearly enjoyed the work that seemed a kind of painful ordeal to a lot of recluses along those halls.

I've known a great many writers who deeply enjoyed talking about their own work. But I've known very few who liked to talk about their subjects quite so much—who thought of other artists as their natural companions. Musicians, I think, are often capable of noncompetitive listening, but I've never known a writer as generous as Ren—he was born to write profiles, and then to bring his subjects together to meet each other, and learn from each other, and to go on to do more work. He is a one-man Chautauqua, and I can think of very little higher praise than that.

—*Bill McKibben*

Weschler's text commentaries on the visual works of Hockney and Ryman transform them into a species of comic-strip. These works can now be experienced as a series of discrete dramatic chapters with a generous human voice punctuating their otherwise mute presence. For me, Weschler's words elevate these works out of the art world into this world.

—*Ben Katchor*

Lawrence Weschler has been a consulting editor to my magazine, *The Threepenny Review*, for the vast majority of its thirty-three years, and in that capacity he has brought us a range of exciting new writers, running the gamut from Rachel Cohen to William T. Vollmann. (If these two, in particular, sound like familiar names to longtime *McSweeney's* readers, that may be because Ren has been a consulting editor there, as well. In fact, I think he can fairly claim to be the only person who embodies that exact position of intellectual overlap between the old Berkeley and the new San Francisco: you might think of him, in this respect, as Ren the Venn.)

But at least as important to us as Ren's long-term consulting has been his own writing for the magazine. He has, in effect, been our Current Events man. As a quarterly, *Threepenny* often finds itself out of step with the teeming world of up-to-date information, but Ren, with his finger always eerily on the pulse of history, has repeatedly counteracted that tendency. Without sacrificing one iota of our literary standards, we have been able to print the words of a keen-eyed world reporter monitoring important events as they happen. In 1990, for instance, he wrote for us about the astonishing developments in Eastern Europe and the then-still-alive Soviet Union, making an analogy between the reawakening of those slumbering populations and Oliver Sacks's book *Awakenings*. (I wonder now if the German director of *Goodbye Lenin!*, a 2003 film premised on a very similar analogy, had actually read Ren's essay.) By the summer of 1991 he was already commenting dourly on the Gulf War: he was among the first to notice the connection between alienated technology and emotionally distanced warfare. And in 1994 we got his eyewitness report on the recent Los Angeles earthquake, rendered in his inimitably ironic style.

Even when Ren was writing for us about something else—the art of Ann Hamilton or Sharon Lockhart, the nature of scientific photography, his grandfather's musical career—a certain topicality gracefully emerged. For instance, his piece on his grandfather, Ernst Toch, a prominent Austrian-Jewish composer who wrote many serious pieces and also a funny song called "Popocatepetl," came to us upon the occasion of that volcano's latest eruption. Even when Ren looks firmly into the past, as he did in his contribution to our recent symposium about Breugel, he does so with a visceral, present-tense sense of what it means to stand in a museum *now*, looking at one or more of those ever-timely canvases.

For those of you who have never published Ren, let me say that a lot of blood gets spilled over his perfectionism. Sometimes it is Ren's blood; more often it is the editor's. I recall a pitched battle we had over a featured section on Helen Levitt, when Ren—unsatisfied with the selection of Levitt photos we had obtained, and wishing instead to write about another—wanted me to go out and get that additional picture from her, complete with complicated rights and permissions. I balked, but in the end I gave in. (One usually does, with Ren.) And now, looking back through that old issue of the magazine, I am very glad he won, because the photograph he insisted on is the best of the lot. That's usually the way it is, with Ren. It just takes the rest of us a few decades to catch up.

—Wendy Lesser

Ren! That's how I think of him and what I call him now. It's how I heard other people refer to him in the years before I knew him— and it always bugged me. It also bugged or bugs me when I heard or hear people talk about Max (W. G.) Sebald, Sasha (Aleksandar) Hemon, and Caz (Caryl) Phillips. Even if you know the books well, the author's nickname (or diminutive or whatever it is) makes you feel excluded from some quietly advertised but widespread intimacy. People probably felt similarly irritated, in the early twentieth century, when mention was made of Tom (Eliot) and Morgan (Forster). Needless to say, I never miss a chance of referring to Hemon as Sasha and Ren as Ren now that I've met them.

I'd first read Weschler before I had any idea that he was Ren. It was in 1987 or 1988, I was working part-time for a publisher in London and was asked to consider a submission called *Shapinsky's Karma, Boggs's Bill, and Other True-Life Tales.* It was such an obviously brilliant book that I recommended we publish it. This advice was not acted on, but, looking back, I struggle to think of a single recommendation of mine that did make its way into print. I think lobbying from me became an easily decoded warning of impending commercial failure. Still, this exercise in powerlessness had the useful effect of lodging the name and work of Lawrence Weschler in my mind. And so, years later, when the collection *Vermeer in Bosnia* was in the works, I jumped at the chance to blurb it as a way of making good that earlier impotent enthusiasm. What struck me was the character and energy of the author's intelligence. Reading certain writers one gets the impression that their brains only come to life when they're behind their typewriters (and sometimes not even then). With Weschler I got the distinct sense of a brain that never turned off, that was fizzing, buzzing, and joining dots—"only connect," as Morgan famously put it—noticing stuff and making the world seem a more interesting place even when he was fast asleep.

This impression of crackling intellectual energy turned out to hold true of the man too when I finally met him—when he went from Lawrence to Ren—in 2006, at a conference he'd organized in New York called "Comedies of Fair U\$e." It was about copyright and sounded like a total bore but because I am a serious professional writer in the sense that I will do pretty much anything to get out of the house I went anyway. I'm glad I did, because the tacit subject turned out to be nothing less than the nature of creativity in the twenty-first century, an investigation of the ways in which something assumed to protect the rights of artists—intellectual copyright—can end up serving the interests of corporate capital, thereby hobbling the inventiveness it is supposed to encourage. It was one of the most intellectually stimulating weekends of my life—and tremendous fun, too. Ren wasn't just a writer, he was an impresario, curator, performer, and connector—not only of ideas but people. His writing, I realized, was a sort of side effect, offshoot, or aspect of this larger phenomenon of Ren-ness.

He is also, I see now, his own worst enemy, a victim of his prodigious talents and enthusiasms. His standing would be more assured if he had confined himself more narrowly, if he'd only done the art stuff, if he'd only done *this* rather than doing *that* and a multitude of others as well. The abundance and diversity of the many segments of his work—that ongoing cabinet of wonders—perversely and unfairly diminish the value of the whole. Needless to say, this abundance, recklessness, and multiplicity are exactly the things his admirers value so highly. They're all compressed into—that's what we mean by—that monosyllable Ren.

—*Geoff Dyer*

Ren sat at my kitchen table, eating a bowl of black bean soup. He was talking about a recent convergence—where two seemingly unrelated events come to rhyme with one another. This one dealt with two trees, on two different continents, that had both been victims of homophobia, or homophobia-phobia. He gestured emphatically as the winter sunlight lit his hands like two birds unable to settle on a branch together.

—*Bill Morrison*

The portrait on the following pages places Ren in a kind of camera obscura, standing in the beam of a pinhole lens. The projected picture is the interior of the Earth as imagined by the seventeenth-century Jesuit scholar Athanasius Kircher. Kircher was one of the preeminent intellectuals of his time; music, biology, geology, geography, Egyptology, history, philosophy, and physics were only a few areas of his accomplishment. It is no surprise that Weschler's personal stationery bears images from Kircher's work.

The cat's cradle in Weschler's hands is made out of collaged strips of longhand notes taken while conducting the reporting for *Vermeer in Bosnia*, his account of the events in 1979 that led to the Solidarity movement. The cradle mimics the pattern of light rays as they pass through a pinhole camera, (as discovered by Ibn al-Haytham in the eleventh century). The Arabic symbols in red denote the action of the beams. Ren holds the cradle in such a way that it connects the light of the exterior world (through the pinhole/lens) with the chamber of the interior (underground/brain). The paper "rays" and the fragments of Earth projected onto his body cause him to serve as a bridge between inner and outer realities. Ren's tie is decorated with the Tree of Life (*Etz HaChayim*) from the *Kabbalah*, which maps the connection between mind, body, and spirit.

—*Riva Lehrer*

FOLLOWING PAGES: *"Totems and Familiars: Lawrence Weschler, P.T. Barnum of the Mind,"* by *Riva Lehrer, page 210; posters from four of Lawrence Weschler's events at the New York Institute for the Humanities, page 212; "Two Trees" (portrait of Ren Weschler) by Bill Morrison, page 214; drawings by Lauren Redniss, page 216; Ben Katchor's cover drawing for Weschler's* A Wanderer in a Perfect City, *page 220; "Lawrence Weschler," 1989, oil on canvas, 16½" × 10½", © David Hockney, page 222.*

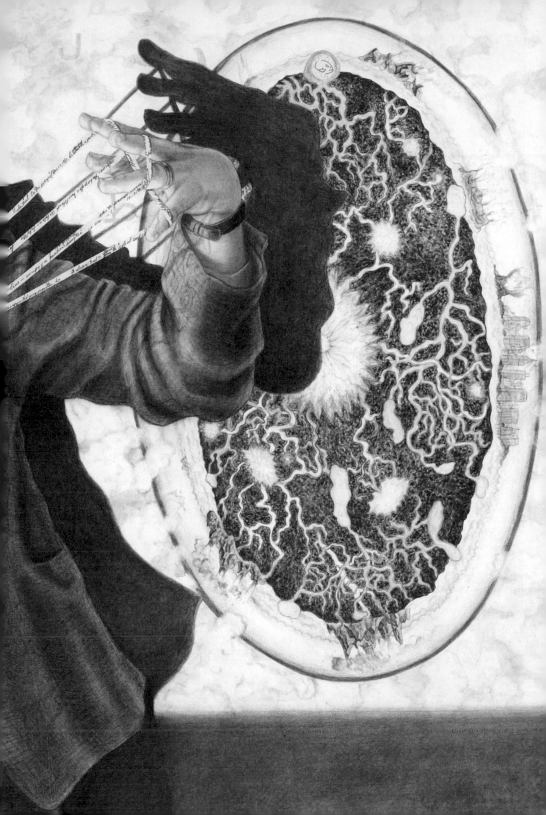

The New York Institute for the Humanities at NYU presents

Library of Dust

Responding to David Maisel's
remarkable photographic excavation
of a warehouse of ashes
otherwise lost to time

with
Ulrich Baer
Rachel Cohen
Jennifer Michael Hecht
Karen Lang
Jonathan Lethem
David Maisel
Geoff Manaugh
Joel Meyerowitz
Ted Mooney
Bill Morrison
Gilles Peress
Michael Roth
Luc Sante
Vijay Seshadri
Lawrence Weschler

Monday, April 13, 2009 at 7pm

The Angel Orensanz Foundation
172 Norfolk Street (south of Houston)

Free and open to the public

For further information visit nyih.as.nyu.edu
or contact nyih.info@nyu.edu or 212.998.2101

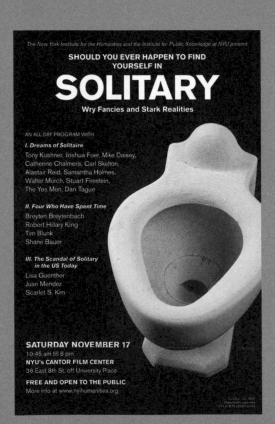

The New York Institute for the Humanities and the Institute for Public Knowledge at NYU present

SHOULD YOU EVER HAPPEN TO FIND
YOURSELF IN

SOLITARY

Wry Fancies and Stark Realities

AN ALL DAY PROGRAM WITH

I. Dreams of Solitaire
Tony Kushner, Joshua Foer, Mike Daisey,
Catherine Chalmers, Carl Skelton,
Alastair Reid, Samantha Holmes,
Walter Murch, Stuart Firestein,
The Yes Men, Dan Tague

II. Four Who Have Spent Time
Breyten Breytenbach
Robert Hillary King
Tim Blunk
Shane Bauer

**III. The Scandal of Solitary
in the US Today**
Lisa Guenther
Juan Mendez
Scarlet S. Kim

SATURDAY NOVEMBER 17
10:45 am till 8 pm

NYU's CANTOR FILM CENTER
36 East 8th St, off University Place

FREE AND OPEN TO THE PUBLIC
More info at www.nyihumanities.org

The New York Institute for the Humanities at NYU, in association with The Humanities Council at NYU present

a weekend long symposium

COMEDIES OF FAIR U$E

A Search for Comity in the Intellectual Property Wars

Ceci n'est pas une Magritte

The title of this 1937 painting (in the collection of a Rotterdam museum),
"La reproduction interdite," which is to say "Forbidden to Reproduce,"
initially gave us pause. But then again, we weren't proposing to reproduce
the painting by Rene Magritte but rather a third-or-fourth generation
reproduction of that painting from a book, which of course is not, precisely
speaking, a Magritte at all. And as the painting itself is doing, we were trying
to make some sort of a point. Was this okay? Is this fair use? We won't deny
it: It can all get very confusing.

featuring
Lawrence Lessig
Susan Meiselas
Joy Garnett
Siva Vaidhyanathan
Jonathan Lethem
Judge Alex Kozinski
Art Spiegelman
Geoff Dyer
Joel Wachs
Lewis Hyde
Errol Morris
Robert Boynton
Lawrence Ferrara
Carrie McLaren
James Boyle
and others

Friday April 28
7:30 pm – 9:30 pm
Saturday April 29
9:30 am – 6:30 pm
Sunday April 30
9:30 am – 1:00 pm

**NYU's Hemmerdinger Hall
100 Washington Square East**

Free, first come, first in
Further details and schedule
visit www.nyu.edu/fas/nyih
or call 212-998-2100

COMICS — Ten Minutes After the Big Bang!

POST BANG

FRIDAY, JUNE 6, 2008, CANTOR FILM CENTER AT NYU, 36 EAST 8 STREET

OVER THE PAST FEW YEARS COMICS HAVE ESCAPED FROM THE *SHTETL* AND ENTERED THE SALON. A BIG BANG HAS EXPLODED THE ASSUMPTION THAT THE MEDIUM IS INHERENTLY IMMATURE, AND COMICS HAVE HURTLED INTO THE WORLDS OF BOOK PUBLISHING (AS LITERATURE FOR ADULTS *AND* CHILDREN), CONTEMPORARY ART, THE ACADEMY AND LITERARY CRITICISM.

THIS ONE-DAY PROGRAM WILL SPOTLIGHT MAJOR CREATORS OF AND COMMENTATORS ON COMICS, HIGHLIGHTING KEY TRENDS AND DEBATES FACING COMICS IN THIS NEW, "POST-BANG" ENVIRONMENT.

11:00–12:15 COMICS AND CANON FORMATION
Rob Storr (moderator), John Carlin and Dan Nadel

1:30 – 2:45 COMICS AND KID'S LIT
Françoise Mouly (moderator), Lisa von Drasek, Leonard Marcus, Mo Willems and Sara Varon

3:00 – 4:15 COMICS AND THE LITERARY ESTABLISHMENT
Jeet Heer (moderator), Hillary Chute, David Hajdu, and Douglas Wolk

5:30 – 6:45 COMICS AND THE INTERNET
Kent Worcester (moderator), Sarah Boxer, Shaenon Garrity, Hope Larson, and Siva Vaidhyanathan

7:00 – 8:00 ART SPIEGELMAN and GARY PANTER in conversation

8:15 – 9:30 Hillary Chute interviews LYNDA BARRY

Sponsored by THE NEW YORK INSTITUTE FOR THE HUMANITIES AT NYU with THE MUSEUM OF COMIC AND CARTOON ART (MoCCA).
This event is being held in association with this year's MoCCA Art Festival, June 7-8, taking place at the Puck Building at Houston and Lafayette in lower Manhattan.

For more information, visit nyih.as.nyu.edu/page/home or contact the New York Institute for the Humanities at NYU (212-998-2100).

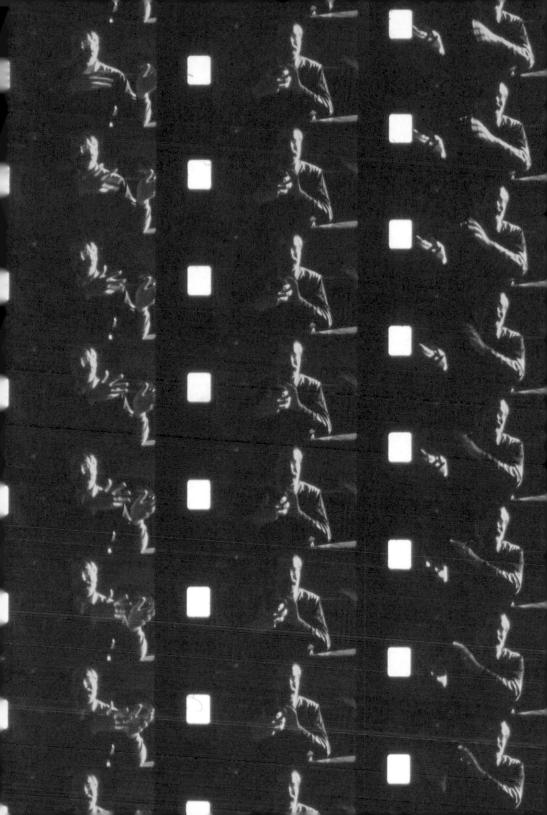

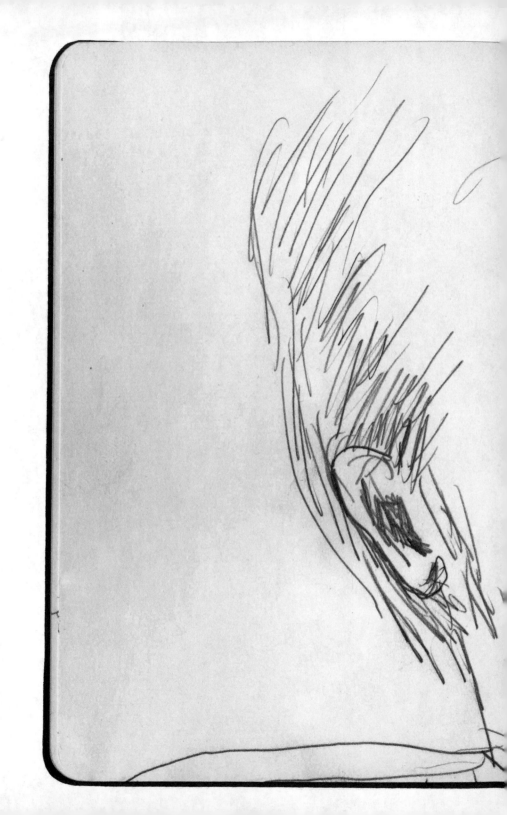

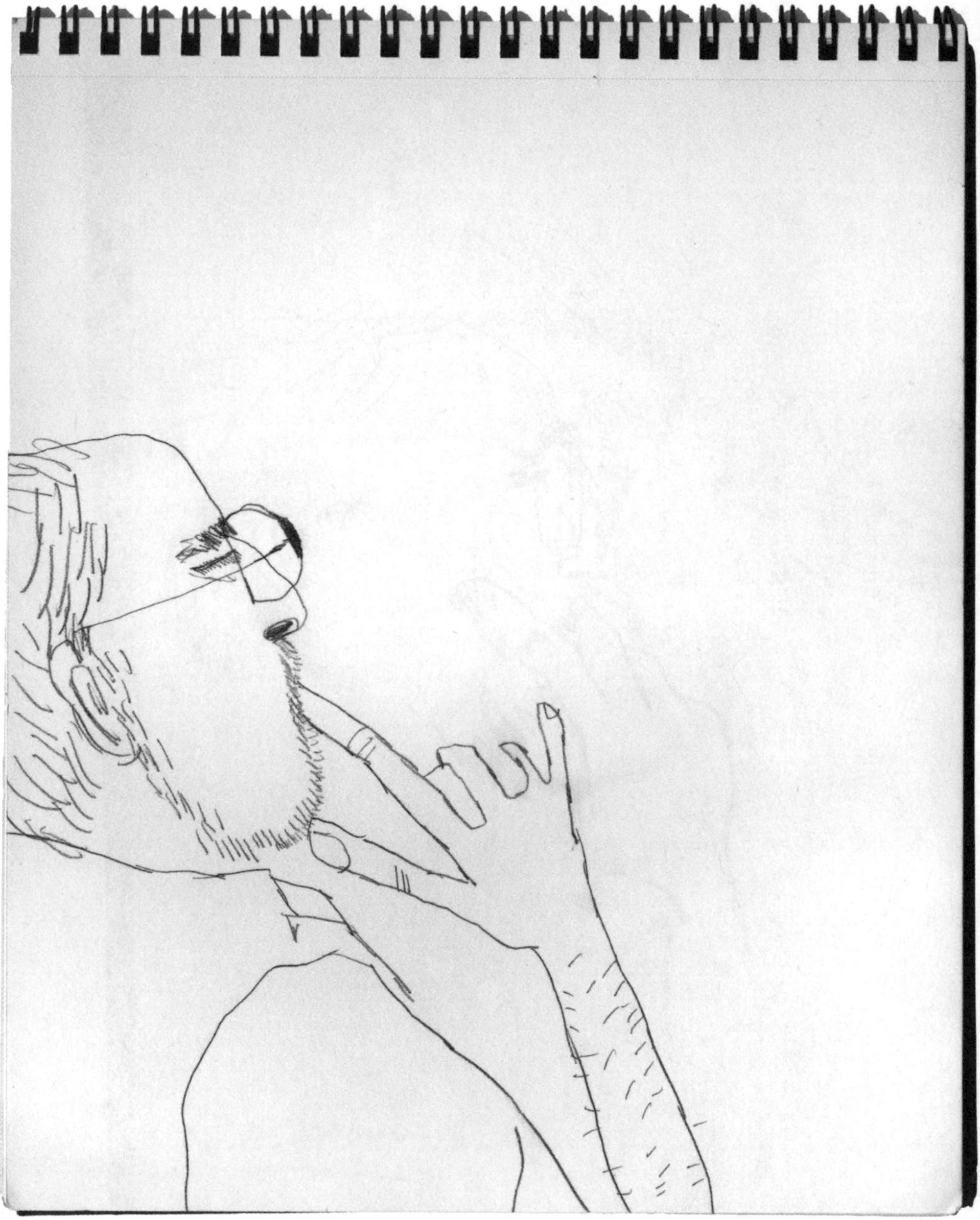

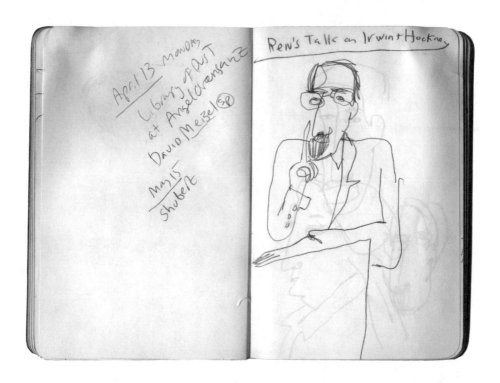

April 13 Monday
Library of Art
at Angel Orensanz
David Mezel ℗

May 15
Shubert

Ren's Talk on Irwin + Hockney

IMPOSSIBLE THINGS
BEFORE BREAKFAST
OR, THE MAN
WHO WAS THIRSTY

by JONATHAN LETHEM

THE FIRST INKLING, the first jot of the connect-the-dot contour indicating the presence of a clandestine Megamind lurking a step or possibly ten thousand steps ahead of yours, is announced in the fact that when you stumble upon the storefront art-installation-museum, that alchemical gnomic curational dream-zone devised for your secret enjoyment, which is outposted in a Los Angeles backwater where none of the natives even seem to know what you're talking about when you say you're going to visit, some other guy has *already written a book about it*. You could almost resent him for that.

Impartiality is a pompous name for indifference, which is an elegant name for ignorance. The way to love anything is to realize that it may be lost. The Bible tells us to love our neighbors, and also to love our enemies; probably because generally they are the same people. I would maintain that thanks are the highest form of thought; and that gratitude is happiness doubled by wonder.

You drop what you really ought to be doing because he told you not to miss today's thing that he can't quite name. After the scheduled presentation in which he unveils the requisite fifteen or twenty brilliancies, and everyone's sated and exhausted except him, he pulls you and a couple of other idlers into his office because you've got to see this, it's really cool, never mind all that other stuff, look at this YouTube video. The clouds at high altitude, crashing against the mountaintop, when accelerated at just the right rate, turn out to be a kind of gaseous surf, waves crashing on a rocky coast. Everything is everything.

No time for transitions, we're on to the next. No time for introductions or small talk, so let's pretend we've already met and we already know what we're talking about and we're actually deep in the middle of this inquiry, not pausing to nibble around its edges—okeedoke?

You're doing things you never did before: debating copyright with a federal judge live onstage in a crowded auditorium, then reading a Donald Barthelme story aloud on the same stage to a scattering of dedicated stragglers an hour later. Megamind's grabbed hold of you again, and you like it, you like it.

The secret's in the corrosion on these copper canisters. The fuzz on the dice. The words said that weren't yours to say but mean more coming from you than from the guy who thought them up. The sample, the glitch, the edge of the coin. The scribble and scrawl revealed when you blow the cross-hatching up to a suitable resolution. The space between the pictures, not the pictures themselves. God is in the gutter. You see more from the valley than the peak. Seeing is forgetting the name of the thing one sees. You Seymour, Me Julian Jaynes. I hear somebody talking, bicameral don't see anybody here? You talkin' to me?

The idea of being reasonable, to me that's the real jewel in the human crown. And part of being reasonable is being responsible. To think something through without the compromises of personal ambition or personal bias. Ideas are very potent elements that can radically change your life. Nothing is the same once you accept an idea, and you can never return to the place you left.

"Alice laughed. 'There's no use trying,' she said: 'one can't believe impossible things.'

'I daresay you haven't had much practice,' said the Queen. 'When I was your age, I always did it for half-an-hour each day. Why, sometimes I've believed as many as six impossible things before breakfast.'"

PASSION PIECES

by PETER VERMEERSCH

O NE DAY BACK in the early 1980s I was marveling at a sticker on our corkboard in the kitchen. Pinned down between random notes and shopping lists was a shiny slip of white paper with one word written on it, hastily so it seemed, in red letters. Curiously, one of those letters carried a flag. The word was *Solidarność*.

"What does that mean?" I asked my mother.

"We have to support the people of Poland," she said solemnly.

I was nine. The only thing I knew about Poland was that it was far away, somewhere in the shadow of the Soviet Union.

But I would soon know more: Poland had started to emerge from the anonymity of the Eastern bloc. All over Europe, as in my home in Belgium, people were following the events in Poland with growing fascination and concern. International news headlines carried word of one of the most efficient military coups of the postwar period. On

December 13, 1981, General Jaruzelski had proclaimed martial law, thereby effectively crushing the revolution of Solidarność, a trade union with ten million members, and turning its leaders—ironically, because some of their activism had relied on Catholic imagery—into martyrs. The entire leadership of the movement, including former electrician Lech Wałęsa, was now in jail or under house arrest. The regime had demonstrated how encompassing its power still was. Poland was a gripping black-and-white story of good against evil, where, for the moment at least, evil prevailed.

Or did it? The military government's repression may in fact have been a sign of its weakness. As it happens, it was also in Poland that, through the introduction of partly free elections in June 1989 and the ensuing meltdown of the Communist power structures, a situation arose that would foreshadow the demise of the entire Eastern Bloc. In 1990, Wałęsa won the Polish presidency, and the story of Solidarity could now be told as a biblical tale of Passion: Christ-like suffering leading to ultimate victory. Clearly, Poland was a country to watch. This was a place where things changed overnight, where white turned into black, strength into weakness, electricians into martyrs, and martyrs into presidents. Where history happened.

This past July, I visited Warsaw. My first trip to Poland had been in 1990—as a first-year student of Eastern European Studies, I had wanted to see some of the political developments firsthand—and I lived in the Polish capital in 1996 and 1997. But now, I was in Poland with another purpose: to read a book. Or to be precise: to re-read it. I've always loved Susan Sontag's dictum: "Literature is what you should re-read." In my bag I carried Lawrence Weschler's *The Passion of Poland: From Solidarity Through the State of War*.

I remembered from reading it the first time, some ten years ago, that the book functions as a brilliant lens through which one can clearly see all the ways Poland was affected by the experience of having lived through the extraordinary Solidarity movement and Jaruzelski's coup. *The Passion of Poland* consists of the essays Weschler had written for the *New Yorker* while in Poland between May 1981 and September 1983, and it's still one of the most detailed accounts of that period available.

I often recommend it to students of political science at the university where I teach now, not only because it's about Eastern Europe in those crucial years of change, but also because it's a skillful study of democracy in the making.

Weschler's method is that of an anthropologist of everyday political life: he sticks around and listens, and from seemingly random bits of conversation with a highly diverse group of people he is able to draw a detailed portrait of the mechanics of popular resistance. After a few days of wandering around at the First National Congress of Solidarity Delegates in September 1981, for example, he provides the following description of the double bind that Solidarity is facing. "Ten million people belong to Solidarity," Weschler writes, "because it is democratic and participatory—but if ten million people were really to start behaving democratically, if differences over fundamental issues were allowed to lead to the formation of hardened factions, then the union's very existence could come into jeopardy." This was the sort of dilemma that other democracy movements would grapple with around the world in the years to come.

In Poland, there was already a lot of uncertainty associated with democratic change at these early stages. Weschler observes it in detail, although he could not have known where things were going. "It feels like I've been writing on quicksand," he admits about halfway through the book, at the moment when martial law is about to be imposed. In order to make sense of what was happening around him, he records meticulously what he sees, and to interpret what he sees he relies on what should perhaps be called his visual intuition. On the final pages of the book, for example, Weschler zooms in on a poignant bit of graffiti in the streets of Warsaw, the logo CDN, which stands for Ciąg Dalszy Nastąpi and means, "to be continued." Weschler writes: "These are the initials one finds, for example, at the ends of installments of serialized writing. The Western press has a tendency to focus on news stories during climactic developments and to fade out during the interim — the long, slow periods when revolutions gestate—so that we may expect Poland to be receding, further and further, into the back pages of our news journals during the months ahead. We should not, however, be misled. The saga of Poland is definitely CDN." His intuition was right.

I've always admired Weschler's book for its precise observations, but that's not the only reason why every once in a while I feel compelled to take it from the shelves and read it again. What makes this book, in Susan Sontag's definition of the word, *Literature*, is its meandering narrative, its elegant flow, its eagerness to tell, and, above all, its ability to let its reader, this reader, see the world around him differently, each and every time he looks up from the pages.

Early July in Warsaw was calm. European Championship soccer had just ended, summer holidays were beginning, and many shops were closed—but luckily not The Gentle Barbarian. A small bookstore and café in the neighborhood of Mariensztat, it is a nice place to sit and read, and it always carries a decent collection of Polish art books and graphic novels. Poland has a rich tradition of animated film, and I remember that a few years ago the store hosted an evening with Piotr Dumała, the most impressive Polish animator around, known for his film adaptations of Kafka's diaries and Dostoevsky's *Crime and Punishment*. His technique is as unusual as it is effective: he draws by scratching white lines into surfaces of blackened plaster. I quickly browsed through The Gentle Barbarian's current collection, sat down with a cup of coffee and a notebook, and thumbed through Weschler's book, which, it occurred to me now, had brought to life the black-and-white world of Cold War Poland in much the same way as Dumała's animations had brought movement to images etched into that black plaster.

The first words I wrote down in my notebook were *visual arts*. From the very first pages of *The Passion of Poland*, it's striking how much importance Weschler attaches to the role of visual arts: films, drawings, street art, animation, posters. Take his meditation on the logo of the Solidarity trade union and how that was, he felt, the perfect expression of the movement's political predicament. The logo was designed by two graphic artists during the August 1980 strike at the Gdańsk shipyards, and immediately it was recognizable to everyone everywhere. But what did it stand for? The word *Solidarność* was unquestionably a reference to the country's history of labor activism. But if you looked carefully, so Weschler tells us, you could also see that the letters were drawn in such a way that they looked like a crowd, so there was the suggestion of mass protest. The red and the white surely referred to Polish national identity. But perhaps the red was also blood. In 1968, 1970, and 1976, previous attempts at organizing mass protests against the authorities had ended in deadly violence. Weschler writes: "Everyone agreed the letters formed a crowd, but part of the time people saw the crowd as surging forward, led by the S and the C; while much of the time, people saw the letters standing around, milling, the A and the R leaning into each other, waiting to see what was going to happen."

Such details are important; for Weschler the visual aspect of a political movement is not some sort of accidental byproduct; it must stand at the center of our attention, along with political stories and the vignettes of everyday life. This book brings across, perhaps for the first time, that important Weschlerian insight that colors all of his later work: that many things that are primarily thought of in terms of aesthetics—be it a logo, a picture, a poem, or any other work of artistic representation—have strong ethical and political implications.

The aesthetics of Poland's opposition movement helped to form some of the country's history. In particular, as Weschler learned from reading Halina Bortnowska's essay on Solidarity, the signs and logos of Solidarity expressed the "subjectivity" of Polish society, by which was meant the capacity of ordinary Polish people to act as the subjects of their own history and not passively remain the *object* of the history of the official rulers of the country. Poland in the 1980s was a place where certain historical questions were suddenly and forcefully opened up for re-examination. What did it mean, for example, to belong to the Polish nation? The Communist leaders, even though they had secured their power in various ways, were incessantly concerned with seeking legitimacy from the population, and did so through the use of national symbols: the state, they argued, is the people. But with the arrival of Solidarity they found themselves trapped in a competition with the opposition, who also, perhaps even better, understood the strategic value of articulating national belonging and did so through all sorts of newly designed symbols of their own. The nation is Solidarity, they claimed. Hence the red and white of the logo.

I wrote down the word *subject* in my notebook, looked up at the posters in the bookstore (film posters, no political ones), and was struck by something else. By devoting so much attention to logos, graffiti, stamps, films, and other visual expressions of political subjectivity, Weschler had not only found a useful way of analyzing Poland in the 1980s, he had also discovered an approach that would inform much of his work to come. *The Passion of Poland*, which is of course on every page a work of political reportage, is at the same time a broad and ambitious literary project that studies people's capacity to act in unexpected, courageous, and creative ways. A few months earlier, I had interviewed Weschler about his writing in his office in New York City. He said, "I used to distinguish between the things that I did as either political tragedies or cultural comedies, but in fact they were all what I called 'passion pieces': they were about people or places that caught fire." In *The Passion of Poland*, he had begun to realize he was "reporting on what it is that comes alive when a place—any place—comes alive, and then what it is that gets repressed when a place, any place, gets repressed." That kind of reporting finds its continuation in his essays about Vermeer, Polanski, and Spiegelman, or in his reflections on human rights activism, politics, and poetry (Weschler wrote terrific pieces about the poets Wisława Szymborska, Czesław Miłosz, and Zbigniew Herbert). Underlying a broad range of specific concerns is a universal story of people finding their subjectivity. And of course, Weschler himself, too, is a protagonist of that story. *The Passion of Poland* is not only about a population catching fire, but also about an American reporter catching fire while writing about them.

Later that afternoon, I felt it was time to look up from the book and compare two Polands: the one described by Weschler and the country around me. I decided to follow Weschler's method of study, by which I mean: I took a walk. I left The Gentle Barbarian and wandered through the center of Warsaw. It was a humid day; it felt like the rain would come soon. I passed by the neatly renovated buildings in a street called New World (the buildings really look new), by that strange and out-of-place artificial palm tree in the middle of Aleje Jerozolimskie (a contemporary artwork by Joanna Rajkowska), and by the old House of the Party (not an art piece but a Communist building from the early 1950s, which for a while in the 1990s was home to the Warsaw Stock Exchange). To me such architectural rhymes and accidental ironies are the poetry of Warsaw. "The country is its own best poet, it is always singing itself," Weschler wrote in 1981; it was still true now. I walked farther to the other side of the Palace of Culture and Science, that gray Stalinist wedding cake at the very heart of the city, only to wander off—was I now actively searching for another one of those accidental ironies?—into the prewar Jewish quarter of town. I say irony because, after all: in my bag was a book whose title invoked the overwhelming presence of the Catholic tradition in Poland, written by someone whose Jewish grandparents had fled Central Europe in the 1930s.

Along the way I kept thinking about how different Warsaw must have looked in the past. Even in the early 1980s it must have been another world. I looked at some of the graffiti and logos on the walls and found a chaotic mosaic of tags and slogans and frivolous colorings, all in all not unusual for a contemporary European capital. While the Solidarity logos of the 1980s were small and sober, a lot of the current graffiti seems to have spiraled out of control; it covers large surfaces, shouts out its messages loud and clear, but somehow does not have the same sense of urgency, or the same power, as it did thirty years ago. But then, how could it? It's hard to recall the extremity of the political climate of that time. Weschler manages to convey it with an anecdote:

> One afternoon, I was talking with a village priest, a fairly radical, longtime activist. When our conversation came to its end, like all the others, I asked, "So what do you think is going to happen?" He leaned forward and quietly said, "A miracle," rolling his eyes toward Heaven and smiling. I wrote the word down in my notebook and then leaned forward and asked, "Like what?" He leaned even closer, his face now a mixture of anticipation and serenity, and whispered, confidentially, "The Third World War."

Weschler tells this almost as if it's a joke. Almost. It's not a joke, of course, and he knows it. He takes it seriously. That's the only way to get to the reality of a place. The outrageous remarks, the chats in the streets, the jokes, the irrational statements—all that is just as important a source of information as films, music, and graffiti. Everything is a potential source. Everything matters.

As I walked I saw a few graffiti symbols that referred to the times of Solidarity, but their meaning has blurred. The Solidarity logo, and other signs associated with the opposition movement of the 1980s, now frequently figure in electoral campaigns, in particular in those of conservative groups like the Law and Justice Party. The images had perhaps always been somewhat nationalistic—always red and white, always bearing references to Poland's history—but now they're often used to buttress a political agenda that is far removed from both the historical context in which they were first used and from the aims of the original struggle of the Solidarity trade union. That these symbols are still capable of mobilizing a public is to some extent related to the images themselves, which still look powerful, but also to the clever ways in which contemporary politicians try to simplify the political landscape of the present. They try to suggest that the dichotomy between "us" (the people) and "them" (the state), well known from anti-Communist protests, is still valid. Some sections of the conservative electorate may still be persuaded to cast a vote for politicians who claim to be "against the state." For the foreign visitor, the effect is disorienting. The old symbols have become overburdened with too much history, and one can easily be confused about which political views exactly they represent.

By now I was entering what used to be the walled-in Jewish ghetto, though there was nothing left to suggest that the ghetto had once been there. I saw the same new buildings as elsewhere in town, the same busy roads. No doubt still affected by the Weschlerian tendency toward free association, I was now thinking about how different the Warsaw of the 1980s must have looked from the Warsaw of the 1930s. But then I entered Ulica Próżna, and there, suddenly, I had a glimpse into how it must have been. Próżna is the only street of the former Jewish ghetto where the original prewar brownstone blocks have been preserved. *Preserved* is not quite the right word: the houses had been empty for years and had fallen into disrepair—with facades crumbling to pieces, with broken windows, with pigeons flying out and bricks falling. I had walked down this street before, and I had never been sure what to make of its decay. Letting a street fall to pieces was perhaps not such a bad way to commemorate the disappearance of a population, to deplore the loss of an essential part of Polish national history, of a whole world destroyed. Would it have been better to build a monument in remembrance of the Jewish inhabitants of this street, and for the rest simply restore the houses to contemporary standards and go on with life? Others had answered the question for me: as I walked farther I noticed that such decisions had already been made. One side of the street was behind scaffolding. There was also a small new coffee bar, a lonely spot still, a single clear patch on a dark and dirty window, but also a glimpse of things to come. The young woman in the light, flowery dress behind the counter smiled when I entered. "They are going to renovate the entire street," she said.

I sat down in that coffee bar to read some more pages of *The Passion of Poland*. Outside a thunderstorm began. What was it Weschler had written about Jewish Warsaw? Like me now, Weschler had walked around with a book in his bag, in his case *Shosha*, a novel by Isaac Bashevis Singer, who had lived on these very streets before the Second World War. Like me, Weschler compared two Polands: one described in a book and the other the country around him. "I sat reading Singer," he writes, "and wondered in what sense one could even construe this to be the place he had been writing about. Virtually nothing of the Jews remains; all that persists—strangely unaltered by their disappearance— is the surrounding anti-Semitism."

Poland had once been a place of many cultures, but, by 1981, it wasn't anymore. And today the streets around Próżna, Chłodna, Leszno, and Krochmalna still shock for what's not there. Weschler described the neighborhood in 1981: a playground for kids and streets lined with gray concrete blocks. Now one could walk by those same blocks and see the children of those children playing on the same playground. One could try to do as Weschler did then: sit on a bench, observe the otherness in the familiar, be the gentle barbarian asking seemingly naïve questions.

Could diversity ever be restored in this place, as the buildings in Ulica Próżna were now being restored? Could history be rebuilt?

Re-reading those pages in the café, the rain outside coming down heavily, I felt that Weschler's book gives an experience not only of the overpowering quality of people's creativity and courage, but also of melancholy. And maybe melancholy is something that echoes throughout his other work, too. I should check the next time I take another volume from the shelves and re-read it. In the case of *The Passion of Poland* I see it like this: the book reads like an elegy for two Polands. They're both places one can pine for. One is a country of resistance against totalitarianism, a place that was once there, and isn't there anymore, and in some strange, contradictory way, one can feel sad about that. ("One can get homesick for things mattering," Weschler writes.) The other is the multicultural, democratic, tolerant, and open Poland that once could have existed, perhaps never really existed, but one day, just maybe, will exist.

MIDRASHIM ON SOME OF
REB REN'S WRITINGS

by ANDREI CODRESCU

We long to lose ourselves in stories—that's who we are. Well-crafted stories transport us, allow us to soar. One day perhaps, things being close enough for all practical purposes, to soar right over the Uncanny Valley, to traverse the Cusan Divide? I don't know, could be.

> —from Lawrence Weschler's "Uncanny Valley:
> On the Digital Animation of the Face" (2002)

REN DOESN'T REALLY believe this: he serves up the conventional ending of an assignment-essay, then hedges with a wise, "I don't know, could be." This colloquial and rabbinical gesture of ending a lesson by combing a skeptical beard with four fingers of one hand grows more pronounced as we leave the computer-generated anxieties of the fin-de-siècle behind. Already in the last essay in *Uncanny Valley: And Other Adventures in the Narrative* (2011), he has revised his view of stories: he's still asking "who knows?" but from within an opposing contention:

> ...maybe it was the jokes that are the true living entities on this third planet from the sun, and we, the humans, maybe merely the endless flowing medium in which they abide.

Contained in this passage, in addition to a novel theory of language, is a brief history of the fall of the Iron Curtain and the revelation by Kundera and others that jokes were the true common culture of all the countries of the ex-Soviet fiefdom, because they were the tolerated form of dissent. After the fall of the Curtain, jokes continued to travel spore-like, but with a more pronounced Yiddish flavor that connected them to Hassidic mysticism. "The Belgian Army Joke Come to Life" that Adam Michnik whispers into Ren's ear in Cape Town, South Africa, is the Joke restored to its roots in theology, but grounded in the political context that is another of Ren's constant themes.

This is the offhand remark that concludes the book:

> God invented Man, the wise man says, because he loved stories. And maybe the other way around: Man invented God for the same reason. Or maybe Narrative invented both of us: couldn't do without us. Hallelujah. Amen.

Here once again is Reb Ren's abrupt way of finishing a lecture (or essay), without the satisfaction of having said (or discovered) what he *really* thought about the matter.

The twentieth century ended with this equation: God = Logos, therefore humans are circuit breakers in the endless flow of Logos. Or, as Bucky Fuller put it, we are "information-gathering" devices in an "eternally generative universe." Ren doesn't subscribe to this proposition either, but like the good debater he is, he feels obliged to synthesize the century's commonplace wisdom. Only his "Hallelujah" and "Amen" hint at his frustration with this (still) unshakeable assumption.

Ren's questions about the "uncanny valley" that divides our reality from computer-generated worlds, are slight feints—they contain real anxiety. Is what we call reality only an older virtuality? Is the unknown and maybe unknowable author of our world a better storyteller than the animators of new cyber worlds? Is the difference between humans and robots only a matter of technical complexity, or is there a soul somewhere, impossible to replicate? What is language? Though worded with seemingly the same intentions, and in the same literary-critical idiom, these are not the same questions asked by Borges and other literary postmodernists; Ren's questions are premodern. He would like to know why making the Golem was wrong. It's an ethical inquiry. In pure Borgesian terms, making golems is what we have to do, an absurd *imitatio dei* that resolves in aesthetic pleasure. Ren's politically engaged Jewish G-d is not so much into "narrative." He's into justice. Ren pays his respects to narrative, but he suspects the "uncanny valley" to be ethically dreadful.

In his earlier *Mr. Wilson's Cabinet of Wonder* (1996), Ren foresaw the incoming virtualities of the next decade in a more benign light. He admired David Wilson, the creator of Los Angeles's Museum of Jurassic Technology, both for his ability to create intricate and almost-believable fantastic objects, and for doing so deadpan, without dispelling the illusion for people who believe or half-believe his inventions. Ren admired David's lack of irony, and made sure, in his own story about MJT's Wilson, to keep the suspense going. Is it real or is it not? It was a comfortable question for Ren, an intelligent writer conversant with pop art and great cities' constant play with shifting identities and intricate hustles. In New York, the city that saw the transition of the drag queen (is it or isn't it a woman?) into pop art, and Warhol's deadpan translate into big money (is it or isn't it art?), the grounds for the question had been laid by the wartime European avant-garde-in-exile; in Los Angeles, the same (or almost) refugee mix had an even greater reach through the movies. It was a big delight for Ren to discover Wilson's mechanistic could-be-true wonders in the city of movies. Movies told stories that were simpler and more accessible to the down-to-earth garage-tinkering practices of middle America than the intellectually anguished abstractions of New York. Here, in Wilson's museum, were horned humans, for chrissakes (to coin a geegosh), who were more purely Jewish, pre-Freud devils, Golems without shame. The storytelling of movies or of kitsch (no matter how clever) was good to enjoy, like folk tales, marketplace magic, the circus. Ren discovered (or rediscovered) America. The suspension of disbelief was understood: it was the obvious basis for enjoying the show.

Mr. Wilson's Cabinet of Wonder is Ren's most enjoyable book; his pleasure in the physical mechanics of creating a fabulous illusion found the perfect storytelling style. The reflexive combing of the doubting beard was unnecessary in the agora, though doubts persisted. Soon enough, *Shrek*, *The Truman Show*, Alvy Ray Smith, and *Avatar* would show up. The innocence of the "why not?" world, which had always been understood by irreverent spectators to be "entertainment," farcical, crude, and liberating, would make room for the pretentions of another kind of virtuality, a "competitor" to "reality."

(I'm quoting here an early founder of VR, whom I interviewed around the same time, 1995–1996, pursuing more or less the same line of inquiry as Ren's. I also discovered the Museum of Jurassic Technology around the same time Ren did, and was thrilled by it, but I think that I was a lot more spooked. I'd been anxiously watching the computer revolution, too, and I knew that MJT wasn't just pop surrealism, but also a foreshadowing of things to come. The apocalyptic always had a seat at the table in California, but until VR became technically possible, no one was sure who exactly was sitting there.)

"It can get downright weird." (That's the first sentence of "Mr. Wilson in Belgrade" from *Uncanny Valley*.) *Mr. Wilson's Cabinet of Wonder* was translated into Serbian for a Belgrade publisher that was also publishing a translation of a book by Fabrizio Rondolini, an Italian who'd written a biography of Madelena Delani, who was (or was she?) an invention of David Wilson's. Perfectly postmodern, right, but just as the book came out, a planned in-the-flesh meeting of the three people who fictionalized each other (Wilson, Weschler, and Rondolini) was canceled because NATO started bombing Belgrade. So much for the delightful part of the postmodern game: reality had the last word. It's only Ren's humble genius that makes this story more than exhibitionist hubris; he turned it instead into a morality tale about the dangers of mistaking one's mind-blowing coincidences for universal truths. Maybe. (My turn with the beard.) The way Ren tells it, the anecdote is actually a story about memory and forgetting. The memory of all that postwar existential European, Jewish anguish was just about to vanish in the pastel-colored forgetting of postmodern Los Angeles, when... Here, another question rears its freaky dragon head (No. 1 redux):

> And indeed, now there it came looming into view: an austere blockwide low-slung hive of graphite-gray monoliths, monoface rectangular plinths arrayed in a regular perpendicular grid over gently undulating terrain—over three thousand of them spread over nearly five acres, some (near the perimeter) as low as a foot and a half, some further into the hive, where the terrain fell into some of its deeper undulations, as high as ten feet, the entire expanse crisscrossed by narrow paths between the parallel rows of vaguely pitched concrete plinths, paths that veritably beckoned those passing by on the busy city sidewalks above into this uncanny maze of vaguely determinate remembrance.
>
> —from "A Berlin Epiphany" (2006), in *Uncanny Valley*

It's a freakishly factual sentence that lineates with chilling exactness Peter Eisenman's *Memorial to the Murdered Jews of Europe* in Berlin. It's a sentence that describes a monument, but could also be a scale rendition of the Nazi mind, and a self-critique of Ren's own surrender to fantasy. It's a merciless sentence that the rest of the essay tries its best to mitigate, ameliorate, soften. The living city of Berlin goes about its noisy joyous present all around and, as it turns out, when playful schoolchildren invade it, inside the monument to the unimaginable, as well. It's a sentence that divides, like a ghost Berlin Wall, artistic intention (and the use of it by the innocent) from historical reality. That history has never been forgotten, by Ren or any thoughtful person, but this artistic expression of it makes it at least partially possible to replace the anxieties history has left behind. And that's as it should be; life must continue. Ren makes a powerful argument for this in "Life Against

Death" (1997), a reflection on Rembrandt's *The Anatomy Lesson of Dr. Nicolaes Tulp*, a painting seen in a number of grim historical contexts that is, in the end, "about living." He goes on to explain that "it's not, as we are sometimes given to recalling, a morbid dwelling upon death but rather a celebration, a defiant affirmation of life and liveliness and vitality generated, as it happens, at a moment when the world was choked with death and dying."

Reb Ren's pendulum swings back and forth between the facts of history and the necessities of forgetting and fabulation. At its core it's an old quandary, but Ren has always insisted on finding new ways to look at the blackbird. Some of the old fables, he notes, have become real. The Golem is barely a metaphor anymore: it's about as close as my laptop. The moral attached to it is not the same, however. In sixteenth-century Prague, the Golem was supposed to defend the Jews against the anti-Semites. In 2012, I don't know… it's supposed to shine your shoes in the morning and be a first responder, or maybe its job is to make more golems. And the job of those golems may be to bomb the shit out of people without golems who hate you.

By 2006's *Everything That Rises: A Book of Convergences*, "to soar right over the Uncanny Valley" has become more suspect, while "I don't know, maybe," has, possibly, become the subject. (Note that my "possibly" also harbors a tiny doubt as to whether one—anyone—can conduct the most focused investigation in the midst of essayistic commerce. My sense of Ren's integrity and genuine (re)search is total, but I do wonder at times if the *New Yorker*'s fact-checkers and grammar orderlies haven't removed some of the accumulated disorder that would naturally occur; I mean, you don't tramp in your boots through the bloody mud of Bosnia and come up with perfectly perfect sentences… Okay, that's just the downtown me having a little problem with the uptown Ren.)

Can there be an ethical probe into virtuality? Ren's writing about art and artists answers that question with a resounding: "Yes. Maybe." If Ren's ethical inquiry was prompted solely by history, there would be no "Maybe." A secular ethics is sufficient for any reader of the past, but Ren keeps a channel open to G-d. Paraphrasing his beloved Nicholas de Cusa, he writes:

One could never achieve knowledge of God, or, for that matter, of the wholeness of existence, through the systematic accretion of more and more factual knowledge.

—from "We Join Spokes Together in a Wheel,"

in *Everything That Rises*

Ren is still trying to understand, if not reconcile, the divine (symbolized by the circle) and the proliferation of historical horrors (symbolized by increasingly complex polygons within the circle). This is the Cusan paradox: the circle becomes more distant the more multifaceted polygons one tries to fill the circle with. Virtual worlds may be the perfect objects that try to imitate Creation (the circle) but do no more than increase the distance to it.

At the start of internet virtuality, "making a world" seemed close to the original act of Creation. Why not? If Wilson or Alvy Ray Smith could make a new animal or a humanlike animation, weren't they close to the great mystery? Weren't they telling the same kind of story? Any narrative needs the requisite act of faith, the quasi-religious reflex that doesn't correspond with anything historical or scientific except, maybe... the brain. From suspension of disbelief to neurology there are bridges: Irony (Ren is a master ironist) and the Ideal (Justice). Neither Irony nor its nonironic opposite, Justice, is a straightforward link from Belief to the Brain, but some artists provide a workable simulacrum that resides easily in all possible realities. The Fringe events caused by Art, and the unexpected juxtapositions that only Irony can deal with, are what Ren targets over and over. Of course, his writing experience makes some images more apropos than others. Ren's search for angel flesh in art (the in extremis position of the captive human), finds and nails many traces of it. When he does find a live paradox, he knows that he is close to the divine, but he either argues it in aesthetic terms or throws it back to... the brain.

Oy, Reb! I made a typo. (Hit *b* instead of *n*, fixed it, and then decided to keep both—hence, "Reb Ren.") You can take the Reb out of Prague but you can't take the Golem from Ren. Ren takes the Golem from Reb. Ren flirts with the Reb but doesn't consummate. This is useful and interesting and good, but is it real? I mean, is it real Now? Does the zeitgeist that is making such a cozy virtual prison for everyone possess the organ for the older virtuality (of G-d) that Ren often speaks for? And what about History? And what is Justice in a virtual world? Is Irony an escape from History? An escape to what? In addition to the irreconcilables of divinity and virtuality, justice and irony, Ren offers (and critiques) another possible solution to the endless dialectic: Wonder. The blessing of innocence. Alas. In Wilson's Museum one returns to childhood despite the certainties of one's education or skepticism. "Wonder" is good when you don't know what all those "marvels" in the *wunderkammer* are. But when you find out? Can you still wonder even if you know? Reb Ren Jacob-wrestles this question, too, in almost every essay. He flirts with metaphysics in a world that won't hear of it: his best study samples are artists like Magritte, poets like Szymborska, or forgers like Wilson, all of whom make nonexistent-but-they-do-exist things. Even when writing about Richard Diebenkorn, for example, abstraction becomes a soon-to-be-fact, but never (and this is high praise) a *fait divers*.

> Abstraction: to be lost in thought, lost to thought, transported out of oneself. But out of oneself toward what?
> —from "Gazing Out Toward," in *Everything That Rises*

HOPELESS MARVEL
THE PHILOSOPHICAL REPORTING
OF LAWRENCE WESCHLER

by BAYNARD WOODS

THERE IS A certain frumpish devilry to the bearded, bright-tied Lawrence Weschler as he spins a multi-sided top on a glass mirror. The mirror reflects one of Weschler's eyes as he stares at the spinning toy, which now seems to be a circle. "Is that cool or is that cool?" he says, grinning, his eyes lit up behind his glasses.

Before that he showed me: a series of miniature books about Napoleon, a painting made by an elephant (abstract), a shape he invented, and countless sets of blocks that he uses to think through the structure of his stories. He likes telling how his daughter used to insist that her friends weren't allowed to play with her father's blocks.

He darts around from wonder to wonder in the living room of the suburban Pelham home he shares with his wife, a human-rights monitor, who calls it all "Ren's crap." But for Weschler, the room is a machine designed to encourage what his daughter Sara calls his "loose-synapsed moments," when perceptions converge to create a kind of narrative philosophy that borders on theology or mysticism.

Every object in the room triggers a story which leads to another object, until they all intersect, just like the books that weigh down the shelves lining every wall, arranged alphabetically by author, whether fiction or nonfiction.

That's always a sore point for a writer like Weschler, who calls what he does writerly nonfiction, conceives of it as literature, and yet finds his work, if he finds it at all, scattered throughout bookstores based on the ostensible subject. And yet, Weschler himself is always at the center of his stories—there is always an "I" observing. "It is so stupid when someone writes *he said to a reporter*. Is that you, or is there a third person in the room?" he asks with rhetorical incredulity. "You use the 'I' not because of the ego, but to avoid it. It is more modest, it is not claiming to be the voice of god."

Weschler began writing for the *New Yorker* in the 1980s, in part because it was the only way to continue the kind of ruminative philosophical thinking he was interested in. He quit under Tina Brown to run the New York Institute for the Humanities at NYU—where he has long taught a class called The Fiction of Nonfiction—because it seemed the only way to keep writing the way he likes.

But without a popular venue like the *New Yorker*, one only discovers Weschler by accident—or as he would have it, grace.

For me, it was in a big chain bookstore one Sunday when I was studying Classics in graduate school and trying to write fiction. I picked up *A Wanderer in the Perfect City*; flânerie was my favorite pretension and pastime back then. I opened it at random and found this sentence: "Nicolas Slonimsky is continually driving his daughter crazy, and it's not just because he named her Electra, although that certainly didn't help."

This seemed to me a perfectly uncanny sentence for the opening of a nonfiction story—I had been translating Euripides and listening to Coltrane, whom I knew made his bands learn the Slonimsky method, though I didn't know what that was. A couple sentences later, when I learned that Slonimsky only talked to his daughter in Latin, I bought the book and loved it. I never saw anything else Weschler did until a grad school roommate left *Mr. Wilson's Cabinet of Wonder* on the toilet.

After I finished a PhD in ancient philosophy, I decided to become a reporter because it seemed like the only life for a modern Socratic. And of reporters, Weschler struck me as the *most* Socratic. Later, when I asked his friend, the film editor Walter Murch, about him, Murch called Weschler a "cosmic gadfly," and it was precisely that quality that compelled me to write him an email. I explained the kind of writing I wanted to do and told him I was not enrolled in NYU and had no money. "But I will take the bus to New York from DC every week for the class," I assured him.

It was rather insane—for both of us. From his perspective, I was certainly a weirdo and a freeloader and from mine, well, I was a weirdo and a freeloader. But I thought he might have something to say, so each Friday for sixteen weeks I left home at six a.m. and returned at two the next morning.

After I finally gained entrance to the university on the first day—the guards wouldn't let me in without an ID—I found that Weschler did indeed possess a decidedly Socratic demeanor. His speech is not exactly elegant—his voice is nasal and high-pitched and punctuated by frequent humming pauses—but it is uniquely captivating and authoritative.

"Let us pray," he said beneath hunched shoulders at the front of the room, before reading a poem at the beginning of every class. Gary Snyder, Szymborska, Herbert. He read the poems like a theologian.

When the class finally reached *Joe Gould's Secret*, Joseph Mitchell's last masterpiece about Gould's nonexistent epic *An Oral History of Our Times*, Weschler said: "This is the holy of holies. This is no longer literature. This is theology. It is hard to imagine that it was written by a human."

He is talking about a mystical theology that leads, curiously enough, to reporting as the sacred action: every aspect of the world must somehow be reflected and glorified.

Once you notice the theological bent in Weschler's work, it is everywhere. In an early "Talk of the Town" piece in the *New Yorker* (August 26, 1985), he explained why he could not write fiction: "For me the world is already filled to bursting with interconnections, interrelationships, consequences, and consequences of consequences. The world as it is is overdetermined: the web of those interconnections is dense to the point of saturation." His reporting, he wrote, is about taking "any single knot and worrying out the threads, tracing the interconnections, following the mesh into the wider outlying mesh."

The mesh he is after is essentially the web of being itself—to the extent Weschler is a reporter, his beat is existential, his peg the ever-present mystery.

This vision has remained constant over the last quarter century. In *Uncanny Valley* (2011), he once again elevates narrative to a theological level—using "the late-medieval number-mystic Nicholas of Cusa," as his touchtone. "Faced with the ever more positivist claims of the Scholastics of his own time, Cusa likened true knowledge of God and the infinite to a circle, within which was slotted a regular compounding n-sided polygon." Cusa argues that you can keep adding sides so that it seems you are getting closer to the circle "whereas a circle has no angles and only one 'side.'" It is pure grace that brings us from the million-sided figure to the circle—grace that allows a representation, a story, to open the world to us.

Watching the top spin on the mirror in his living room, Weschler says, "See, when it's spinning, it appears to be a circle. That motion is like narrative. It makes the polygon seem like a circle."

The movement that drives his narrative, Weschler calls it passion; it's the way a person either affects or is affected by the world and manifests itself either as political tragedy or cultural comedy.

"The dark makes you marvel all the more," he says as the top comes to a rest against the mirrors with a series of clicking sounds. "I do find that a very odd feeling: to see the world as very dark and to marvel at what remains as long as you can. Wonder without hope—to marvel hopelessly."

Weschler walks away from the top, now lying flat on the mirror, to a set of Swedish blocks. "Now these are cool," he says, picking them up off the shelf.

LAWRENCE WESCHLER'S
CABINET OF WONDER

by WALTER MURCH

O UR PATHS FIRST crossed back in 1989, when Ren and I inde-
pendently discovered David Wilson's newly opened Museum
of Jurassic Technology in Culver City. Unfortunately, it was
only our paths that did the crossing—it seemed as if we were in and
out of the museum on alternating weeks, never actually meeting in
person. The place always left me weak-kneed and speechless with
perplexed admiration, but in 1996 Ren distilled his delight into *Mr.
Wilson's Cabinet of Wonder*.

It is a marvelous book, but the title is particularly apt, since *Cabinet
of Wonder* would be a good description of Ren's take on life itself, with
some grisly bits jostling alongside the more enchanting slices of human
enterprise and achievement.

My wife Aggie actually met Ren before I did, interviewing him in
1998 on KPFA Berkeley for his book *Calamities of Exile*; five years later

we finally connected when I was in New York previewing the film *Cold Mountain*, and Ren was jockeying his literary/visual journal *Omnivore* through its first printing. One of my translations of Curzio Malaparte's short stories had made it across Ren's threshold, and it appeared in the journal's premiere (and regrettably, so far, only) issue.

That was almost ten years ago, and if Ren and I don't meet somewhere, or at least correspond every few months, we both think that something might be amiss. His curiosity about the world is indeed omnivorous and inspirational: the subjects of his fifteen books over the last thirty years vary widely from politics in Poland, to the aesthetics of David Hockney and Robert Irwin, from torture in Brazil, to the work of counterfeiter/artist J. S. G. Boggs, to the hidden resonances that lurk in the visual blizzard that envelops us these days.

The last item, taken up in *Everything That Rises: A Book of Convergences*, is a comprehensive gathering of visual rhymes profound, upsetting, witty, and mysterious, and anyone leafing through it can immediately grasp the appeal of Ren's sensibility to someone like me, an editor whose work is similarly the mining of whatever film I am working on for these same kinds of visual reflections.

As director of the New York Institute for the Humanities and artistic director of the Chicago Humanities Festival, Ren also combines his curiosity with the most engaging and irresistible way of making you understand that this next thing—whatever wonder he happens to be writing about or organizing—is going to be the most interesting and important yet. And then over and over again you find out he is right: a recent day-long event last November was an exploration of solitary confinement—with testimony from Breyten Breytenbach and others who had been there—and the reasons why this form of torture has become routine in American prisons.

Personally, I am multiply indebted to Ren: first, for often including me in his annual Wonder Cabinet events, often with my theories about planetary orbits and the music of the spheres. In fact, I feel sometimes like one of the exhibits at the Museum of Jurassic Technology, displaying my "mice-on-toast" peculiarities to the mystified gaze of the patrons. But perseverance furthers, as the *I Ching* reminds us, and recently Ren linked me up with a professor of astronomy who seems to take me seriously, and things are moving to the next level, whatever that might be.

And then I am also indebted to Ren for encouraging my translations of Curzio Malaparte over the last ten years, and for recently putting me in touch with Jack Shoemaker and Charlie Winton of Counterpoint Press in Berkeley, who have just published *The Bird That Swallowed Its Cage*, a collection of Malaparte's short stories, translated into English for the first time.

But I am mainly indebted to Ren for simply existing and being part of the larger discussion. I am certain my case is typical of anyone who is lucky enough to mesh gears with Ren: he is a catalyst and *encourageur* for all that is best (and frequently most off-beat) in the humanities—in the deepest, most all-embracing and wonder-full sense of that word.

CONTRIBUTORS

TOM BARBASH is the author of *The Last Good Chance* and *On Top of the World*. His short story collection *Stay Up With Me* will be published by Ecco/Harper Collins in September.

ANDREI CODRESCU's newest books are *Bibliodeath: My Archives (with Life in Footnotes)*, *The Poetry Lesson*, *whatever gets you through the night: sheherezade and the arabian entertainments*, and *The Posthuman Dada Guide: Tzara and Lenin Play Chess*.

RACHEL COHEN is the author of *A Chance Meeting: Intertwined Lives of American Writers and Artists*, winner of the PEN/Jerard Fund Award. Her essays have appeared in the *New Yorker*, *The Threepenny Review*, the *Believer*, and *Best American Essays*. Her new book *Bernard Berenson: A Life in the Picture Trade* is forthcoming in October 2013.

ROB CURRAN has written about high-speed hedge funds, Cuban movie-poster art, Irish builders, Peruvian roads, and Sid Vicious. He has blogged under the pseudonym Sarah Palin and once crashed a steamroller. He is planning to self-publish his first novel, *The Crap Terrorist*, in the fall.

REBECCA CURTIS is a writer and holistic nutritionist who lives in Brooklyn. Her collection of short stories, *Twenty Grand and Other Tales of Love and Money*, was a finalist for the Pen Hemingway Prize and the Los Angeles Times Art Seidenbaum Award for best first book of fiction.

STUART DYBEK is the author of three books of fiction and two books of poetry. His work has appeared in both *Best American Fiction* and *Best American Poetry*, and his awards include a Guggenheim Fellowship, a Lannan Award, and a MacArthur Fellowship. Two new books of Dybek's fiction are scheduled for publication by Farrar, Straus & Giroux in Spring 2014.

GEOFF DYER's many books include *Zona* and *Jeff in Venice, Death in Varanasi*.

WILLIAM FINNEGAN writes about politics, war, poverty, race, organized crime, international trade, immigration, and surfing. He is a staff writer at the *New Yorker* and the author of four books.

STUART GLOVER teaches at the University of Queensland in Brisbane, Australia. He publishes the literary site *Bumf*. He writes about literary culture and for little magazines.

JESSICA HOPPER is a music and culture critic based in Chicago. She is also the music editor for *Rookie* magazine and the author of *The Girls Guide to Rocking*.

RICKY JAY is a sleight-of-hand artist, actor, and author. He is the subject of the new documentary *Deceptive Practice: The Mysteries and Mentors of Ricky Jay*. His latest book is *Celebrations of Curious Characters*, published by McSweeney's. This broadside for Ren was designed with Coco Shinomiya-Gorodetsky, an award-winning art director and graphic designer.

BEN KATCHOR's latest book, *Hand-Drying in America and Other Stories*, is a collection of strips from *Metropolis* magazine on the subjects of design and architecture. He teaches at Parsons The New School for Design in New York City.

RIVA LEHRER's work focuses on issues of physical identity and the socially challenged body. It has been shown at the United Nations, the National Museum of Women in the Arts, the Smithsonian Museum, the Chicago Cultural Center, and elsewhere. She is currently adjunct professor at the School of the Art Institute of Chicago, and visiting artist in Medical Humanities at Northwestern University. She is represented by Printworks Gallery of Chicago. Her work can be seen at rivalehrer.com.

WENDY LESSER, the founding editor of *The Threepenny Review*, is the author of eight works of nonfiction and one novel. Her tenth book, *Why I Read: The Serious Pleasure of Books*, will be out next year from Farrar, Straus & Giroux.

JONATHAN LETHEM is the author of *Dissident Gardens* and eight other novels, including *Girl In Landscape* and *Chronic City*. His writing has been translated into over thirty languages.

BILL MCKIBBEN was a staff writer at the *New Yorker* from 1982 to 1987, and has been a freelance writer since.

ERROL MORRIS is a filmmaker and writer. He has never understood why he prefers dogs to humans, but believes he is making progress.

BILL MORRISON is a New York–based filmmaker whose work often combines rare archival material with contemporary music, as with "Decasia," "Light Is Calling," "The Miners' Hymns," and "Spark of Being." Icarus Films will release "The Great Flood" in Fall 2013.

WALTER MURCH is a film editor, sound designer, director, translator, and amateur astronomer. He has contributed sound- and picture-editing work to films including *THX-1138*, *The Conversation*, *The Godfather*, *Julia*, *Apocalypse Now*, *The English Patient*, *Cold Mountain*, and *Jarhead*. His latest film work was for *Particle Fever*, a documentary on the Large Hadron Collider.

LAUREN REDNISS is the author of *Century Girl: 100 years in the Life of Doris Eaton Travis, Last Living Star of the Ziegfeld Follies* and *Radioactive: Marie & Pierre Curie, A Tale of Love and Fallout*, a finalist for the 2011 National Book Award. She received a Guggenheim Fellowship in 2012 and is currently Artist-in-Residence at the American Museum of Natural History. She teaches at Parsons the New School for Design in New York City.

JOE MENO is a fiction writer and playwright who lives in Chicago. A winner of the Nelson Algren Award, a Pushcart Prize, and a finalist for the Story Prize, he is the author of six novels and two short story collections including *The Great Perhaps*, *The Boy Detective Fails*, and *Hairstyles of the Damned*. His latest is *Office Girl*.

RYAN MROZOWSKI's work has been exhibited internationally. He is represented by Pierogi in New York City.

ANDREW PALMER is a 2013-2014 Fellow at the Fine Arts Work Center in Provincetown. He is writing a novel about *The Bachelor*.

SIMON RICH has written for Pixar, *Saturday Night Live*, and the *New Yorker*. His latest book is *The Last Girlfriend on Earth*.

MIKE SACKS has published three books: *And Here's the Kicker: Conversations with 21 Humor Writers About Their Craft*; *SEX: Our Bodies, Our Junk*; and *Your Wildest Dreams, Within Reason*. A sequel to *And Here's the Kicker* will be published by Viking/Penguin in June 2014.

JENNY SHANK's novel *The Ringer* won the High Plains Book Award and was a finalist for the Mountains and Plains Independent Booksellers Association award. Her work has appeared in *Prairie Schooner*, *Alaska Quarterly Review*, *Santa Monica Review*, the *Onion A.V. Club*, the *Rumpus*, and *Bust*.

JIM SHEPARD is the author of six novels, including most recently *Project X*, and four story collections, including most recently *You Think That's Bad*. He's at work on a new novel.

WELLS TOWER is the author of *Everything Ravaged, Everything Burned*.

PETER VERMEERSCH is a professor of politics at the University of Leuven, Belgium, and a former visiting scholar at Harvard University. He has published widely on Central and Eastern Europe. He is also an essayist and a poet. His website is petervermeersch.net.

BAYNARD WOODS is the author of *Coffin Point: The Strange Cases of Ed McTeer, Witchdoctor Sheriff*. His work has appeared in the *Georgia Review*, *The Millions*, and the *Rumpus*. He is a librettist for Rhymes with Opera and plays rock 'n' roll with the Barnyard Sharks. He lives in Baltimore.

DISAPPEARING ACTS

by Ryan Mrozowski

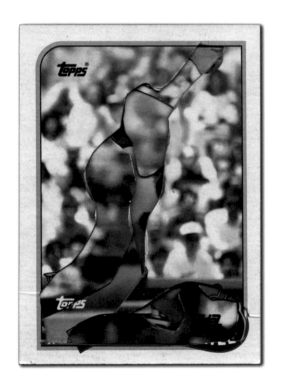

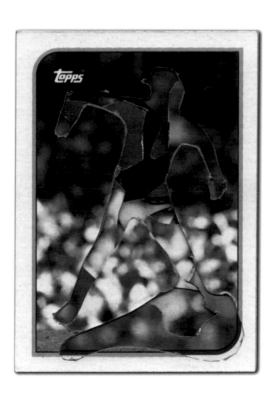

Ryan Mrozowski made the preceding collages for *McSweeney's* as part of an ongoing series called "Disappearing Acts." Each collage is a stack of seven 1989 Topps baseball cards from which the players and identifying graphics have been cut out, leaving only the backgrounds and borders. The seven cards in each stack are as follows. (All cards are listed top to bottom.)

I	II	III	IV
#331—Curt Wilkerson	#8—Dave Eiland	#603—Frank Tanana	#543—Damon Berryhill
#333—Bob Ojeda	#337—Calvin Schiraldi	#497—Pete Stanicek	#185—Claudell Washington
#306—Tracy Woodson	#517—Greg Brock	#637—Joe Magrane	#16—Ron Robinson
#694—Les Lancaster	#334—Steve Lyons	#103—Tim Birtsas	#223—Jay Buhner
#539—Barry Jones	#240—Greg Maddux	#317—Jack Armstrong	#553—Luis Salazar
#439—Frank DiPino	#701—Storm Davis	#562—Danny Cox	#530—Nolan Ryan
#690—Doug Jones	#18—Rick Rhoden	#525—Chili Davis	#101—Les Straker

V	VI	VII	VIII
#708—Chuck Finley	#250—Cal Ripken, Jr.	#197—Neal Heaton	#537—Pete Smith
#259—Larry McWilliams	#57—Alejandro Pena	#614—Joe Hesketh	#182—Bob McClure
#271—Jay Tibbs	#420—Joe Carter	#425—Jay Howell	#644—Lloyd McClendon
#262—Jeff Pico	#247—Shawn Hillegas	#355—Mark Langston	#108—Fred Manrique
#172—Frank Williams	#736—Jeff Hamilton	#192—Paul Mirabella	#621—Rick Mahler
#695—Carlton Fisk	#466—Chuck Crim	#621—Rick Mahler	#647—Kevin Bass
#775—Jeff Reardon	#615—Robin Yount	#4—Andre Dawson	#169—Mike Jackson

HOW MUSIC WORKS
by David Byrne

How Music Works is David Byrne's remarkable and buoyant celebration of a subject he's spent a lifetime thinking about. He explains how profoundly music is shaped by its time and place, and how the advent of recording technology forever changed our relationship to playing, performing, and listening to music. Acting as historian and anthropologist, raconteur and social scientist, he searches for patterns—and tells us how they have affected his own work over the years with Talking Heads and his many collaborators. *How Music Works* is a brainy, irresistible adventure and an impassioned argument about music's liberating, life-affirming power.

ONE HUNDRED APOCALYPSES
AND OTHER APOCALYPSES
by Lucy Corin

Lucy Corin's dazzling new collection is powered by one hundred apocalypses: a series of short stories, many only a few lines, that illuminate moments of vexation and crisis, revelations and revolutions. An apocalypse might come in the form of the end of a relationship or the end of the world, but what it exposes is the tricky landscape of our longing for a clean slate.

At once mournful and explosively energetic, *One Hundred Apocalypses and Other Apocalypses* makes manifest the troubled conscience of an uneasy time.

HIGH-RISE STORIES
compiled and edited by Audrey Petty

High-Rise Stories sheds light on the human cost of one of America's most ill-conceived and catastrophic civic programs: the Chicago housing projects. As the buildings themselves are slowly being dismantled, leaving thousands of residents in flux, this issue is as critical—and underreported—as ever.

In these gripping first-person accounts, former residents of Chicago's public housing describe the consequences of relocation, poverty, and gentrification. Their stories of community and displacement give voice to those who have long been ignored, but whose hopes and struggles exist firmly at the heart of our national identity.

FROM MᶜSWEENEY'S

A MILLION HEAVENS
by John Brandon

On the top floor of a small hospital, an unlikely piano prodigy lies in a coma, attended to by his gruff, helpless father. Outside the clinic, a motley vigil assembles beneath a reluctant New Mexico winter—strangers in search of answers, a brush with the mystical, or just an escape. To some the boy is a novelty, to others a religion. Just beyond this ragtag circle roams a disconsolate wolf on his nightly rounds, protecting and threatening, learning too much. And above them all, a would-be angel sits captive in a holding cell of the afterlife, finishing the work he began on earth, writing the songs that could free him. This unlikely assortment—a small-town mayor, a vengeful guitarist, all the unseen desert lives—unites to weave a persistently hopeful story of improbable communion.

EMMAUS
by Alessandro Baricco

The secular and the pious. The rich and the poor. Those with "a capacity for destiny" and those who "cannot afford it." *Emmaus* is a world of stark contrasts, one in which four young men—all from proud, struggling families, and all lusting after Andre, a hypersexual woman—are goaded from adolescence to manhood in a torrent of exploits and crises, sexual awakenings and morbid depressions, naivety and fatalism.

A brilliant portrait of the perils and uncertainties of youth and faith, *Emmaus* is a remarkable novel from one of the very best writers in Europe.

THE BOSS
by Victoria Chang

Written in "a breathless kind of fury," the poems in award-winning poet Victoria Chang's virtuosic third collection *The Boss* dance across the page with the brutal power and incandescent beauty of spring lightning. obsessive, brilliant, linguistically playful—the mesmerizing world of *The Boss* is as personal as it is distinctly post-9/11. The result is a breathtaking, one-of-a-kind exploration of contemporary American culture, power structures, family life, and ethnic and personal identity.

Coming this fall

THE BEST OF MᶜSWEENEY'S

The Best of McSweeney's is a comprehensive collection of the most remarkable work from *McSweeney's Quarterly Concern*. With full-color contributions from some of the pioneering artists and illustrators featured in our pages over the years, and a breathtaking array of first-rate fiction (and some incredible nonfiction, too) from:

JONATHAN LETHEM	JOHN HODGMAN
A.M. HOMES	ADAM LEVIN
DEB OLIN UNFERTH	KEVIN MOFFETT
SHEILA HETI	ANDREW SEAN GREER
DAVID FOSTER WALLACE	DAN CHAON
RODDY DOYLE	KEVIN BROCKMEIER
RICK MOODY	LYDIA MILLET
JESS WALTER	SAM LIPSYTE
GEORGE SAUNDERS	JONATHAN AMES

This is a book to be pored over, and lasting proof that the contemporary short story is as vital as ever.

ALSO AVAILABLE IN A DELUXE SLIPCASED EDITION, FEATURING A BEVY OF THE BEST-LOVED OBJECTS——PLAYING CARDS, COMICS, MINIBOOKS, AND LOST NOVELS——THAT HAVE APPEARED IN THE QUARTERLY OVER THE YEARS.

ALSO AVAILABLE FROM McSWEENEY'S McMULLENS

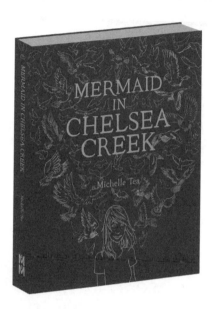

MERMAID IN CHELSEA CREEK

by Michelle Tea · illustrated by Jason Polan

Everyone in the broken-down town of Chelsea, Massachusetts has a story too worn to repeat—from the girls who play the pass-out game just to feel like they're somewhere else, to the packs of aimless teenage boys, to the old women from far away who left everything behind. But there's one story they all still tell: the oldest and saddest but most hopeful story, the one about the girl who will be able to take their twisted world and straighten it out. The girl who will bring the magic.

McSWEENEY'S McMULLENS

NEXT ISSUE

HITCHCOCK AND BRADBURY FISTFIGHT IN HEAVEN

FEATURING STORIES BY
RAY BRADBURY
FREDRIC BROWN
SIDNEY CARROLL
JOHN CHEEVER
ROALD DAHL
J.C. FURNAS
JOSEPHINE W. JOHNSON
FRANZ KAFKA
HENRY KUTTNER
JULIAN MAY
JACK RITCHIE
JOHN STEINBECK
AND MORE

Subscribe at mcsweeneys.net